WHILE WE RUN

by Karen Healey

LITTLE, BROWN AND COMPANY
New York   Boston

WHILE

WE

RUN

Little, Brown and Company

Hachette Book Group
237 Park Avenue, New York, NY 10017
Visit our website at lb-teens.com

Little, Brown and Company is a division of Hachette Book Group, Inc. The Little, Brown name and logo are trademarks of Hachette Book Group, Inc.

The publisher is not responsible for websites (or their content) that are not owned by the publisher.

First Edition: May 2014

Library of Congress Cataloging-in-Publication Data

Healey, Karen.
  While we run / by Karen Healey.—First edition.
    pages cm
  Sequel to: When we wake.
  Summary: "It's the year 2128, and Tegan Oglietti, the world's first successfully revived cryonics patient, and her maybe-boyfriend, Abdi Taalib, are on the run from the government and from a dangerous rebel group. When they uncover shocking new information about the cryonics program, they are faced with an impossible decision that will put thousands of lives in their hands"—Provided by publisher.
  ISBN 978-0-316-23382-8 (hardcover)—ISBN 978-0-316-23383-5 (electronic book) [1. Cryonics—Fiction. 2. Science fiction. 3. Australia—Fiction.] I. Title.
  PZ7.H3438Wj 2014
  [Fic]—dc23
                                                                    2013022281

10 9 8 7 6 5 4 3 2 1

RRD-C

Printed in the United States of America

For Kieran Hartley York,
who gives me hope for the future.
And for Willow, who fights for it.

CHAPTER ONE
Sanguinante

They always wanted me to sing "Here Comes the Sun."

It used to be one of my favorite Beatles songs. The lyrics capture so simply the longing for light. The singer talks about the cold, the ice that hasn't melted in a long time, but he repeats over and over that the sun is coming soon.

In 1969, over a hundred and fifty years ago, George Harrison was having a hard winter. He'd been arrested, he'd had his tonsils removed, and he was being forced to comply with the corporate demands of the Beatles' record company. He'd even temporarily quit the band.

Then, one winter's day, he walked around a friend's backyard with an acoustic guitar and wrote "Here Comes the Sun."

It's supposed to be a love song, and I know the audiences heard it as one. But to me it's not about romance. If anything, it's a dedication to hope, to the fragile, delicate possibility of things getting better before the long winter swallows us all.

Once, I sang "Here Comes the Sun" for Tegan Oglietti. She died a hundred years ago, in 2027, and was cryonically preserved to be revived in our time. She was the first person who'd returned to life from the long winter of death. She chose that song to sing to our classmates, and when her voice cracked and faded, I sang it with her.

She says she loved me for that, so maybe I'm wrong about the lack of romance. But I know I'm right about the hope.

Six months after I first sang that song for Tegan, I sang it for a number of well-dressed people gathered in a hotel ballroom in Brisbane, Australia. The people I was singing to wanted me to give them hope. Earth was overcrowded, overpolluted, and fast running out of resources. The oceans were beginning to die, and humanity on Earth would go with them. But my audience wanted to buy a second chance, on another world. Cryonics offered them that chance—cryonics and the gigantic starship currently under construction in orbit. If the revival process could be perfected, these fortunate ones could escape the dying world and sleep while the starship traveled to its distant destination. They could wake, centuries later, to a new sun.

I finished embellishing the final notes as the backing track died away and raised my hands to acknowledge the applause. In the last six months, I'd performed for all kinds of people, but this was my most common audience: wealthy Australians who wanted to secure their places on that ship. Body mods were popular in Australia, but here there were very few flashing lights set into teeth or heat-reactive tattoos flashing slogans.

2

Instead, there was a lot of subtle surgery designed to disguise the signs of aging.

"Hello," I said, pitching my voice over the applause. "Thank you all for coming!"

They applauded again, but their eyes widened as the wall behind me lit up. The main attraction, and she wasn't even here in the flesh.

"I'm Abdi Taalib," I said. "And this is Tegan Oglietti."

Tegan's face swam into view on the wall.

She looked beautiful and composed. Tegan was actually in Japan, the final stop on her two-month world tour before she came home.

"Hi, Abdi," she said, and blew me a kiss. I caught it, smiling, and pressed my palm to my heart. "And hello to you," she went on, beaming at the gathered people. "Let me tell you a story."

The audience settled down.

"Over a hundred years ago, I died," she began, and I had to concentrate on looking interested. I knew the rest of the story by heart—I'd witnessed most of it and knew just how much of this retelling was actually true. But I had to look alert and nod as Tegan told the rapt crowd how she'd been shot dead in a tragic error, a sniper's mistaken target. She'd been revived by the Australian army in 2128, the first—and so far only—successful revival from cryonic suspension. When she'd foolishly run from her government protectors, she—and I—had been kidnapped by the Inheritors of the Earth, religious zealots who wanted to deny her the right to her second life. Those zealots had filled her head with lies. They'd used a government

3

secret to confuse her: The Australian government had been at work on the starship, getting it ready to send sleeping settlers to a bright new land. The Inheritors told her that the refugees who crowded Australia's borders had been imprisoned and frozen, slave labor for this new world.

The audience shifted uncomfortably, but Tegan continued, describing how the Inheritors considered giving people new life to be blasphemy. They'd planned to destroy the ship and destroy second chances forever. And the signal for that destruction was to be—

"—the suicide of Tegan Oglietti," Tegan said.

The crowd knew this story. The whole world knew this story. But they still gasped, right on cue.

Tegan went on to tell how we had escaped from the Inheritors. She'd thought that the army and government were exploiting those refugees and that exposing their plans could save thousands. So she'd told her story, in a livecast viewed by millions all over the world. Everyone had known about the refugees then. Everyone had known about the starship. And the Australian government had been besieged by angry voters wanting to know the truth.

"But here's what I didn't know," Tegan said. "The refugees were volunteers, not prisoners. Those poor people were driven to Australia by war and hunger and thirst. It's a sad fact that we can't care for them here; Australia simply doesn't have the resources."

Keeping my face from showing what I really thought about that particular line had taken a lot of practice. But I'd been drilled, and now I drew my mouth down at the corners and nodded solemnly.

"The refugees weren't coerced," Tegan went on. "They agreed to cryosuspension, and they agreed to keep it secret, for fear of sabotage. A fear that was well founded, thanks to those extremists from the Inheritors of the Earth. Fortunately, the starship was protected. And over the last six months, piece by piece, it's been taken into space and reconstructed."

"On a new planet, these refugees can care for themselves," I broke in. "As a citizen of a poor African nation, I can tell you that people from less wealthy countries want to contribute to the project however they can—in this case, with their labor. They want to build their new home."

Tegan nodded. "A new home to become everyone's home," she said. "Isn't that amazing?"

The crowd agreed that it was.

Someone stepped into the background of the 'cast and bent over Tegan's shoulder. It was her handler, Lat.

The skin along my spine tightened. I propped up my smile again and hoped the tension didn't show.

"I have to go," Tegan told us all. "But I'll be back in Australia soon! Abdi and I are hosting the President's Ball in a few days. Won't that be fun?"

"I'm looking forward to it with all my heart," I told her, and returned the blown kiss. She laughed, her voice light as a feather, her dark eyes sparkling with barely tempered joy, and caught the kiss in her hand.

As the 'cast faded out, she pressed her palm to her lips.

The moment I stepped off the stage, my handler appeared.

"Abdi, that was great!" Her eyes were shining with suppressed amusement.

I ignored it as best I could. "Thank you, Diane."

"You simply must come and meet some people," she said, and introduced me to my first target for the evening, an elderly woman whose name I promptly forgot.

"That was a wonderful story," she said.

"Thank you."

"My grandnephew tried to tell me that the thirdie refugees were being forced onto the ship, but I said don't be silly, Callum. I wish he'd come tonight." She leaned in close to confide, "I think he's a bit crushie for you."

Diane laughed. "Oh, everyone falls for Abdi. The serious boys always get the interest, don't they?"

"You're a very good-looking young man. And your voice! No wonder Callum's all abuzz. But these Save Tegan people he's fixy with don't seem very nice."

My interest spiked. "He's socializing with people who...do they claim to speak for Tegan, ma'am?"

"Oh, it's that group they've been fussing about on the 'casts." She waved a beringed hand. "Troublemakers, you know."

I hadn't had access to unfiltered news for six months. I didn't know, and with Diane watching me, I didn't dare ask.

"They think Tegan's in some kind of trouble with the government," the nameless woman said. "Ridiculous. Look at you both, so healthy and beautiful. It's lovely that you could spare the time to meet us here. When do you go home?" She meant Melbourne—not my real home, a terra-cotta house in Djibouti City.

"The day after tomorrow," Diane said, her smile glittering like knives. "Abdi has loved visiting Queensland, though."

"It's very beautiful," my mouth said. "It reminds me a little of Djibouti, with the beaches."

"I thought Djibouti was a desert," the nameless woman said. Her tone was sharper. The people at these parties didn't like being wrong or uncertain. And it was harder to get money out of them when they were.

"A coastal desert," I told her. "The Red Sea and Gulf of Aden are full of life. There are thousands of species in the water." The space under my ribs was expanding with homesickness. I wanted very badly to go down to the Red Sea again, to strap on a snorkel and float, peaceful in warm salt water. My younger sister, Sahra, would tag along, but she wouldn't bug me, too entranced by the movements of fish. She wanted to be a marine biologist, which would mean a lot of study abroad. My mother was reluctant to let her last baby go, but my money was on Sahra. She was stubborn, my little sister. Like Tegan.

The nameless woman was looking at me. If her face had been able to wrinkle with concern, I think it would have.

"Are you all right?" she asked softly.

I rose out of that empty space and met her eyes with baffled good cheer. "Of course."

Diane touched her EarRing with her second finger; a signal

to me, not a response to any call someone had made. "I'm afraid we have to move on," she said, and I summoned an apologetic smile before we turned away.

"Less talk about Djibouti, more about the refugee camps," Diane said as we moved out of earshot. "Lots of positive statements. Hit the talking points. How the camps are fine as a short-term solution, but refugees are embracing the long-term opportunities the Ark Project has provided."

I stumbled. Diane adjusted beautifully, her grace turning the misstep into a pause, a carefully choreographed beat in a dance. But her eyes stared into mine, measuring.

"I don't know if I can do that convincingly," I said. There was a trace of fear clouding my voice, like a drop of ink in a still pool.

Diane leaned in, close enough that I could feel her breath on my cheek. "Of course you can, Abdi. You're very good at being convincing. Why do you think we sent you to the camps? Why do you think you're here?"

Because I'm African, I thought. *Because I'm a thirdie. You want me to tell these people that the refugees* want *this, that what the Australian government is doing to people who come here out of fear and desperation is just and noble. And you want me to persuade the refugees they should file into their cryopods as docilely as sheep into a pen.*

I thought it very deep down and let none of the thought show on my face.

Diane straightened the line of my somber green shirt, long fingers dancing down the lapels. I stayed still, a small creature playing dead in the presence of a predator. "You can tell them everything we need you to if you try. You're here because these are serious people. You're good at being serious, Abdi."

The people here didn't look serious. One of the men a few feet from me was loudly discussing, in great detail, a horse he'd just bought and whom he intended to beat with it. If Australia allowed migration, the money he'd spent on that horse could have been loaned to the people in the camps, setting up a family in a business they could maintain. If he'd been willing to make the money a gift, not a loan, it could have contributed to another medical center or a shower block, or another appeal to the World Court.

But he'd stood there and nodded as Tegan told them that Australia *didn't have resources.*

"I can be serious," I said, holding her gaze. I wasn't allowed to break eye contact.

"Serious and convincing," Diane said, and the back of my neck exploded.

The pain coursed down my spine, every nerve in my body flaring red-hot. My skin felt as if I were rolling in broken glass. My scalp tightened over my skull like an iron band, and my mouth flooded with the taste of copper. I made a high, sharp sound, then forced my teeth to clench.

Making noise in public had to be punished.

From the outside, I must have looked a little unwell, perhaps momentarily dizzy. Faces turned toward me, then politely away.

Diane laid her free hand on my wrist, her face composed in concern. Her other hand was hidden in the folds of her outfit, clutching the implant controller, and that was the one I watched.

It felt like eternity. It always did. Realistically, though, it was only a few seconds that I suffered, while Diane touched me and smiled, her hidden hand drawing pain from me until I thought my bones would burst through my skin. When she finally turned off the controller, I almost collapsed with relief, locking my knees at the last second.

"There we go," Diane murmured, and stroked my sweating palm as if she were soothing a fretting pet. "Do you think you can talk about the camps for me now?"

"Yes, Diane," I said, and hated myself.

"And if they mention Save Tegan, you brush it off. They're malcontents who have no idea what they're talking about, understand?"

"Yes, Diane."

"Good boy," she said, and pointed me at the next target, her fingers stroking at my shuddering pulse. "Fetch."

CHAPTER TWO
Tremolo

I made it through the rest of the night without further incidents. The morning was spent in rehearsal, the afternoon in what Diane called "nap time."

I didn't sleep. I stared at the ceiling and counted the tiles in my hotel room—six vertical, four horizontal—and wondered, clinically, when the horror might end.

It was hard to believe everything had begun with something as simple as a song at my cousin's wedding. The bride's family was from Somalia, and I'd been showing off a little— there were some nice-looking girls I hadn't seen before. My brother could impress them with his shoulders, but I had to rely on my voice, and I was making it do a lot of work for me that day.

I didn't get anywhere with the girls, but the firster who caught it on camera was certainly impressed. Her 'cast (imaginatively titled "Local Boy Sings!!!") hit the tubes at just the right moment; whatever alchemical formula makes instant celebrity kicked in, and I was suddenly famous.

It was funny, how quickly it blew up. At home, my flute lessons and singing were only hobbies. My family was proud of me, in their way, but they made it clear that it was my studies that I was supposed to concentrate on, my brain that was going to earn my place in history. Music was a part of me, but only a small part. But to firsters, my voice was all they knew of me. My singing was everything.

Barely an hour after the 'cast hit the tubes, the first offers came. I ignored the interview requests and politely refused the recording contracts. No, I wouldn't record an album. No, I wouldn't open for their band on tour. It was very flattering, but I needed to concentrate on my schoolwork.

Then the scholarship offers came. Ifrah and Halim, my older siblings, stopped teasing me for having a big head, and my little sister, Sahra, stopped whining that she could sing, *too*, and no one had 'cast *her*. My parents stopped being serenely amused about the whole situation. School offers—*that* was serious business.

At the top of the pile was an invitation from the prestigious Elisabeth Murdoch Academy. It came with a near guarantee of one of the rare student visas to cover my time in high school and university. In Melbourne, Australia, where almost no outsiders were permitted to go.

Most of the other schools, I could have gotten into on my own merits. But Australia was forbidden territory and attractive because of it. And my mother didn't underestimate the glamorous effect that returning from an impossible-to-reach world power could have on my political ambitions at home.

I could vividly remember our final discussion about it. In the inner courtyard, in the cool of the evening, Hooyo had folded her hands in her lap and looked at me, warm eyes unblinking.

"It will be difficult," she said. "Australia is prejudiced."

"But there are benefits, too."

"Yes. Your father and I agree that this must be your choice. Whether you stay or go, Abdi, it's your decision."

I had decided.

And now I was here, under circumstances more *difficult* than either of us could have imagined.

"Time to get up, lazybones," Diane said, and tossed me tonight's outfit. "Put on your smiling face!"

Δ ʃ Ω

Another night, another party. I smiled until my cheeks ached. I talked about the camps, just as Diane wanted. I said things like *amazing opportunity* and *best possible solution*, and the next time someone mentioned this Save Tegan movement, I dismissed it as being disgruntled political dissidents with an ax to grind. I smiled at these people, and I told them all about what wonderful work the Ark Project was doing.

And I deliberately forgot their names.

As I passed from one group to the next, Diane nodded at me. I felt the warmth of her approval and immediately afterward was disgusted by myself. I hated Diane, but for my own safety,

I needed her to like me. And because I usually liked the people I wanted to like me, my own emotions seemed determined to mess me up. The inside of my head felt like a viscous ball of melted tar.

"You've been doing well, Abdi," she murmured. "We've noticed a marked improvement in your conduct. It's been two months since your last major incident."

The last major incident had involved my trying to communicate with Tegan by tapping a message on her hand as we sang in Adelaide. I'd only wanted to know if she'd been eating enough; she'd looked dangerously thin that evening. I'd also wanted a warning, if I could get one. The first time she'd gone on a hunger strike hadn't been pleasant for me, and the second time had been horrific.

But that time, Tegan hadn't been defiant. She just hadn't been hungry. On the train back to Melbourne after the benefit, she reported that I'd tried to communicate outside approved channels, in a voice as flat and dead as her eyes.

And after they punished her right in front of me, she'd looked up from the floor, directly into my eyes, and said, *This is your fault.*

They'd praised Tegan. They'd said she was *adapting well.* She'd become a perfect puppet, and I couldn't tell if it was a role she was playing to fool them or if she'd broken under the unbearable pressure, or some unstable mixture of the two. Either way, she'd betrayed me, and it burned.

I'd decided that if it were pretense, I had better pretend, too.

So while Tegan was on her international tour, traveling

14

around the world to talk about the Ark Project and the *AUS Resolution* and find rich sponsors who wanted to give the Living Dead Girl lots of money, I had also become the perfect guest of the Australian government. I'd dressed, eaten, and spoken exactly as I was told. I hated it, but there were benefits to playing along, such as no more nights of being forced to watch Tegan cry because I'd stolen a guard's computer and tried to get blueprints of our prison and they took it out on her. No daylong stints of being woken every time I began to drift off to sleep because Tegan was fasting again.

Nowadays, Diane didn't use the implant controller that often. Her suspicions, I thought, had been lowered. I kept telling myself that if I could just keep being good, my chance to escape would come.

It was so easy to give in and do what I was told. It scared me so much, how easy it was.

"Next, we have a very special dinner party," Diane said. "You're the guest of honor of the guest of honor, and I want you on your best behavior. And tomorrow morning, we'll call your parents." She twinkled at someone across the room, waving coyly. I wasn't fooled; I knew exactly how deadly she was. Her formal lavender culottes and blouse floated around her lean brown frame, and she looked clean and stylish, but I knew that elegant, billowing fabric concealed at least three weapons beside the implant controller: A bolt-gun, a sonic pistol, and a buzz-whip were standard for her, and I'd be surprised if she didn't have a couple of thin knives, too. She liked showing me the knives. "Abdi, I must say I'm growing tired of calling your mother and father every week. Persistent, aren't they?"

"They only want to know that I'm all right."

"Of course they do. And that's what you'll tell them."

"Yes, Diane."

"Good boy."

My empty stomach churned, but long practice kept my face smooth.

"Not long now," Diane said, and stroked my shoulder. "And then you can have something to eat."

Δ ∫ Ω

The very special dinner party was hosted by Valda Simons, Australia's most notoriously untouchable criminal. Where there were extortion, racketeering, illegal arms dealing, cybercrime, and human trafficking, there was Mrs. Simons, taking a cut and ruling the roost, her smile as tight as her short blond curls.

And here she was now, shaking my hand, nodding at Diane, and ushering me into the hotel's private dining room, where a table had been laid out in black and gold, crystal glasses shining in the soft candlelight.

Candles were greatly looked down upon in Australia, where burning things was considered a savage Earth-killing practice for thirdies, but like so many things, it was different for the wealthy. Besides, if you were Valda Simons and didn't balk at ordering murder or kidnapping, you probably didn't have many qualms over a few candles.

"I'm so glad you could make it, Abdi," Valda said gently. She didn't sound like a ruthless crime lord. Her hand was soft and manicured, her aging face sweet. But her blue eyes were cold. I couldn't see anything of the person behind them. "Ruby is very much looking forward to meeting you—ah, there she is now."

I looked across the length of the room to see a young woman make her entrance and instantly knew that the dining room's decor had been chosen to set her off.

She was stunning.

Her golden skin—actually golden, the result of an expensive skin mod that bonded light-reflecting particles into the top layer of the epidermis—glowed, and her short, spiky hair was a deep, rich red. The long black trousers and matching vest were really the background for the piece of art that was her body. She had a black cord tied around her upper arm with long dangling ends, a fashion trend I'd seen on some of the younger people in my audiences. As she moved closer, I saw the red stones embedded in the loose ends glitter. Rubies, of course.

Valda smiled. I thought it might have been genuine pleasure. "Ruby, darling. Meet our special guest."

"Abdi Taalib," Ruby said, her voice smoky, her accent indeterminate. She reached for my shirt lapel, but I caught her hand before she could touch me, bowing over it.

"Enchanted, madame," I said, and wondered where her accent was from. After nearly three decades of the No Migrant policy, I was usually the only person in the room with an accent out of the norm. Ruby's accent must be as contrived as the rest of her.

"Madame? No. Call me Ruby." Her gaze drifted down my tailored suit and back up to meet my eyes, deliberately slow. "Call me anything you like."

17

Aware of Diane's eyes on me, I flirted back. "It's a delight to meet you, Ruby. It's clear why you were named for a treasure."

"Oh, stop," she said in a laughing way that meant *please keep going*, and moved a little closer.

"We're on a schedule," Valda said, her tone mild, but Ruby snapped to attention.

"Of course, Mother. Abdi, come sit with me. I want to hear everything about you."

I glanced at Diane, who inclined her head. There was a smirk hovering around the corners of her mouth, and I braced myself for whatever horrors the evening might hold. When Diane was this happy, I was usually about to become very sad.

Δ ʃ Ω

It was a select group—five couples, including Ruby and me, who were seated at the head of the table. Valda flew solo at the foot, Mr. Simons having died in a regrettable incident over twenty years ago when he'd tried to lead a coup against his wife's interests.

The food was excellent, the conversation trivial. Ruby might have pretended to want to know about me, but while my presence was clearly a triumph for her, she was much more interested in herself. I sat through story after story about snubs she'd received and personal victories she could gloat over—this fashion show she hadn't been invited to, that social event she'd kept a rival from.

It wasn't so bad, really. I'd been trained to handle this kind of mindless small talk since I was very young, when my mother first decided on me as the natural heir to her political ambitions. My older sister, Ifrah, was too outspoken, and my brother, Halim, couldn't master the ability to feign interest. They went into engineering and medicine instead. But I'd loved the "pretend game" my mother played with me from when I was four. Hooyo would say outrageous things, and I had to keep a straight face. Or she would tell me two truths and a lie, and I had to pick the lie from her facial expression—or entirely from her tone, with my eyes closed, straining to pick up the minutiae of inflection. She started taking me to political functions when I was seven. It's amazing, the things people will say in front of a quiet child.

Ifrah grumbled that I was my mother's favorite, and Halim rolled his eyes whenever she praised me, but it wasn't my fault I had the skills they didn't.

Unusually, Diane wasn't signaling me to keep talking, which meant that the Special Australian Defence Unit must have already gotten the money it wanted from the Simons women. My presence was their reward. I was an ornament for the occasion.

"Here, Abdi," Ruby said, and speared a lump of something in a creamy sauce with her golden fork. "Open wide!"

"What is it?" I asked.

"Pink handfish!" she said triumphantly. "Cooked to a special recipe."

My family never ate fish. At home, it was considered a disgusting animal that only the most desperate people would touch. But I couldn't let my revulsion show for a second. As

Ruby maneuvered the cold lump into my mouth, I closed my lips around the fork and smiled, swallowing hard.

"Delicious," I said, making my accent stronger. I knew what Ruby wanted to see. The exotic thirdie, suitably civilized, but provokingly different.

"Yes, you are," Ruby said, and wiped a smear of sauce off my lower lip. Her touch lingered possessively, and my gaze jumped to Diane, who was calmly standing at the other end of the room.

Diane only left me alone with people who were rich when they wanted something from me. Sometimes it was an assurance that I was fine and had really changed my mind about the Ark Project. More often, it was sex. Sex sold ideas as much as it ever had products.

Of course, SADU would never take the risk of letting me move out of their hands and into a secluded area, no matter how much they wanted my would-be seducer's money. But the tease of thinking that it might be a possibility had managed to get extra sponsorship out of quite a few people who were curious to try out the government's famous thirdie. I was willing to bet that Ruby Simons was in that category.

Diane was smirking again. The fish settled in my stomach, the cold lump growing there.

Valda Simons stood up, and everyone quieted immediately. I couldn't deny the woman had presence. "I'm delighted you could all be here to meet our special guest," she said, and I acknowledged the light murmur of agreement by lifting my water glass. "And I have to eat a little bit of crow. You see, when Nathan Cox first told me about the Ark Project, I was dubious.

'Nathan,' I said, 'this might be all right for thirdies who need someplace to go, but you're never going to get real Australians as paying passengers on that ship. It's too much of a risk.'" She laughed, and the guests laughed with her.

I laughed with them, burning inside. So the president of Australia was on first-name terms with Australia's biggest crook. Well, I wasn't naive—my mother's campaigns had donations from people whose hands weren't clean, either. But Cox's confidence in future elections suddenly made more sense.

I'd been to the camps that held the people Valda dismissed as "thirdies who need someplace to go." The children there had lined up with their parents to sign the forms volunteering them for cryonic suspension and indentured labor, far, far away. I'd smiled for the bumblecams and cracked jokes in French and Arabic and Somali and nodded solemnly as carefully selected and meticulously coached refugees had made their statements to the gathered media about being grateful for an amazing opportunity, about reaching for the distant stars.

There had been a group of teenagers hanging around, staring at the SADU uniforms my escorts wore. The kids muttered to themselves, then began to talk more loudly. When they started to shout, the camp guards took over and SADU ushered the journalists out.

But I'd seen what had happened next: the blood, the broken teeth. Nothing deadly—but enough to show those kids what happened when you tried to disrupt the story the government wanted to tell.

My head was pounding. Valda had said something else about

the starship, about her arguments against it, and I'd missed it. Now she shook her head mockingly. "Nathan just looked at me and said, 'Valda, my dear, you're not thinking of the future.' He was right! I'm an old fuddy-duddy, but our young people are the brave ones, the pioneers. And I'm very pleased to be able to tell you that my beloved daughter, my darling Ruby, is one of them."

Ruby stood up, her black cord dangling gracefully. "That's right!" she said. "Welcome to my going-away party! I undergo cryonic suspension tomorrow morning."

I gasped, and the other guests gasped with me—a massive inhalation that could have been funny if it weren't for the seriousness of the situation. Ruby Simons was choosing to die?

There was real emotion in Valda's eyes as she looked down the table at her daughter. "I love you, darling. I'm going to miss you more than I can say. And I admire you more than you can imagine."

The guests broke into applause. I clapped with them, but my mind was whirring. Most of the wealthy benefactors of the Ark Project who'd gotten themselves frozen had been ill or old. Ruby Simons didn't seem to be sick. And she looked about twenty-five, which was far too young to be worried about anything that might destroy brain function before her doubtlessly well-drilled cryo team could spring into action.

Ruby waited for silence. "I love you, too, Mother," she said, and then with an elaborate sweep of her hand, "but I have to claim the future! Tomorrow is the day before my thirtieth birthday. I'll go to sleep and wake up somewhere wonderful, and I'll be ready to take on the world. And I won't be old and boring." The guests, some of whom were fairly old themselves, laughed politely at that. Ruby's teeth glittered at me. "Will I see you there, Abdi?"

The guests gasped again.

In a world built on slave labor? The thought was appalling.

"We'll have to see," I teased.

She laughed and kissed my cheek as she sat down, her painted lips moist against my face. Dinner became noisier after that, as people came up to congratulate Ruby and admire her bravery. Valda watched her daughter with sad eyes. Once, Ruby hugged her and I thought both of them might have shed tears, if it wouldn't have spoiled their careful eye makeup.

Abandoned, I took a moment to have my water glass refilled and drifted closer to the balcony wall, open to the warm night air. I could see city lights outside, a long way down.

A shiver of pain ran down my spine in warning, and I stopped six feet away. Diane wasn't going to let me get that close to any kind of freedom.

When I turned around, meaning to rejoin the party, Ruby was there.

"Running away?" she asked.

"From you? Never."

She smiled, moving even closer to me, and brushed her hand down my arm. My skin crawled at the cool stroke of her long fingers, but I made myself sway toward her. "So, Tegan's away," she said. "How long has she been on this international tour?"

It was the first time she'd mentioned Tegan all evening. I should have noticed that earlier. Usually, all anyone wanted to talk about was the Living Dead Girl. Now the resentful note in Ruby's voice set off all my warning bells.

"She's been gone two months."

"Two whole months! You must really miss your lady love." Ruby paused. "Unless you don't love her anymore?"

"Tegan and I are very good friends," I said, giving the rote response that had been drilled into me. "But we prefer to keep our private lives private." I looked up at her from under my lashes, putting a promise into my eyes.

"Really?" Ruby said. "I'm fond of privacy myself. Shall we go and find some?"

That was usually the moment Diane would turn up again with an apology for the interruption. She'd stay with me until Ruby left frustrated. But Diane was loitering by a couple some distance away.

"Abdi," Ruby whispered. She draped herself artistically over my shoulder. Her breath was warm on my ear. "I want to show you something. Let's get out of here."

Diane could hear everything. I knew she could. Why wasn't she stopping this?

The realization was a blow to the head, leaving me sick and dizzy, a low throb at the base of my skull. She'd told me to be nice to Ruby. Diane wanted me to be *very* nice to her. After all, what was the risk? Ruby was going to die tomorrow, to sink selfishly into her icy chamber, waiting for the dawn of a new world to thaw her out. Ruby wouldn't risk her future on the word of a handsome boy, whatever he told her about what was really going on. But she might make a final donation for the chance to bed him.

24

Please, I thought, staring across the room, willing Diane to hear me and rescue me at last. *Please don't do this to me, too.*

Ruby followed my gaze, and her tone sharpened. "Why are you looking at her?"

Diane turned away.

My tongue was thick, moving like a sluggish snake in my dry mouth. I made a noise that couldn't be mistaken for words, while I groped for self-control. I couldn't say an outright no to this woman. I couldn't even be unpleasant in the hope that she'd reject me.

"We could dance," I suggested, my stomach flopping around like a dying fish. I summoned a smile that strove to be playful.

Ruby smiled in return, taking the gesture as compliance. "There's no music," she said. "We can dance in my hotel suite." Which was no doubt being monitored by SADU. They'd be recording everything. Did Ruby know? Did she even care?

But I could think of no escape. Even the balcony behind me was too far away. Perhaps inspiration would strike on the way to her rooms.

In the elevator, Ruby leaned against me. She'd drunk a lot of the wine during dinner, but I didn't think she was that intoxicated. "I'm going to miss my mother," she said.

"I miss mine," I said, unable to keep the sadness from my voice.

"But I won't miss anything else," she continued, blithely ignoring me. "All these boring people, these boring parties...I want something new, Abdi. I want an adventure."

And that was what I was to her—an adventure, not a person. As we moved out of the elevator and into the penthouse suite, her hand slipped under the hem of my shirt, stroking up the plane of my belly. I stared into that beautiful, blank face and wondered if it might not be so bad.

I saw the white bed over her shoulder, lush and soft.

No. No matter what it cost me, no matter what it cost Tegan when I didn't comply, I couldn't do it.

I caught Ruby's wrist. "No," I said simply.

She blinked. "What?" I was guessing people didn't say no to Ruby Simons. "Is this about Tegan? She'll never know. You can keep your little girlfriend; I'll be gone tomorrow. I thought you wanted to have some fun."

My mouth wasn't working properly again. "No. I can't do it."

Ruby leaned in and kissed me.

I shuddered, a full-body rejection that I couldn't disguise, and pushed her away from me, almost violent in my disgust.

"Hey!" she said. "I don't like that. They told me you'd be *nice*."

And that was it. The dams that kept my anger curbed burst, and rage flushed through my body, hot and roiling.

If I was going to be punished anyway...

My fingers bit into the soft flesh of Ruby's arm. "Don't go," I said.

She stared at me, right on the edge of panic. "What?"

"Don't freeze yourself! Don't board the starship. You'll be profiting off slave labor, making money out of human misery. Don't do it, Ruby!"

"But I'll get *old*," she said.

The former Abdi could have found an argument to persuade her. Appealed to her vanity in some way, made her think about

26

the fame she'd acquire if she tried to stop the *Resolution* and find a better solution for the dying world. But all I had now was fury and despair, and I was clumsy with it. The last two months' work, of making Diane think I was being good, of trying to lower her suspicions and curb my rebelliousness, had just been utterly wasted.

Only my mother's training could save me now. I was reaching for the answer, grasping for any rhetorical strategy I could muster, when Diane activated the implant and my world exploded into pain.

I hit the floor, the taste of my own blood sharp in my mouth as I writhed. Ruby screamed for help, even as she knelt by me.

"It'll be okay," she was saying, hands frantically patting at my cheeks. "What's wrong, Abdi? Stop it! Stop it now! Somebody help him!"

"Holy crap!" an unfamiliar voice said, and then there were shiny shoes around me as hotel staff and SADU security surrounded me, calm voices soothing Ruby's distress.

The last thing I saw was lavender silk and Diane's angry eyes before my nervous system overloaded with agony. I passed out on Ruby Simons's pretty, pretty carpet.

CHAPTER THREE
Elegy

When I came to, I was strapped onto a narrow float-bed, back in my gray Melbourne cell. There was an IV sticking into the back of my hand, and I recognized the empty, dizzy feeling of being fed liquid nutrients for a while.

"Did you hear?" Diane said brightly from where she was perched at the foot of my bed. She was dressed in her SADU uniform now, no flowing lavender silks. "The Save Tegan campaign tried to poison you as a traitor to their cause. You went into convulsions in the middle of the dinner party. It was deeply shocking. Lucky I was there to administer treatment and get you airlifted to safety."

Experience had taught me that people were willing to abandon hard truth in favor of comforting falsehood in almost every circumstance, but it was still hard to believe anyone would believe such a huge lie. But people *liked* big lies, lies that were so big they couldn't believe they were lies—because who would dare to tell such a big lie?

"What *is* the Save Tegan campaign?" I asked, risking the question on her good mood. She was always in a good mood after I'd been severely punished.

Diane shrugged. "Reckless, dangerous idiots intent on overthrowing the democratically elected leaders of Australia." Her smile flashed. "And as of last night, terrorists. I don't think you'll be hearing much more from them."

Before two nights ago, I'd never heard of them at all. Eavesdropping at these events had been my only way of gathering information in my media blackout. Apparently, I should have had more faith in humanity—and not the part of it that came to those parties. Someone cared. And was making enough noise that even selfish, self-absorbed people had noticed.

Diane must have seen the hope in my eyes, because she stopped smiling. "Did you and Ruby have a nice talk?" she asked.

My hope died. "I'm sorry, Diane," I said mechanically. "I won't do it again. I was just surprised. I didn't understand."

She stood up and sauntered to the head of my bed. I flinched when she reached for me, but she only stroked my head, long fingers gentle on my scalp. "I forgive you," she said. "It was a brief impulse. The heat of the moment. And I smoothed things over with Ruby. She went into her cryocontainer this morning."

So Diane's attempt to prostitute me had been unsuccessful—but so had my efforts to persuade Ruby to stay alive in the present day. Diane would have plenty more opportunities to carry out her plans. Would I?

"Unfortunately, Abdi...you missed your catch-up with your parents. And one of the waiters got footage of you flailing about on the floor and 'cast it on the tubes. He was fired, of course, but your parents saw the 'cast. They're very worried."

"I'm sorry," I said dully. I was sorry for the waiter, mostly. I hoped SADU wouldn't take any further steps.

"They asked all sorts of questions. I explained that we were in hot pursuit of the perpetrators, but they keep insisting that you'd be much safer back in Djibouti. We've set up another call for tomorrow morning. You're going to have to be very convincing."

"I can do that," I said.

Diane smiled. "I know you can." She pulled her computer out of her pocket and snapped it open. "But you might need some extra motivation."

Tegan appeared on the computer screen. She was standing in a luxury aircraft with pale cream walls and plush furnishings. Her bright blue gown was beautiful and her dark hair elegantly arranged, but the expression on her small face radiated sheer ugly terror. I tended to freeze when I knew punishment was coming. Tegan was more kinetic, though, and her reaction was to move. She never tried to hit them anymore, but she couldn't be still, either. She twisted and tugged in her handler's impassive grip as if escape wasn't a futile option, never quite daring to strike him.

"No, no, no," she was saying, her voice distorted with her terror. "I've been good, so good. I'm a *good girl*."

"Are we ready to go, Lat?" Diane asked pleasantly.

Tegan's handler held up his controller. "Ready."

Tegan's breath sobbed out, and she went dead still, her eyes fixed on the camera. "Abdi," she said.

My eyes were trained on Tegan, but I spoke to Diane. "Please don't," I said.

"You know how this works, Abdi." Diane sighed. "I'd hoped you'd learn a little faster. I really don't enjoy having to do this."

That was a lie. Diane loved her job. It was in the mocking slant of her smile as she held the screen in front of my eyes. Sometimes I wondered what had been done to her to make her like this. Surely she hadn't been born evil. But most of the time I couldn't spare the energy to care.

"You'll watch," she said, her voice quiet and clear. "You'll watch and you'll remember. Tomorrow morning, you will convince your parents you love Australia and need to finish your work here before you can even think of going home. And tomorrow night you'll go to the fund-raiser with Tegan and President Cox, and you will turn in a perfect performance."

"Please don't hurt her," I begged, and then, more desperately, "Please don't make me watch." I hated the tone of my voice, the sick churning in my belly. And I couldn't stand the shame of the second plea being more important to me right now.

Tegan, on her SADU-controlled plane, with her SADU handler gripping her arm, wouldn't have the luxury of passing out. Over the last six months, the tiny tendrils attached to the implant core had worked their way around nearly every bundle of sensory nerves in our bodies. If we went off script in public, Diane and Lat could shut us down immediately and claim convulsions or terrorist attack. But in SADU-observed privacy, when it didn't matter what we said or how loud we screamed, they didn't give us the oblivion of unconsciousness.

Tegan would suffer for a long time because of what I'd done. And I would have to watch.

"Diane, please!" Nothing I'd said had ever made any difference, but I still had to try.

She hesitated. "Well...you have been quite good lately."

I was already bracing myself for the inevitable denial, and it took me a second to realize the opportunity. "Yes!" I said. "I talked about the camps."

"That's true." Diane's eyes shaded over. "And it is understandable that you panicked when you were supposed to go with Ruby. You didn't know what I wanted."

"Tegan's behavior has been excellent," Lat rumbled. He was looking at me with disapproval. "Not a single incident all tour."

Tegan looked at him, then through the computers at Diane. "That's right," she said eagerly. "I've been very good."

"It seems a pity to punish her," Diane agreed, tapping her lips. "And you'll cooperate next time, Abdi?"

I swallowed hard. I knew what she wanted. I'd have to let her pimp me out without voicing a protest or whispering a word about the horror SADU had trapped us in.

Eventually, they'd make me do it anyway; with enough time and pain, they could make me do anything. And until I did, they'd hurt Tegan for my disobedience. I looked into her wet eyes, huge with hope, and couldn't face being the cause of her agony again.

But I couldn't face what Diane wanted, either.

Lie, I thought. *Pay for it later. Lie now.*

"I'll do it," I said, and met Diane's amused eyes, pushing sincerity into my own gaze. "I'll do whatever you want, Diane. I promise. I'll do anything."

Diane's smile was a slap. "That's nice, Abdi. But I'm afraid Tegan has to pay for the mistake you've already made. Lat, go."

Lat looked displeased, but he held up the implant controller, and Tegan's face crumpled into terror again.

I lunged for the computer, but Diane held it out of reach. As Tegan's screams began, I stared into Diane's mocking face and hated her with every part of me.

"It's very easy, Abdi," she said, tilting the screen so it was in front of my face. "Just stop screwing up. Now, watch what you did."

$$\Delta \int \Omega$$

When it was over, I had lunch. My appearance was as carefully planned as a battle and subject to the same military discipline; every calorie had to be accounted for, every muscle worked and streamlined and pushed into the appropriate size for the image they'd created for me.

After what I'd just witnessed, the food sat like a lump of stone in my stomach. I had to force each mouthful down and keep it down, but I knew better than to refuse to eat. Tegan had managed four hunger strikes; I'd only tried once before the pain and humiliation of force-feeding made me give in.

After lunch came the exercise routine, then bathing, hair depilation, skin conditioning, costume fittings, and all the other inescapably dull activities required to keep me looking good. Before, I'd enjoyed fashion and taken pleasure in finding bright colors to contrast with my skin. But I didn't get to do anything now. It was all done to me. I stood for half an hour while the SADU tailor moved around me with memory cloth and clips, trying not to think about how Tegan had looked as Diane had ripped her hope away.

It didn't work; my memory was too good to dismiss the way agony stretched her features, the way her body strained as the convulsions hit. It was harder to remember Tegan as she'd looked when she'd still been defiant, still resisting the process of becoming a puppet. It was harder still to remember her before we'd been caught. She'd been so strong then, the frozen girl reborn, facing her future with determination and a yen for justice and a reckless disregard for her own safety. She'd faced down a hostile media and school bullies, she'd defied religious zealots and her army handler, and she'd confronted head-on the dangerous truth of the real reasons behind her revival. They'd tried to make her a tool and a spokesperson, and instead she'd escaped to tell her own truth.

That wild courage, that fierce strength. I could have spent days kissing her for that.

Instead, we'd had two nights. One night, locked in darkness under the Inheritors' compound, I'd told her about my ambitions: that I wanted to be a lawyer, then a politician like my mother. I'd told her about my family and the way they guided my choices—but that the choice to come to Australia had been mine, and helping to smuggle vaccines into Africa was my decision and mine alone. I'd listened to her memories of a world gone by, and her hopes for the future.

And on the second night, I'd promised a speech-shy Tegan that she could tell the truth about the Ark Project. And she did. She talked until dawn to tell the world everything she'd discovered about the frozen refugees and the secret starship. We'd thought everything was going to change. In that long night, I'd allowed myself to hope.

In the gray light of the new day, SADU had come to take us both away. And we'd discovered that up till then, the people in charge had been playing nice.

"Don't move," the tailor said irritably, jolting me back to the present.

"Sorry."

She snapped the fabric tight. "You're still growing." It was more complaint than observation.

I glanced at the full-length mirror, something I didn't do much anymore, because it was so hard to look myself in the eye. I looked good; it was true—a tempting morsel for people like Ruby. High cheekbones; full lips; and dark, polished skin, dark even for a Somali boy. Under arched black eyebrows were my light brown eyes, an odd color that caught yellow light in the sun—golden, Tegan had called them. Amber, said Ifrah, the time I'd complained about them. I'd wanted eyes like hers and my mother's—deep brown and soft. My face hadn't changed too much in six months; a little stiffer maybe, the jaw a little more defined.

But my shoulders had broadened, straining against the dark blue cloth. The muscles in my thighs were clearly outlined in the tight pants, exaggerated to a point that looked almost obscene.

"The exercise routine," I said. I'd been lean before, fit enough to play a game of soccer without getting winded, but not bulky. Now I had a lot of new muscles, and new strength and nothing to do with it. Sometimes the trapped energy fizzed beneath my skin until I thought I would burst.

"You're getting taller, too." The tailor sighed and shook her black curls. "We're going to have to give Tegan higher heels again."

"Sorry."

"Not your fault," she said, and met my eyes. I blinked. Most of the time the tailor treated me as an inconveniently fleshy mannequin. She'd never even told me her name. "I'll fix it. Getting taller isn't your problem."

I felt my rusty political instincts creak into gear. This was the closest thing to genuine sympathy I'd heard for six months.

"I'm sorry I'm making more work for you," I tried, and caught the wry lift at the corner of her mouth.

"That's my job," she said. "Everyone's gotta do their job."

And you're becoming less comfortable with yours, I thought. I knew better than to make the same mistake I'd made with Ruby and push too hard, too fast. But while I kept my mouth shut, I couldn't stop my mind from jumping ahead. It would be very useful to have someone inside who was unhappy about what SADU was doing to us, especially someone who had access to both Tegan and me. Eventually, she might be willing to pass messages or get word out to this Save Tegan movement.

It would take patience and time. A lot of time.

I wasn't sure how much time I had left. SADU's endgame was obvious; break us to the point where they didn't have to break us anymore. They'd like nothing more than for us to believe the lies we were telling, rather than just repeating them.

But somebody knew. Somebody wanted to Save Tegan—and presumably, her thirdie sidekick. No one in Australia would ever pretend I was the first priority. I was along for the ride; the person pulled out to perform when Tegan wasn't available.

I made sure to thank the tailor when the fitting was over. She told me her name was Natasha.

Δ ʃ Ω

More food, more exercise, then rehearsal for the President's Ball tomorrow. Diane didn't bother to stick with me for every minute when I was inside the Melbourne facility, but she always turned up when I sang. It wasn't because she enjoyed my voice; she just liked watching me squirm as I performed on command.

She didn't seem to be getting her usual thrill today. As I sent my voice through the umpteenth rendition of "Blackbird," she was actually frowning.

"Music, stop," she said, and the house computer cut off the audio. My skin tightened. Interruptions were never good.

"Tell me about Joph Montgomery."

Joph? "What about her?"

She sighed. "Don't try to be clever, Abdi. It doesn't look well on you."

I *was* clever. Her condescension scraped at my nerves. "I'm sorry, Diane," I said humbly. "I don't understand the question."

Diane held up her fingers, ticking off points. "She was your classmate at Elisa Murdoch Academy. She was the chemist making the drugs for you to smuggle back to your filthy little country. She had a starring role in Tegan's political temper tantrum, helping you two and Bethari Miyahputri break into that cryostorage facility so you could get footage of frozen refugees and fill my life with many, *many* problems."

Joph had been shot in that cryostorage facility, a bullet going through her thigh. The last I saw of her, she'd been telling Tegan and me to run. I had no idea what had happened to her since.

I'd asked, of course. But no one had given me answers.

"Is she all right?" I ventured.

"*I* ask the questions, Abdi. Are you two friends?"

Though it would have been a catastrophically bad move, I nearly laughed in her face.

Until Tegan woke from her death sleep, Joph had been the only person at school who had seemed to like me for me. I'd been there on a music scholarship, half celebrity, half curiosity, but I'd been secretly working on my own goal of getting vaccines out of Australia, and therefore trying to keep my profile as low as possible.

So, while Bethari and her political crowd had been elaborately respectful, I hadn't wanted to risk getting close to them. And some of the other students had done their best to make me pay for the massive mistake of setting my thirdie foot inside their privileged firster walls. The rest had been busy with their own lives and ignored me.

But Joph was different. She was kind and funny, and listened to me. In a quiet way, she cared about the world as much

38

as I did. In her tiny, hot haven in the janitorial closet off the main hallway, Joph and I became something much more important than friends. We were allies.

Joph made thousands of little pink pills in her home chemistry lab, and she gave them all to me. I passed them to my Australian shipping contact, the man who called himself Digger Jones. And he got them to Northeast Africa, to the people who could not afford the patented, name brand, incredibly expensive cure for the deadly Travis Fuller Syndrome. Joph didn't look much like a hero, but she was one of the smartest people I had ever met, and she was responsible for saving thousands of lives.

"We were friends," I said cautiously.

Diane's mouth creased. "Well, this *friend* has scored an invitation to the President's Ball. Her mother's a member of Parliament for Victoria, and she's the plus one."

Joph was alive and some form of free, or Diane wouldn't be concerned about her presence at the ball. I started to have some thoughts about where the Save Tegan movement might have come from.

"I'm telling you this in advance, Abdi, because I want to be very clear about my expectations. You'll be given a chance to chat with Joph Montgomery in private, and you will be very sorry you haven't been in touch and absolutely sincere about the importance of the Ark Project."

I kept my face schooled to attentive blankness. I had to be very careful. "Yes, Diane."

"I know you, Abdi. I know every thought that goes through your devious brain. You're right now thinking that you can take advantage of this, and I'm here to tell you that you can't and won't. If there is a whisper, a tiny gesture, anything I don't like, Tegan will pay. You will pay. And Joph Montgomery will pay." She stepped right up to me and pulled the microphone out of my hands. "Joph is a traitor, Abdi, and she massively violated medical patents. She got away with it because she's rich and her mother's powerful. But with a girl like that, no one would be surprised if we found more evidence of different crimes. We could find evidence that even a mother couldn't deny."

Or you could plant it, I thought. Neither of us had to say it. Diane's threat was clear.

"I won't," I said, feeling ill at the thought.

"She'd be in an ordinary jail," Diane went on, drifting one of her long fingers down my cheek. "Not your plushy setup. Terrible things can happen to people in jail, *do you understand*?"

"Yes!" I said. For a moment, the room wavered around me and I saw Joph instead. Joph stabbed. Joph beaten. Joph's sweet smile and calm voice cut off forever. "I understand, Diane! I won't do anything. I promise."

"There's my good boy." She hooked her fingers into my collar. "Now, come to bed. You have a long day tomorrow. We have to make sure you're ready for it."

CHAPTER FOUR
Cadenza

Even in the sound-insulated waiting room, I could hear the noise from the event hall. I'd thought the public's greed for this kind of function might have been sated, but Tegan's tour had apparently whetted their appetite, and they were ready to see her triumphant return.

But not as ready as I was. When Tegan came through the door, I was on my feet so fast Diane actually reached for one of her hidden weapons.

Normally, we wore similar clothing—sharp-cut shirts and pants, impeccably tailored. Tegan was nearly always in blues, me in greens and yellows. We had to look serious, after all, like responsible young people championing a bright future. But tonight was supposed to be a glittering event, with President Nathan Phillip Cox here to lend his blessing to the fund-raising efforts. Tonight I was wearing a sleeveless chrome vest over dark trousers, an elaborate gold cord tied around my upper arm like the black one Ruby Simons had worn.

And Tegan looked like a European princess. They'd dressed her in a long white gown, with a shimmer of iridescent dust over her bare collarbones. SADU didn't want to remind people too much of the real, risk-taking girl who had thrown herself off a two-story building to escape a military hospital. At an event like this, it made sense that they'd try to make her look like a fairy-tale figure instead—Snow White or Sleeping Beauty. She was supposed to play the role of a naive ingenue wakened from a deathlike sleep, with the future itself cast as a handsome prince, giving Tegan a second chance at life.

It was a lovely tale.

And much, much safer than the real one.

"Abdi," Tegan said, and walked toward me, swaying gracefully in her heels. Before the tour, she'd still been unsteady, but now she handled her shoes as easily as she did her guitar.

Her minder was right behind her. Lat was youngish, and short, and muscular, and he had a scar through the left cheek that my older sister, who liked swashbuckling stories, might have described as "rakish." His eyes were a solid dark brown that seemed black, and they were as flat and merciless as the eyes of a tiger shark I'd seen in the Red Sea. I hated him almost as much as I hated Diane, and I feared for Tegan in his hands. Her old minder had vanished after Tegan's third hunger strike, never to be seen again. After Lat's arrival, Tegan had very quickly *adapted*.

I put out my hand, and she grasped it tight. This was the

single kind of touch we were allowed. Hugging was too close; we might whisper to each other then. "I'm so sorry," I said, trying and failing to put out of my head an image of the way I'd seen her on Diane's computer—crying helplessly on the ground and begging Lat to stop.

Tegan's hand was thin, but the grip was strong, and her exposed collarbones didn't have that sunken appearance I'd learned to fear. "I understand," she said. "I know you won't do it again. Tonight you'll be perfect, won't you?"

She said it without a hint of sarcasm. That was the worst thing about being constantly observed, constantly exposed; we never knew if the other was being sincere or saying what we thought would keep our handlers happy.

"Joph's coming tonight," I said, watching her face.

Her expression didn't change. "Lat told me. It will be nice to tell her a little about the work we've been doing."

My stomach roiled. Diane smirked. "How was the tour, Tegan?" she asked.

"It was interesting. We went to a lot of places. Canada wouldn't let us in, of course."

Canada maintained that Australia's No Migrant policy was a contravention of human rights and wouldn't allow an Australian citizen to cross its borders except as a refugee seeking asylum. Diane shifted; this conversation was too close to topics we weren't allowed to mention.

"So I performed in a cruiser anchored in international borders," Tegan said quickly. She'd noticed Diane move, too. "It was fun. Lots of sponsors came. How are you, Abdi?"

"I'm fine. I missed you," I said, ignoring Lat's disbelieving grunt.

"I missed you, too," she said. "Planes are much fancier than in my time. Before it was cramped and noisy. And no food. On tour, it was like a restaurant in the air."

My face stayed smooth, no matter that I wanted to curl my lip. "Some people can afford luxury."

"Ahem," Lat said.

"It was an observation, Lat. Abdi wasn't being seditious." Tegan said it with the tiniest hint of irritation in her voice, and I could have wept at this signal that she was still in there somewhere, that this smooth, shiny creature wasn't entirely remade to SADU's exacting specifications.

"Courtesy, Tegan," Diane reproved. "Goodness me, have you lost your manners on tour?"

"Tegan was very good," Lat said, and bestowed a smile upon his charge. She smiled back, her dark eyes lighting, and I hated him a little more.

"Well, no need for her to become lax now! And, Abdi, do you really think such observations are helpful?"

"No, Diane. I'm sorry."

"Good." She touched her EarRing and nodded. "We're up. Walk."

Tegan and I shifted our grip so that we could hold hands side by side and walked the short distance from the waiting room to the stage entrance. President Cox was doing the standard spiel: new wonder, new borders, new phase for humanity. Tegan's hand shifted, damp with sweat, and I could feel the slight tremor. She still had stage fright; she probably always would. Tegan's true love was for the music itself, but they'd warped that into making her a showpiece. I'd always loved to perform; when I was too mired in my head to talk, I could always reach people with music. So they demanded performance of me on their terms, not mine, and had stopped me from reaching anyone at all.

The people in charge had imprisoned us and hurt us, and they'd done it so that we'd fix the public-relations problem they'd so richly deserved.

"Break a leg," Diane whispered, and gently stroked the back of my neck. "And remember what I said about Joph."

Yes. I would have to lie to her.

I would have to look into the face of my one Australian friend and tell her that everything she'd done to help me had been pointless. That her being shot had just been a little mistake, that the frozen children in the cryocontainers we'd recorded had chosen freely and happily to give up their lives here so they could work on a distant planet. If I went onto that stage, I would have to betray Joph, and myself, and Tegan, and I would have to keep doing it, over and over and over.

It would never stop.

It felt as if despair had grabbed my legs and pulled me under the surface of my turbulent emotions, stealing my breath and tightening my muscles. Tegan felt it through her grip on me, and her body language shifted in response. She caught the look on my face and whispered, "Not now."

"…now, I am pleased to present to you the ambassadors for the Ark Project, Tegan Oglietti and Abdi Taalib!"

45

Tegan stepped forward and jerked to a halt, motionless on the end of my outstretched hand. I knew I had to plaster a smile on my face and walk onto the stage, but my feet were rooted to the floor.

"Abdi," Diane said behind me. It was a command.

"I can't," I said. "I can't do this anymore."

Tegan twisted to face me. "Don't do this to me," she said. "Abdi, please don't! I can't take it!"

Months ago she'd shouted her defiance in their faces. *I'm glad he tried to escape. I'm glad! Hurt me all you want, I hope he does it again!* The Tegan I'd come to know, the girl I'd kissed and fought for, would have screamed it now.

Instead she looked over my shoulder and said, "Lat, I'm being good! It's not me. He's doing it. Don't punish me. Not tonight!"

But there was nothing special about this night. It was just another performance, like a hundred we'd done before, like a thousand more we'd do until SADU decided the Living Dead Girl wasn't useful anymore and found a convenient accident to get rid of her and her thirdie boyfriend. Or, even worse, until we truly became what we only appeared to be, the insides of our heads changing to match the veneer of their perfect puppets.

"It's too much," I said, shaking my head. "It hurts too much, and it'll never stop. I can't do it."

"Please, Abdi," Tegan said. "It'll be fine. Please trust me."

But I didn't trust her. I couldn't.

It was a horrible realization; for six months she'd been my only ally, the only person I could count on to understand how I felt and empathize with my pain—and vice versa. Now I didn't know how much of the strong Tegan I'd loved was still in there. And I couldn't trust what might remain.

Lat bent down by my ear, while President Cox made jokes about stage fright and how shy and humble we were.

"You will move, or I will hurt her in new ways," he whispered, his voice deep and pleasant. "And I'll make you watch it all." He chuckled. "Maybe she'll even enjoy it."

It felt as if he'd wrapped his hands around my throat and squeezed all the air out. They'd never threatened her with that before. I couldn't let it happen.

But I also couldn't continue as I had.

Stretched thin between the two impossible choices, I gave in to Tegan's insistent tug on my hand and stepped forward, into the light of that enormous room and the hundreds of greedy eyes that waited to devour us until we were nothing but empty husks.

Nathan Phillip Cox, president of the Republic of Australia, was waiting to greet us. His face was broad and rugged, a handsome, sturdy kind of face. You could imagine it on the first European pioneers trying to cross the Australian desert or running sheep over the rounded hills. His wrinkles had been superbly tweaked to suggest seriousness, but not sternness, and his crow's-feet proclaimed that this was a man who laughed as often as he frowned. He was laughing now, but the emotion didn't reach his eyes. He'd want to know the reason for our hesitation.

Tegan strode forward to shake his hand, a gesture the

president turned into a one-armed hug. He beamed down at her, a kind uncle, then solemnly shook my hand in a man-to-boy gesture that would look great on the 'casts. The noble firster president of superpower Australia, in common cause with the savage thirdie boy from tiny Djibouti.

Tegan was waving and smiling, happily ignorant of Lat's threat. "Hello!" she yelled. "It's so great to be back! Did you miss me?"

The crowd roared.

"I missed you," I said again, only this time it was part of the script. I didn't have to pay attention; the words spilled out easily, my every gesture rehearsed and fine-tuned.

"Well, I've been traveling the world talking about something really important," Tegan said. "You all know about the Ark Project. You all know about the *Resolution*. You know that we're sending humanity to the stars for the first time. And everyone can be a part of it! Everyone can donate something or spread the word."

"The world is in a slow decline," I said, looking grave. Among the solemn nods and sad faces, I saw pursed lips and heads shaking, and wanted to punch something. This was the one part of our spiel that was true, and it was the part a few people always wanted to deny.

"The first travelers are the brave pioneers of our future," Tegan said. "They're taking on the challenge of finding a new home for humanity! And as soon as the revival process is perfected, we'll all take on the challenge of getting them on their way."

"They had faith that we'd help," I said. "Will you keep faith with them?"

"Will you pledge what you can pledge?" Tegan asked. Her excitement looked so real. Was it real? Had she broken that hard? I felt a flash of curiosity before the intense gravity of my despair crushed it down to the soundtrack of the cheering crowd.

"That's enough politics!" Tegan yelled over the noise.

I held up my hands, the golden cord swaying from my forearm. I was doing everything as perfectly as if Diane were tugging directly on that dangling string to manipulate my movements. Tegan couldn't be punished for this. "How about a song?"

They clapped and laughed, while Tegan was handed her guitar—not the third-hand instrument she'd named Abbey and loved with fierce devotion but a custom-made guitar that had been covered in a white skin of memory fabric, glittering like her dress. She checked the tuning, nodded at me, and began picking the opening notes.

It was "Here Comes the Sun."

They always wanted me to sing "Here Comes the Sun."

From the corner of my eye, I could see President Cox, smiling and nodding along to the beat, and Diane in the wings, looking bored. She was looking at the crowd, scanning them idly.

But Lat was watching Tegan.

His eyes were trained directly on her face, and I felt that fear rise within me again. He'd do it. He'd bend her body to his will. The one thing I'd learned to depend on when it came to SADU is that no matter what we did or how good we were, they would always find a reason to hurt us.

As I looked away, unable to bear the possessive fervor in Lat's face, my eyes snagged on a lump under the president's jacket. Probably ninety percent of the people in that room would never have seen it, but over the last six months I'd become hypersensitized to those lumps and what they indicated.

Cox was armed.

Almost idly, I considered the possibilities. I could finish the song and go over to shake his hand again, grab the weapon, aim for Lat, aim for Diane if I got a second shot....

Cold sweat prickled in the curve of my back as fantasy condensed into a viable plan.

I really could do it. The only drawback, as far as I could tell, was that I would definitely die. And they'd punish Tegan afterward—but I wouldn't be around to watch.

I might be able to save her from Lat, though. Perhaps my death would be able to save her entirely. Questions would be asked; people would want to know what had happened and why. My parents were already unhappy, and with me dead they wouldn't have to step carefully around the need to appease my current guardians; they could cause the outcry I knew they wanted to make. Perhaps the furor would give Tegan an opportunity to escape and tell the truth. Perhaps these Save Tegan people would gain some political traction. Perhaps the Ark Project would be revealed for the horror it was.

I wouldn't be around to see it, but it might happen.

And I wouldn't have to commit that final betrayal and lie to Joph.

That was it, I decided. It would be better if I had a way to warn Tegan, but there wasn't any time for hesitation, and if there was anything of the real, brave Tegan left, I thought she would understand that—she'd always been the one who leaped fearlessly into action. Funny, almost, that I would die in my attempt to do the same.

We neared the end of the song, and I poured joy and power into the final chorus, drinking in my final moments. I would go down singing—that felt right; that was proper. The crowd brightened in response to my sudden effort, and I smiled, my gaze sliding around the room. I felt almost sorry for those excited, happy people, who would soon be scared and shocked.

My gaze caught on a slender girl with short tan hair, pushing her way forward to the front row. She was staring directly at me, her brown eyes lit with the same reckless joy that was rising in me.

I smiled at Joph, wishing that I could say good-bye.

Jump, she mouthed.

I frowned, confused. Joph grimaced and beckoned extravagantly. "Jump!" she shouted, her voice cutting clear across the moment of silence at the end of the song.

And as all the lights went out and the startled murmurs began, I launched myself forward, into the dark.

CHAPTER FIVE
Volante

Without being able to see the floor, I landed hard, slamming into a body on the way down. I rolled off and crawled a few paces, striking out in the darkness toward where I thought I'd leaped from. This blackout wasn't part of the performance. If I could just get Tegan off the stage, we could conceivably make a run for it.

Someone grabbed my upper arm, and I gasped.

"Abdi, it's me," Joph whispered, and pulled me up into a crouch. "Stay still."

I was bracing against the pain that should be blasting through my skull, but it hadn't come. Why hadn't Diane put me down? She didn't need to see me to stop me.

"What's happening?" I whispered back. I was taking a chance, but since the implant wasn't causing me pain, it also might not be picking up everything said around me. Besides, I had plenty of cover with the panicked yells all around us. Had these people never encountered a blackout before?

Or maybe this was something else. In a blackout, I'd expect to see people using their computers as flashlights, but there were no lights cutting through this velvet darkness.

"EMP," she said, and there was a thread of something in her voice, a tone that wasn't entirely happy. "We've knocked out all the electronics."

I could barely process the implications of that. "Tegan," I said too loud. "You have to save Tegan."

Joph clapped her hand over my mouth and yanked back hard, as a whisper of fabric passed over my outstretched hands. A fleeing audience member? Or Diane on the prowl? I could sense her moving out there: fluid, silent, and dangerous, like the big cats I'd seen in zoos. I felt that if I strained I could catch the vanilla and jasmine scent of her perfume. I'd liked the smell of vanilla, once upon a time.

"Tegan knows. She's coming. This way." Joph seemed to have no trouble seeing her way through the panicked crowds, but I blundered into people rushing through the darkness, tripped over the limbs of people lying huddled on the floor.

Excitement was racing through me—excitement and fear. This was the rescue I had dreamed of for so many nights, and now that it was here, I was afraid the reality was also a dream. The adrenaline and the darkness pulled at my head, until I was seeing colors that weren't there, while Joph went inexorably onward. She could have been walking in a circle, for all I knew. She could have been leading me into Diane's open arms.

Or worst of all, I could have gone for Cox's gun and died, and this was my brain's last attempt to comfort me as I lay in a pool of blood and shattered bone. I shivered, my hand tightening on Joph's shoulder. Either way, I'd been ready to die to escape. I'd make them kill me before I let them take me again.

Joph suddenly ducked, and I went down with her. "The guards outside are coming in," she whispered. "They have dark vision, too. Move with me."

She began to crawl, and I followed, more confident now that I knew she had dark-vision lenses in her eyes to guide our way. There were shouts over the crowd, loud orders for everyone to freeze. But this panic wasn't so easy to stifle. Whoever was behind this rescue had planned it well.

Joph stopped and I kept going, prompting a pained noise as I stumbled over her legs.

"Are you…"

"I'm fine," she said breathily, and I remembered, again, the wound to her leg.

"Door's here. Once we're through we have to move fast. Okay? Go."

I went, stumbling after her through the door. It was just as dark in here, but much warmer, and I could feel walls on either side with my outstretched hands. A corridor of some sort.

Joph rustled, something snapped, and there was abruptly light glowing in her hands, a yellow sphere filled with fluid. She tossed it to me and grabbed another from the cleavage of her long dress. "Run."

Running was no problem. I'd wanted to run for months, and my new muscles stretched out into that familiar rhythm, relishing the smooth speed. Joph, on the other hand, was limping slightly, lurching to one side, and I felt a killing rage surge inside me again. They'd shot her; they'd killed children; they'd hurt Tegan and me; they'd—

"Here," she said, and banged through a door marked CAUTION: ALARM. I flinched instinctively, but no alarm went off.

We burst out into one of Melbourne's alleyways, complete with the collection of garbage, compost, and humanure bins that were stacked behind every commercial building. It was dark, and it was raining, a warm, soft drizzle that wouldn't do anything more than dampen the city's depleted dams. Except for the camps, it was the first time I'd been outside for six months, and I took one deep breath of unsanitized, uncooled, unapproved air.

Then I noticed the body lying by the door. It was very definitely a dead body, since it didn't have a head.

Joph saw it, too, and jumped.

In the chemiluminescent glow, I could see something black all over the cobbles, trickling into the gutter that had formed in the middle.

"He's dead," I said, very intelligently, and held the glowing sphere down lower. He was wearing a SADU uniform. "Is he a guard? Did you kill the guards?"

"No!"

"I hate them." I poked the body with my foot. "I think I'm glad he's dead."

"Don't do that." Joph clutched at me. "We have to go, Abdi. Come on!"

I straightened. Somewhere in the back of my head a voice

that sounded very much like my mother's was insisting that this would be a bad time to go into shock. "Where's Tegan?"

I heard screeching wheels, but whatever was responsible for the sound was out of range of our lights. I reached for Joph, meaning to pull her behind me, but she let out a relieved noise and went toward the vehicle. I followed, to see a large white van that looked like an ambulance. When I climbed in after Joph, I saw it was an ambulance: twin narrow float-beds, equipment, and all.

Tegan was lying motionless on one of those float-beds. Lat was holding her down, one hand planted in the middle of her back. His other hand held a knife.

Red fury flung me at him, my hand sweeping the blade away. I smashed him against the back of the driver's seat, prompting a yell—a driver, I should be wary of the driver—and then whirled to throw him against the ambulance wall itself. The vehicle rocked as I dug my thumbs into the hollow of his throat.

"Wait," Lat choked, his shark eyes wide. I squeezed harder, stopping his voice with his breath. I crushed him against the wall with my body when he kicked, then ducked to take an elbow strike on my forehead, not in the eye. My head rang with the impact and skin tore, spilling warm fluid down my face. But he was losing strength. He couldn't stop me now. No one could stop me now.

There was blood dripping over one eye, blood dribbling into my mouth as I gritted my teeth and locked my hands and shoved—

—and something cool and wet sprayed the base of my spine.

56

It traveled the length of my back in a tingling rush, and my limbs went weightless and limp, falling from Lat's neck. I crumpled, and he caught me, carrying me down to the ambulance floor.

"I'm on your side," he wheezed.

My mouth wouldn't work properly. "Ur sah..." I slurred. "Sah hur Teahn..."

Joph knelt by me, blinking the dark-vision lenses out of her eyes to reveal the concerned, warm brown underneath. There was a hypospray in her hand. "We have to get the implants out," she said. "Abdi, there wasn't time to explain."

I could see Tegan over her shoulder. She was motionless, too, but her eyes were open, blinking at me, and I could see her mouth working in the same lazy way mine was.

"Help me get him up," Lat said. His voice was raw and creaky, but he handled me with gentle strength as he and Joph got me laid out facedown on the other float-bed. "Ready, Carl," he told the driver, and the ambulance started to move.

Joph braced herself against the bed, microinjector dropping from her hand. "But the trackers—"

"We're out of time," Lat said, and scooped something up from the floor. It was the knife—a scalpel, really, bright and sharp. "We'll have to do it on the move. Hold him down."

Whatever Joph had stuck me with blocked pain as well. I felt the blade slice through my flesh, and nothing hurt at all.

CHAPTER SIX
Glissando

It was incredibly frustrating, traveling in the back of the ambulance with my brain whirring but my body limp. I wanted to be demanding answers or checking on Tegan, but neither of these were options. Joph's microinjector hadn't held a total muscle paralyzer, obviously—my heart was still beating and my lungs were pushing oxygen to my brain—but it had been remarkably effective at shutting down most of my motor functions.

"Ah-ee," Tegan said, blinking deliberately at me as Lat turned his scalpel on her. I blinked back, about all the conscious motion I could manage, and made myself watch as he cut. He made one precise slice, popping through the skin on the back of her neck. Blood welled up, and he traded the scalpel for a suction tube. Joph leaned in with a long device with a flat, round end.

She yelped as the ambulance swayed, sending her sprawling onto the float-bed. Tegan grunted at the impact, and Lat grabbed Joph's arm. "Steady."

"I'm trying!"

"We're right on the edge of the dead zone, Joph. We can't keep dodging around like this; they'll catch us."

"I know." Joph let out a deep breath and slid the device smoothly into the incision. She twisted her wrist slightly and pulled, and the implant was out, stuck on the end of her surgical probe.

It was so small for something that had caused us so much agony. Just a vaguely rectangular white blob of plastic and metal. Smeared with blood as it was, I couldn't see the thin wires that bristled around it. Those wires had spun themselves deep into our nervous systems, pushing their tiny tendrils everywhere. Joph must have cut all those connections when she pulled the implant out.

Even with the implant out, there were wires still inside me, clinging to my nerves like barbed wire wrapped around a fence. The thought made me sick, but I couldn't do anything about it. I watched as Lat took the suction tube away and bound the wound with autostitch and skin spray. The standard medium brown shade of the fake skin looked very dark against Tegan's skin; I knew from previous experience that it looked pale against mine. I was so dark that my mother had joked about losing me at night. But she'd lost me in the gray light of the Australian dawn when SADU had first taken us away; it was at night that I was taking the first steps back.

Lat climbed into the passenger seat beside the hidden driver while Joph sat cross-legged on the ambulance floor and took my limp hand. I rolled my eyes around to watch her.

"It's all right. Everything will make sense soon," she said, and gave me that peaceful smile. But her face was weary, and she was kneading her thigh with the heel of her free hand—a gesture that looked so unconscious as to be habitual. How often did her leg cause her pain?

My fingers twitched as I tried to return her comforting squeeze.

Joph looked sharply at me. "Did you just move?"

I concentrated fiercely on my fingers. There was no mistaking the motion that time, and Joph bit her lip. "Oh damn."

"Uh?"

"You're bigger than you used to be, and I didn't account for your increased muscle mass. I think the relaxant's wearing off."

"Ooh," I said emphatically.

"It's not good. It's an anesthetic as well, and if your metabolism's burning it up that quickly..." Joph stood up and began rummaging through the cabinets above my head. "Kelleritizene, Lebeaumitol..." Her hand went to her pocket, to a computer that wasn't there. She turned a look of dismay on me. "I should have checked for contraindications beforehand. I don't think I can give you any of these."

"Ih oh-kay." My tongue had gained enough control to make the k-sound, which I was inordinately pleased by.

"You have a bleeding hole in your neck!"

And Diane could never hurt me with that implant again. I didn't have enough muscle control back for a phrase like that, so I repeated, "Iss okay." The back of my neck was beginning to sting, but I felt great. Better than great. Tegan and I were out of that hellhole, I was reunited with a good friend, and Lat was sitting up front, not hovering over Tegan and infuriating me.

And best of all, I had realized this rescue meant people were moving. People had listened to Tegan's story and believed it, people had known better than to swallow the Australian government's lies and the blatant falseness of our feel-good performances.

There were sirens, out there in the night, wailing through the streets. Looking for us, or looking for trouble—I tensed automatically, realized I could, and realized a split second afterward that tensing really, really hurt. My head was aching from the adrenaline backwash and the blow Lat had landed on my skull. That cut over my eyebrow was stinging, and the implant-removal site felt worse than the second-degree burns I'd acquired in my first week in Australia. I hadn't believed that I needed to wear sunscreen— my skin had always been enough protection at home. I'd gone to Williamstown's artificial sandy beach without any covering and stayed there for hours, trying to re-create the feeling of the natural beaches of Djibouti. I'd gone back to my host father's house even more homesick, with a prickling sting on my bare scalp. Djibouti was much hotter, but the UV wasn't so terrible there.

My growing pain must have been obvious, because Joph dropped back down to take my hand. "I should have...they told me not to bring my computer in, but I should have looked it up beforehand. Abdi, I'm so sorry. Tell me if it gets too bad, and I'll try the Lebeaumitol anyway."

"Will do," I said, and then looked across at Tegan, who was still, thankfully, motionless. If muscle mass was the problem,

Joph's dose might have even been slightly too strong for her. "She knew," I said. It wasn't a question; I could put a puzzle together when all the pieces were there.

Lat was apparently on our side, and as soon as he'd turned up, Tegan had started playing nice with our captors. And then she'd gone on tour, where there must have been security holes that could be exploited, and a plan developed. She'd known rescue would come tonight.

Tegan must have nearly lost it when I'd balked at walking onto the stage. No wonder she'd looked so grateful to Lat, when he'd whispered those horrible things to make me move.

"She knew," Joph said. "She wanted to tell you. But we couldn't get word to you."

Tegan had started telling Diane when I disobeyed. She'd *adapted* because she had a plan, because she needed both of us in one specific place at a specific time for this rescue to work.

And she'd left me ignorant and in despair.

I wasn't sure how I felt about that. I could see the sense in it; though Lat was on her side, Diane wasn't on mine. When my captor played with her electronic toy, she could ask me anything, and I'd say whatever I thought she wanted to hear to make the agony stop. I could easily have betrayed the plan then; Tegan had kept quiet to get us both out.

I should probably forgive her silence.

But Diane's hands on me, her mouth against my ear, telling me exactly what she was going to do—

I wrenched my head away from the memories and took refuge in my body instead. I could no longer feel the eyebrow

62

cut; the neck wound had swallowed all my minor aches into its overwhelming mass, like a red giant star expanding and burning up the planets around it.

Someone was saying my name, over and over, and I blinked back to myself. Joph was kneeling by the bed. I was holding her hand so tightly my knuckles were pinkish-gray, but her voice was soft and reassuring.

"We have to change vehicles now," she said. "Can you stand up?"

I discovered I could, and with Joph holding my arm I could even walk, my feet dragging and my neck flaring with every step. There were lights on in this part of town. Tegan was limp in Lat's arms, and the previously unseen driver was opening the door of a dark blue four-seater. I thought that I should probably know who he was, this dark-skinned man with the red locks, but my brain was hazing out again, flashing white across my vision. There was a fumble of movement, and a long high-pitched noise, to my embarrassment, came out of my own mouth.

Then I was sitting down, and Joph asked me a question to which I couldn't respond, and the blessed cool spray of her microinjector hit my shoulder. I slid gratefully into the deep black of sleep.

Δ ∫ Ω

The tattered wisps of dreams clouded my vision, so that when I woke, for a moment I saw plain gray walls and furniture bolted to the floor and Diane's beautiful, horrible face—the only bright thing in that place—and her hands reaching out for me.

Then I woke up the rest of the way, jerking myself upright in the middle of a wooden bed that creaked in protest. I was in a well-lit, dusty room crammed with tarnished mirrors, faded pictures of old landscapes, tiny china people, and dozens of other things wedged onto tiny tables and shoved into shelves. My heart thrummed, but the pain in my neck and the strangeness of my surroundings were reassuring. I had not dreamed my rescue. Joph had come for me, and Tegan had escaped, too.

And Lat had helped us out. That was less pleasing, but I couldn't damp down the wild rush of joy. I *was* free. I could go home at last.

Back to the terra-cotta house with the fountain in the cool courtyard. Back to the yellow earth, and the tang of salt in the air, and the call to prayer five times a day. I'd never thought I'd miss the call to prayer. It was a reminder that I was different, that my classmates and siblings and mother would be talking to their God, while my father and I stayed silent. But that call—God is most great! God is most great!—that was part of home, too. Here, my atheism wasn't unusual. It was everything else that made me a freak, and when I went home, I'd be a freak no more.

I was still wearing the clothes I had worn to the fund-raiser, chrome vest and dark pants entirely out of place in this ancient room. The golden cord had tangled around my body as I slept. Remembering the way Diane's fingers had brushed my skin as she adjusted it, I tried to yank it away, but succeeded only in tugging the whole concoction down to one wrist. The knots were too tight to loosen with my teeth and one free hand; it would take a blade. The air was chill. I found the blanket from the floor and wrapped it around my shoulders, wondering when someone would come to let me out.

Ten or twelve minutes afterward—an embarrassingly long time—it occurred to me that the door might not be locked.

I had been imprisoned for six months. During that time, I had been escorted everywhere, to everything. The nights I had been unpunished, I had been left physically alone to sleep, but I was watched, always. I could carry out no task unless I was given specific orders or permission. I was told when to eat, to wash, to exercise, to rehearse, and to sleep.

And no doors opened to my hand. Trying to force one had resulted in Tegan's most severe punishment of all, and I'd never tried again.

I had not successfully opened a door since the morning they'd taken us away.

But I was safe now, I told myself. Or at least not in immediate danger. The implant was gone, and Diane was not here.

I wrapped the blanket tighter, padded to the door in my silver slippers, and paused, my hand an inch away from the doorknob.

This could all be an elaborate trap. A test of how well I had adapted, with Joph suborned, and Lat on Diane's side all along. And Tegan could be either an innocent dupe or a willing participant in the scenario. After all, what word had she said to me? She had been motionless the whole time. And what had I seen, really? Darkness, and an alley, and the inside of an ambulance that could have driven in circles. I had nothing but Joph's word to rest my hopes upon.

I trusted Joph, I did. I knew I was giving too much weight to baseless fears. But I had to put my left hand on the back of my right and force it to the knob. It turned, easily, soundlessly, and I flung the door back with as much violence as I could muster.

If Diane was waiting on the other side, ready to laugh at me, ready to reclaim me, I did not want to go to her hesitant and timid. I wanted to go fighting.

The door flashed out, rebounded off something set behind it, and slammed back again. I had gained the impression of a room as equally old-fashioned, with a small, rickety table and a small, dark-haired girl in a silver gown seated at it, face turning toward the door in fear and confusion.

I was through the door in the space between heartbeats, as she stood, one hand stretched toward me. I took it in mine.

And then, without speaking, we moved into the touch we'd been forbidden for so long. I wrapped my free arm around her, flattening my hand against the smooth skin between her shoulder blades. Her fingers slipped from mine so that her arms could go around my waist, burrowing under my blanket, thumbs tucking into the waistband under it. The top of her head tucked in under my chin, thick hair warm and soft against my bare throat. I stroked her arm.

That was when I knew we were free. Diane would never have allowed us that hug.

We stood there for a few moments, breathing together, silent in our embrace, and then Tegan muttered something against my chest.

I loosened my grip. "What was that?"

She tipped her head back. "I said, I can't believe you're wearing a blanket. It's, like, a zillion degrees."

I felt a smile tugging at my lips. "I'm cold," I said, as solemnly as possible. "You have thick blood. It's all that Welsh in you."

"What about the Italian part of me?"

"Must be northern Italian," I decided. "Up in the Alps. Practically Swiss."

Tegan laughed, that sudden bright explosion that was her true laugh. Not the mannered chime she'd developed for them.

I had thought I would never hear that genuine laugh again. I kissed her while the sound still spilled from her lips, as if I could share that joy with her if I caught it on her breath. She kissed me back, warm and teasing, and we broke apart to grin foolishly at each other, giddy.

I saw the shadow sweep across Tegan's eyes. "I'm sorry," she said. "I wanted to tell you, but…"

"I understand."

"But they did such awful things to you. They made me watch."

"Let's not talk about it," I said, and kissed her again.

She pulled away when we came up for air. "I really want to apologize for—"

"You're making it up to me," I assured her. I had the uneasy suspicion that I was lying. She'd left me ignorant and hurting, and a simple apology couldn't fix it—neither, I suspected, would her touch. But I wanted to touch Tegan so badly. I couldn't wait for her guilt to fade, nor my forgiveness to be real.

She didn't pull away again, and our kisses turned serious. It was as if we were locked under the Inheritors' compound again, that feeling of being the only two people in the world, with sight and sound gone, and touch the most important sense of all. The feel of Tegan's skin against mine, her hands demanding on my back, the taste of her mouth, the heated gasps of her breath as she kissed a wet line down my throat; that was all there was room for in my head. Her presence crushed the nightmares and the fear and memories of Diane's hands into a tiny white spark, small and unimportant.

I lifted her onto the table without thinking about it, my blanket sliding away. She tugged me in with her heels in the small of my back, her fingers fumbling at the fastenings of my vest as she crushed her mouth against mine. I wanted to touch her, but all that smooth silver fabric frustrated my efforts, slipping against my palms. I found the zipper at the side and tugged it down, my hands greedy for more of her, all of her—

"We eat off that table," someone observed neutrally, and we leaped away from each other as if we'd been electrocuted.

It was the mysterious dark-skinned, red-haired driver—not so mysterious now, when I wasn't shocked and hurting. I knew him.

Carl Hurfest was the only reporter Tegan had known well enough to go to for help when she'd wanted to tell her story. That didn't mean she liked him. Hurfest had a reputation for being incorruptible and unafraid to ask the hard questions, and he'd asked Tegan the hard questions twice—once, just after she'd first ventured into her new world, and again shortly afterward, at a prepared interview the army had set up for her.

I'd watched that interview. She'd melted down on camera,

but not before I saw her, incandescent with rage, alive with passion as she told Australians to wake up.

"You are not the future I wanted," she'd said. "I wanted you to be better. Be better!"

And I'd thought, reluctantly, *I really like that girl.*

And I hadn't liked the reporter who had baited her into this frenzy.

But the third time Hurfest and Tegan had met, he'd helped her tell her story to the world. She still hadn't trusted him. Neither did I.

"Hello, Hurfest," I said, and stood in front of Tegan while she put her dress back together. She was flushing bright red. "Couldn't you knock or cough or something?"

Hurfest shrugged. "I did both, several times. You were busy. Lat went upstairs after my first attempt to interrupt you, but he's more of a gentleman than I am."

I found a certain satisfaction in the thought that Lat had seen Tegan kiss and touch me, but Tegan's blush only deepened. Which was less satisfying.

"I'm sorry to interrupt," he said, and he sounded sorry, or at least like someone making a sincere attempt to sound sorry. "But we need to fill you in on the situation. The information Tegan was privy to was necessarily limited, and I imagine you have plenty of questions, Abdi."

Still keeping Tegan shielded from him, I nodded. I had all the questions in the world. Starting with, where the hell were we?

CHAPTER SEVEN
Chorus

We were underground.

Joph's great-great-aunt, Celia Davies, had been famously eccentric and fabulously wealthy, both traits her descendant had inherited. The complex was on family land, and it had been dug out decades ago, when things had been heating up between China and Japan. Miss Davies had decided to provide a secret haven for her enormous extended family, just in case one was needed. So she'd hired various contractors, paid in cash, and quietly constructed a massive rabbit warren under the old stone cottage that had been her childhood vacation home in Bendigo, about two hours from Melbourne.

"All off the books and untraceable," Hurfest said, leading us through the corridors. We passed a few strangers as we went, people who looked at Tegan and me with concern, or pride, or something that looked startlingly like awe. I automatically smiled at them until I realized I didn't have to. "Celia Davies was really something. And when China and Japan didn't go to war and Australia didn't get pulled into it, most of Joph's family forgot it was here. It was used for storage sometimes, which is why we have all this junky furniture. But it doesn't officially exist."

"Who are these people?" Tegan asked as a bright-haired man pushed himself thin against the wall so we could pass unimpeded.

"Key members of the Save Tegan movement," he said easily. "You really made an impression, Teeg." He smiled at her. She didn't return the smile, and he hesitated a bare moment before resuming the lead.

I'd seen at least nine unfamiliar people, which was interesting, all of whom had been armed, which was even more so. I considered the headless SADU guard I'd seen on our escape route and watched Carl Hurfest's back. His shoulders were set back, his steps sure. And the people in the halls looked at him with respect.

The Hurfest I'd known hadn't been liked, but he'd been respected, especially by political liberals like the ones in Bethari's clique. Famously, Hurfest told the truth, and on a few occasions, he'd told it at some personal risk. There were whispers that he'd managed to outface government threats to confiscate his media license by threatening to go public with every unsubstantiated rumor he'd picked up in twenty years of political reporting. The substantiated rumors, of course, he'd already told.

For no real reason, I'd assumed Lat was in charge of the Save Tegan movement. The evidence indicated I'd assumed wrong.

And Hurfest wanted us for something—or at least he wanted Tegan, or he wouldn't be making such an effort to be nice to her.

My poltical instincts were prickling into life. *Observe*, I thought, emembering my mother's lessons. *Consider.*

What did Hurfest want? Power, probably—after a couple of decdes of political reporting, maybe he wanted to get in on the gme, instead of just talking about it. But there were much safe ways he could become politically powerful; he could have leraged Tegan's story into the government's narrative and rde himself complicit with their lies. Instead, he'd chosen this derground lair and a call to action. That meant something. It would be foolish to trust him completely, but his motives were probably genuine. Hurfest really did think that Cox's government was bad for Australia and that the human-rights abuses it had engineered couldn't be allowed to go on.

It was comforting how smoothly my brain clicked back into motion. SADU had hurt me, made me weak. But they hadn't gotten to all of me.

We hit the end of the corridor and started up a flight of stairs. The girl coming down didn't flatten herself against the wall. She took one look at us and bounded down the steps past Hurfest, her purple headscarf and long gold dress rippling with the speed of her passage.

"Tegan!" she squealed as she launched herself into Tegan's arms.

Tegan staggered under the impact, but her grip was sure. "Bethari! I've missed you so much!"

"You too!" She looked over Tegan's shoulder and caught my

eye, her teeth sparkling in a wide crescent under her long nose. "Abdi, this is so great!"

"It's nice to see you, too," I said, not at all sure about that. Bethari Miyahputri was Tegan's best friend and Joph's ex-girlfriend. She was a journalist, a hacker, a cheerleader, and a steadfast enabler of Tegan's more dangerous ideas. I was happy she hadn't been imprisoned or hurt after our encounter with the guards in that cryostorage facility, but I didn't really want to spend time with her.

Bethari was so earnest it almost hurt to have her around. She was a political idealist—like Tegan, like me—but she seemed to have absolute certainty in the righteousness of her causes, which was both enviable and suspicious. She 'casted long diatribes against the ills of society and told every newcomer to our school to be nice to me.

Bethari Miyahputri was probably a good person, but she was so *loud* about it.

She was focusing back on Tegan, who was still leaning against her. "Are you okay? Stupid question. How are you feeling?"

"Better," Tegan said, laughing. She pulled back, and I saw the tears she dashed away. "So much better, thanks to you."

Bethari's joyous expression abruptly snapped into something harder. She twisted to glare at Hurfest. "Speaking of that—"

"Not here," he said firmly. "Abdi and Tegan need to be briefed." He tilted his head at the hall, a clear dismissal.

Bethari's face twitched, but Tegan tucked her arm into

Bethari's and began blithely walking back up the stairs, making jokes about her dress. I grinned. Clearly, the Tegan who was happy to challenge the illusions of the powerful was still in there. Bethari played along, smiling slightly as Hurfest gave in with a huff.

I brought up the rear, wishing Hurfest hadn't seen me kissing Tegan in that living room. It gave him a handle on me I wasn't sure I wanted him to have.

I probably needed to work out how I felt about Tegan before we did that again. There was something between us, but there was also betrayal and pain. I remembered the perfect puppet face she'd turned to the world, and my anger trembled in my limbs. Rescue had been coming, and she hadn't told me. I'd been drowning, hopeless and hurting, and she'd known. I'd been desperately lonely, left without support, and she'd had an ally. I'd been ready to die to make it stop.

I understand, I'd said, but I didn't.

But I understood the softness of her skin, the sure way in which she'd pulled me closer to her, the ease with which I'd been able to put everything but touch aside. She wouldn't like it if I told her, but Tegan was good at becoming the center of everything, without even trying. The center of attention, the center of a publicity campaign, the center of a movement.

It would be so easy to let her be my center, too.

But if I did that, I might finally lose myself.

CHAPTER EIGHT
Fugue

Tegan exhaled when we emerged from a trapdoor built into a stone floor. "Daylight," she said, pointing to a window.

Thick drapes were drawn across it, but a ribbon of pale light traced the window's edges.

"I thought you liked being underground," Bethari teased. "All that urban exploration you used to do with your best friend, crawling through drains and tunnels."

"Alex liked the tunnels," Tegan said. "I went with her, but I was more into abandoned buildings. Better opportunities for trying out free-running tricks."

"Well, don't try them here," Hurfest said, with a tone that was striving hard to be jovial. "We're trying to keep this place looking abandoned."

"Good job," Tegan told him, and I silently agreed. This was another living room, as dusty and crammed as the bedroom I'd woken in. It was filled with tables and glass-fronted cabinets packed with trinkets and photographs. Faded cotton sheets had been draped over most of the furniture, which looked ancient, and was probably riddled with pests. Certainly there were no spine correctors or memory fabric to shift under your weight to the most comfortable position. When I sat in the chair Hurfest nodded to, I feared that I might fall straight through.

Lat appeared in the doorway, Joph behind him. "All clear," he said. "The flier patrols flew a general pattern over the area, but I think Diane must have taken my bait. She'll be looking toward the northern routes."

"Is Marie here?" Tegan asked.

He smiled at her, and I bristled. "Soon. I just got word that her rescue was successful."

Tegan dropped into the middle of an old couch, which creaked precipitously, and Bethari curled in beside her. Joph took the other side, the three girls sandwiched together there. They all looked so different—Joph's light brown coloring, Tegan's sharp contrast of pale skin and dark hair, the richer hues of Bethari's darker skin. But they all had the same expression of relief and joy.

Dr. Marie Carmen had been captured before we had been, and she was then used as bait to draw Tegan into SADU clutches. I'd never met the woman who'd performed the first successful revival procedure and then taken the subject of that process into her home, but Tegan's foster mother had been such a strong presence in her story that I felt as if I had.

"That's great news," I said, meaning it. Even if Lat had been the one who brought it.

"How many fliers?" Hurfest asked.

"Every one Diane could requisition, I imagine," Lat said. "Which will be several hundred."

Bethari looked as appalled as I felt, but, of course, it was for a different reason. "All that fuel," she protested.

Lat's voice was patient to the point of being patronizing. "They really won't care about the fuel. The president wants Tegan back."

"I'm not going back," she said flatly. "I'd rather die."

I'd thought the same thing. But it was an unpleasant shock to hear it from Tegan, who had, after all, had it easier with Lat. Perhaps I'd better keep the desperation of my final moments in SADU hands to myself. Or Joph. I could tell Joph. "How did you get us out?" I asked, followed by the more important question: "And why?"

Lat and Hurfest exchanged a look. It was a look that said, as the only two adults in the room, they were privy to information that they might or might not dole out to the children. Tegan saw it, too, her eyes narrowing in response.

"As soon as I was assigned to Tegan, a number of opportunities were made available," Lat said. "Having chosen to undertake a dual rescue, the mission plan with the greatest chance of success depended on a nighttime public event with sufficient attendants to provide confusion and panic as a cover, and an operator who could both be permitted to approach Abdi and who Abdi would follow when instructed to do so."

"A triple rescue," Tegan said.

Lat squinted at her.

"You said 'dual'. You rescued Marie as well."

"Dr. Carmen's escape was considered a separate mission," Lat told her. "It was the dual rescue that required the most planning."

No doubt it would have been far easier for Lat to get Tegan out alone. He must have had dozens of opportunities on tour. I had been the problem.

"As it was, public events that satisfied the mission parameters were plentiful. It was likely operators on the ground were thin." He nodded at Joph.

"I got my mum to take me to the party," Joph said. "She's not part of the rescue; she wanted to prove to me that you two were fine. She's a Victorian MP; just a backbencher, but part of the government. She really wanted to believe that you were mistaken. She wants to believe that government is good."

"Depends on the government," I said, thinking of my own mother.

Hurfest snorted.

Joph ignored him and continued. "I had to pester her. Eventually I told her that if she showed me you were both fine, I'd go to whatever chem-research program she chose for me. She told me about that party only yesterday, so we had to scramble."

"Fortunately, contingent on that one point, everything had been planned in tedious detail," Hurfest added. "It wasn't all that difficult to make it work. I stayed outside the dead-zone perimeter in the ambulance, waiting for the lights to go out—"

"How did that work?" Tegan asked.

"That was me," Bethari said. Her voice was very flat, and

she'd looked progressively less happy as the story had gone on. Now she raised her head and stared at Hurfest, a challenge in her gaze.

"It was my decision," he said, sounding oddly kind. "Don't blame yourself."

"I don't," she said immediately, but I caught the inflection change, the shiver at the edge of her eyelids. That was a lie. Whatever had happened, she did blame herself.

"What did you do?" I asked. I was trying to make my voice gentle, but there was dread curling in my stomach. All the lights had gone out, and we'd driven in the dark for such a long time.

Bethari took a deep breath. "I thought we needed leverage. I thought, if we were going to scare the army into letting you go, we had to have something that was actually scary. So I went looking through various places and hunted on some forums and got in touch with some people."

Bethari was a hacker. I automatically translated this as "slid into secret databases and stole classified information" and "talked to criminals about their illegal discoveries."

"Eventually I got my hands on some half-finished plans for a...well, call it an EMP generator. It's not, actually, but it has the same effect. Flip the switch, and it creates an electronic dead zone. Everything in that zone stops working."

"Half-finished?" Tegan asked. "I didn't know you were an engineer, too, Bethi."

"I'm not. I had a lot of help." She glanced at Hurfest.

"I put Bethari in touch with some people who I thought could assist," he said smoothly. "Every time we came across a problem, she was able to crowdsource solutions from her contacts on the tubes—no one person had the complete solution, but by putting together the disparate parts, Bethari got the design for the whole. It was very efficient, really."

It sounded like a good thing. In one blow, they'd knocked out all the technology Diane and her team used to control and keep track of us. At the same time, it had caused enough confusion to make escape viable.

But I still had that feeling of dread. "How big was the dead zone?" I asked.

Hurfest winced. "Twelve kilometers diameter—centered on the event hall, just beside Parliament House."

A hundred years ago, Tegan had died on the steps of Parliament House, hit by a sniper who'd been aiming for the Prime Minister. That reminder flickered across her face, then vanished. Another legacy of our imprisonment; before we'd been taken, Tegan had been very bad at swallowing or concealing her emotions.

"It wasn't supposed to be that big," Bethari said. Her cheeks were flushed, and her eyes were very bright. She kept them fixed on Hurfest. "I wanted to make a smaller, more focused version. The big one was only supposed to be a threat, to show them that we could do it if we wanted to. To make them hand you over peacefully."

"What am I missing?" Tegan asked. "There was a blackout; we got out.... What's the problem?"

Bethari bit her lip. "It wasn't just a blackout," she said. "An EMP doesn't just cut power to machines; it overloads them. A lot of things that were in the dead zone just aren't going to work anymore."

"Like what?"

"Like…" Bethari pulled her hands apart, conveying with that gesture a vast, empty space. "Like everything. Everything that was powered on when the EMP went off just stopped."

My mouth went dry. Almost everything had at least residual power flow, even in standby mode. If the EMP had truly taken out everything, the consequences would be massive.

No electric motors meant no lights, no air-conditioning, no food storage. The entire transport system inside the dead zone would be in chaos: Cars wouldn't start, the safe-transport net that warded against accidents would be down, and the city's trams and trains would have halted, bringing most of the population to a standstill. If the pulse had fried every personal computer in the zone, that meant no digital entertainment or information—not a real problem in itself. But as I knew from my confinement, the loss of a personal computer would be deeply disorienting to people who had used them before they could walk. More important, personal computers used solar batteries. If it had been an ordinary blackout, the computers would have kept going even when the mains went out. But the EMP had fried their circuits. People would have realized that something was very wrong. That explained the panic in the event hall.

That fear and confusion meant that all the people who would ordinarily be trying to find us now had much bigger problems on their hands. The police would have been trying to restore order with only antique equipment like battery-powered flashlights at their disposal. The armed forces would be wondering if this was the preface to an invasion or major attack and be scrambling accordingly, and the state government, based in the central city, would be unable to assist as all their records and communication networks had abruptly disappeared. True, as soon as new equipment could be brought into the dead zone, officials would be able to function again. But while we'd escaped, they'd been in the dark.

My stomach clenched. Enthusiastic, cheerleading Bethari had built the Save Tegan movement a weapon that was tailor-made for targeting a civilian population.

She'd meant it to be a threat only; I had no trouble believing in her intentions. But they'd used it.

Hurfest shifted, his face hard and defensive. "We had to get you out," he said. "We were running out of time. Lat was worried that if we waited much longer there wouldn't be much left of you to rescue. Bethari was doing her best to get the more focused version ready in time, but we just couldn't delay any longer."

I remembered how very nearly I'd come to suicide by bodyguard, bare seconds before my escape. He was right. But he was wrong, too. "Fires," I said. "I heard sirens while we drove. Were there fires when the grids overloaded?"

"Probably," Hurfest said. "That's what the fire engines are for, though. They would have come from outside."

"How would they know where to go, with no one able to call? And...how many hospitals were in the dead zone?"

"Two," Bethari said, squeezing her eyes shut.

Hurfest rubbed the bridge of his nose. "They both have emergency generators; it's standard equipment." .

"But their medical equipment wouldn't have worked," I said. I was so horrified that I had to force the words through my stiff jaw. "The generators would have fired up, but everything that was turned on, everything monitoring patient health or regulating drug administration or keeping them alive wouldn't have worked. My brother's a medical technician; you think I don't know these things?"

Lat held up his hands for peace. "Maybe in your country that would happen. In Australia, the most vital equipment generally has safeguards and there are a number of backup equipment options—"

"Nobody has backup for every life-support system, even in your country," I cut in. "When you flicked that switch, Lat, you killed people."

"Innocent people," Tegan said, her eyes dark with anger. "I wouldn't have agreed to that, Lat. You know I wouldn't!"

Bethari was silent beside her, hands folded tightly against her stomach.

"Now, hold on a second here," Lat said, striving and failing for calm. "I gave up SADU, my career, my family. Tegan, I gave up everything for you."

Hurfest's voice was equally heated. "You have no idea of the risks we've taken, of what they'll do to us if—"

"Oh, I think I do," I said, my hand going automatically to my neck. "And that all sounds very noble. But what you're really saying is that you devastated a huge chunk of a city in order to

83

rescue two teenagers. You're saying that to save Tegan and me, you condemned an unknown number of innocents."

"Casualty estimates were gauged—"

"Who killed the guard, Lat? Joph and I nearly tripped on a body coming out of the hall."

Tegan turned on him, her mouth opening.

"A SADU guard, Tegan," Lat said, before she could speak. "I'm not going to apologize for shooting someone who would have killed all of us if he'd had the chance. And I don't believe you'd cry for him, either, Abdi."

Well, that was true. I was no longer glad he'd died; that had been the shock and anger. But I wasn't sorry he was dead.

"You made me a murderer," Bethari said. There were tears leaking from her tightly closed eyes. "I told you I could make it smaller. I told you twelve kilometers was too much. I didn't even know what had happened until Joph found me here."

Lat sighed. "A smaller version wouldn't have worked, even if there'd been time to make it. We needed sufficient confusion to cover the escape. Bethari, believe me. You saved your friends. Without you, things could never have gone so well."

Tegan's eyes were narrow. "Bethari's right, Lat. Sick people in hospitals aren't acceptable casualties!"

"Tegan," he said, and leaned forward to catch both her hands in his. She went still and I had to fight to keep from snarling. "Trust me, Tegan. We had to get you out. People need you. You're very, very important."

"I'm not saying Tegan's not important," Bethari said shakily, wiping at her face. "I'm just saying—"

"We understand," Hurfest said. "Believe me, it was a hard decision to make. But there was no other way." He sounded so certain.

Abruptly, I couldn't cope any longer. It was so *typical*. People decided that what they wanted overwhelmed the needs of others, that whom they hurt along the way didn't matter. And then when we told them they were wrong, we were dismissed, patronized, and ignored.

"Explain that to the dead," I said, and surged to my feet.

Lat got between me and the door, and my prisoner's training kicked in again. I shied away from him. You couldn't strike a handler: That was *bad*; I'd be *punished*.

Then I remembered where I was, and who I was, and balled my fist.

"Move," I said.

"It's not wise to go ou—"

"Is this how it's going to be?" I asked, directing the question at Hurfest. "You save me from one prison and put me in another?"

Hurfest's eyes slid from me to Tegan and back again. "Of course not," he said smoothly, and jerked his head. Lat stepped out of my way, and I checked his shoulder with mine as I went past. He actually staggered, and I felt the impact with a flush of satisfaction that radiated through my belly.

Behind me, Tegan was shouting at Hurfest. It would be almost worth staying in the room just to witness that battle, but I couldn't stand being trapped anymore. I was moving through a narrow, dusty hall, past a tiny kitchen, and out the back door, bursting onto a gravel path that wound through an overgrown garden.

The sun stood overhead in the pitiless sky.

People died because of you, I thought, and had to swallow back my bile. I wanted to vomit out the horror of that thought, but I couldn't get rid of the knowledge so easily. It had happened—without my knowledge, without my consent, but it had happened for me. So that Tegan and I could be free.

If they had told me, if I had known that my escape would come at this cost, I wasn't sure what I would have done. Would I have been able to refuse this plan, tell them to find another or else leave us there?

I think I would have escaped anyway, I realized, and then my stomach gave in, and I really was sick all over a clump of dry weeds.

I felt better afterward, as if I'd purged myself of some poison. It wasn't as if the situation itself had changed, but I'd confronted the worst about myself and found I could survive it if I had to.

I heard light footsteps crunching on the stones behind me. I turned, expecting Tegan had come to argue with me or cry with me or hold me, but it was Joph. She had my discarded blanket in one hand and a computer in the other. Her soft brown eyes were sympathetic.

"How's your neck?" she asked.

"Fine. Sore, but not too painful."

She nodded and handed me the blanket. I tucked it around my shoulders to be polite, but it was actually much warmer outside. From here, I could see the house was constructed out of uneven lumps of stone. The roof was corrugated tin, flaky green in places, rust brown in others.

The garden was dry. There was what could have been a vegetable patch to one side of the gravel path, and a riot of flashy daisies to the other, their colors even brighter in the unforgiving sunlight. The path itself led to a shed, also made of stone and tin. There were vehicles in there, casually covered with old tarpaulins; presumably the one that had brought us here was one of them. There had been living trees encircling the place once, but now they were dead wood, held upright by the tangles of their desiccated roots.

Djibouti didn't have a lot of greenery. Forests didn't comfort me the way I knew they did Joph; green growing things made me think of slime, of mold cultures grown in gel solutions in my biological-sciences studies. But even I could tell this place wasn't meant to be so barren. There should have been more flowers than just the daisies, colorful survivors that they were. The trees should be rich with summer growth, not bare as dead bone. But trees needed water, and there wasn't enough to go around—for them or for us.

I caught an odd movement and frowned at one of the skeleton trees. After a second, the picture resolved into a woman holding a long rifle and lying across a knobby branch as casually as she might recline upon a sofa. She nodded at me, then returned to sweeping the horizon with her eyes.

I turned back to Joph. "What do people do out here?" I asked.

"Not much, now. Used to be a lot of farming, but the Murray and Murrumbidgee dried up, and most of the new farms are closer to Melbourne, where the transport costs aren't as high. Some people still farm out here, but most sold up and moved, or just moved if they couldn't find anyone to buy. The bush is taking over again. The native scrub can do better without much water—though even some of those plants are struggling." Joph quirked her lips. "Did you really want to talk about horticulture?"

"No."

She waited.

"How's Tegan?"

"Furious. Shouting at Hurfest, demanding to know all the details. It's Bethari I'm worried about."

"Why?" I said, unwisely.

Joph looked reproving. "She's really upset, Abdi. She kept telling them they didn't have the range tight enough yet, and they used it anyway. Bethari's being quiet and sad. It's not like her."

Well, what had Bethari *thought* would happen when she built a weapon like a strong EMP generator? I had enough sense not to ask Joph that, though.

"Did *you* know they were going to use the EMP?" I asked.

Joph jolted, looking straight at me for the first time. "Of course not. I wasn't staying here, you know, until now. When they gave me the okay, I thought Bethari must have gotten the kinks out of that smaller version she wanted to make." She grimaced. "I didn't realize what we'd done until we were halfway out of the dead zone."

"They'd," I said.

"Hm?"

"You said 'what we'd done.' They did it. Not you."

Joph looked over the dying grass. "Pretty to think so." She handed me the computer. "I thought you might like to catch up on what you missed. Don't worry. It doesn't auto connect; it's more like a storage computer. Bethari modified them for us."

"Why is she even here?" I asked, and immediately regretted it. Sure, you didn't need to keep your hacker in the same place as your top secret hiding spot, but only my mother could deliver a disappointed look like Joph.

"She couldn't go home," Joph said briefly. "She couldn't go anywhere. Her mother bailed her out of police custody, gave her all the cash she could scrape up in a hurry, and told her to get out and keep her head down. Bethari was the first one I told about this place, the first one who started working on ways to get you and Tegan free. She knew that you and Tegan would never be saying those things about the camps if you weren't being forced to. She started putting the plans together herself, but she couldn't get all the components she needed, and she didn't have the mechanical skills to put it together. That's why she went to Hurfest for help."

I grimaced. "Poor choice in friends."

"A journalist like him has sources everywhere," Joph said patiently. "He has fingers in a lot of pies. And he did help you that first time, don't forget. Bethari thought she might be able to trust him to help again. There's no way she could have anticipated his taking over like this."

"I suppose not," I said reluctantly.

"You suppose right. I don't know why you don't like her, Abdi, but you need to know you can trust her. She'd been kicked out of her home and her very first thought was wondering how she could help *you*."

I suspected that Bethari's first thought had been wondering how she could help *Tegan*, but I took Joph's point. "I trust her," I said, and I wasn't lying. Bethari's heart was in the right place. It was her mouth I had problems with. I unfolded the computer and snapped it rigid. "So what's on this?"

"Whatever I could grab," she said. "Some news, some music. The rest of that K-drama you like."

"*Double Trouble*," I said instantly, feeling only slightly ashamed. Comedy-dramas from Korea were a guilty pleasure, and one I'd managed to keep from my parents and siblings. My mother would think it was frivolous, to be so invested in silly plot devices and ridiculous coincidences, and my sisters would tease me for liking romances.

But Joph understood. She patted my shoulder. "There's also a lot of 'casts about you and Tegan." She pointed at a wooden bench settled into the gravel. "I thought you might like to see."

I wanted to say, "Screw that stuff," and settle down to find out if Jee Sun and Kyu Hwang had finally told each other their various secrets and actually kissed (as opposed to the three times they'd accidentally kissed by falling on top of each other, being pushed together by raucous fans, or both diving for the last dumpling), but I knew where my responsibility lay.

People died because of you, I thought again, and sat down heavily on the bench. The wood was warm beneath my thighs, a small comfort as I opened the archive marked *Ark Project*.

It was almost worse to see it from the outside. Tegan and

I marched around, smiling and opening our mouths, and the words of our handlers flowed out. Lighting and costuming and makeup conspired to make us look beautiful; we looked fine as we were, but this kind of beauty was beyond reality. I watched myself enthusiastically shill for the Ark Project in dozens of short 'casts, sliced in with footage of earnest engineers and scientists explaining how the Ark Project worked and how the *Resolution* would sail among the stars to its new destination. There were three distant solar systems with good candidates for the colony, and people were encouraged to vote for their favorite.

Several of the richest donors had already had themselves frozen, and this was trumpeted as proof of their commitment and dedication. I thought of Ruby Simons, who had gone gladly to her unwrinkled sleep. She was planning to wake on a world ready-made for her, as if this one wasn't enough.

While some interviewers asked harder questions, most of the footage was positive, objections brushed away with, "We'll have to look into that more closely as the time nears." But the time was nearing, and not just for Australia.

China had announced its own starship-construction project. Korea and South Africa were planning a joint project, with space for colonists from Indonesia and Brazil available in return for resources. But the *Resolution* was the starship closest to completion—one more year of scheduled construction, maybe less. The *Resolution* was what the world was watching. And Tegan and I were its ambassadors.

The next file opened with a shot of President Nathan Cox

sandwiched between Tegan and me. He looked paternal, and Tegan was giving him her brightest smile. I was nodding solemnly, as if I'd just been given some important advice and was letting it sink in.

I couldn't remember when that footage had been taken. It must have been one of the days I'd lost to pain.

When Cox spoke, he sounded mellow and rich; he had a soothing voice you wanted to take care of you. It was a long speech, by 'cast standards, appealing to donors. The conclusion was the only part that touched upon the people I was concerned about. "But this isn't just an opportunity for our wealthiest citizens," he said. "The poorest people from the most wretched places of the world are also leaping to the stars."

And in the video, I smiled and nodded along.

My skin buzzed with the urge to throw the computer from me. *Wretched places.*

The footage of the refugees was sickening. They were lining up to volunteer for the Ark Project, waving at the bumblecams. They were short, tall, dark, light, black-haired, and platinum blond, and everything in between. But they were all thin, all hungry. And they smiled at the cameras, too.

Hands trembling, I turned the computer off.

Joph had wandered into the garden to poke at things with a stick. She looked up when the noise ceased.

"How can this be happening?" I asked. I knew why, but I wanted someone else to say it.

"Because people are selfish," Joph said. "And because... they're like my mum. I love her, but she wants to believe so badly that everything is okay that she's convinced herself it is. And if it's not, if the world's oceans are really failing, if humanity really has no future on Earth, they want to believe that there's an escape clause. They've decided this is it."

I waved my hand at the dry garden, which might never bloom again. "An escape clause to the end of the world."

"Or the end of the species. Geologically, the world will be fine."

I snorted. "You say that calmly."

"I'm a scientist. I can take a longer view." She sat on the bench beside me, tucking her legs up under her.

I rested the computer on my knee. "I'm surprised there isn't any footage of us singing."

"None exists. They're very careful about that. You only get to see the famous Abdi Taalib sing at the fund-raising dinners, and pay dearly for the privilege." Joph hesitated, a very obvious pause.

"What is it?"

"Your mother resigned."

I stared at her. "She...what?"

"The opposition parties put a lot of pressure on the president of Djibouti. You know the kind of thing: 'How can we know Madame Taalib didn't conspire with her son, endangering Djibouti's relationship with Australia—'"

"What relationship with Australia?"

"Well, with firster countries in general. I don't know. I don't speak Arabic, and not all of it is easy to access from here. The media monitors have quietly cut down on a lot of international feeds. But I get the feeling your mother jumped from the party before she was pushed."

"When did this happen?"

"About four months ago."

"But she and my father have been talking to me every week. They never said a thing."

Joph nodded. "That makes sense. Because as long as you never asked about it, they knew that you didn't have free access to information, whatever the project personnel said."

I thought back to those carefully cheerful conversations: them asking how I was, me following the script to convince them I was fine and working for the project of my own free will, knowing that Tegan would pay if I wasn't convincing enough. My father's light eyes had been tense sometimes, but my mother had been serene always. She had a perfect politician's face, one that would never show anything without her permission.

She'd trained me to wear the same face. I wasn't as good at it as she was, but it had helped me survive while I was in SADU hands.

And behind that face, she'd hidden the destruction of all her ambitions. She'd been one of the president's best ministers, helping to balance the allocation of power between Issa Somali and Afar interests at home, slated as a likely Somali candidate when Abdullah Haid, the popular Afar president, stepped down. By now she should be planning how she would help lead Djibouti. Instead she'd had to toss her career into the trash. Because of me.

"Hey," Joph said, and put her hand on my shoulder. Her long fingers were warm. "People make their own choices."

Guilt was sour on my tongue. "I forced her into this one."

"Her opponents did."

"Because of me. Because of what I did, thinking that I could help people. I got you to make those medicines. I knew Hooyo wouldn't like that; I was supposed to be here making contacts, not curing disease. I had no business breaking the law; I knew that would reflect badly on her. I should have thought about the consequences more."

"You saved lives."

"*You* made the medicine, Joph. You saved lives. I was just the conduit."

"I wouldn't have done it without you," she said. "And without your help, Tegan would never have gotten her story out. Without you, Tegan would be *dead*."

I couldn't say I regretted that.

"I could have found another way," I said instead. "I owe my mother everything, and now I've cost her everything, too."

Joph shook her head. "You're her son, and she loves you. From everything you've told me about her, I can't see her blaming you for a second."

I couldn't argue with that, but I wanted to. "Why does Lat think Tegan's so important?" I asked instead. It came out wrong, but she knew what I meant.

"Because she is. I mean...to us, of course, but also to the campaign. Do you remember how people were trying to help you while Tegan told her story?"

I did. It had been a surreal experience; Tegan talking and talking to what became nearly two billion people from every part of the world, and me sitting just out of camera view as the messages came in. Hundreds of thousands of them, moving far too fast for me to follow. People had gathered outside the starship base in Tasmania; they'd hacked government records to find the location of the other frozen-refugee facilities; they'd gathered money for legal fees and put together a dozen nodes campaigning to have Tegan freed—and this before she'd been arrested.

"Save Tegan," I said, remembering. "It started even before we were caught."

"Yeah. Except now it's more like three campaigns in one." Joph was rubbing at her thigh again. "There are the people who started it, the people who think that telling the truth about what Tegan found and what's happened to her afterward is the most important thing. They've been putting up posters—hard copy—and using graffiti to get the message out. Raising awareness, the same way Tegan would have in her time."

"That's..." *pointless*, I thought. A foolish stunt. "Retro."

Joph heard what I didn't say and looked rueful. "We didn't want to speak for Tegan, you know? That would be wrong. But we were using her name, and without her to tell us what she wanted, we were kind of stuck. Then there are the politicals, who want Tegan to speak for *them* and who have their own ideas about what needs to happen. They're pushing for governmental change. Tegan's sort of a symbol to them, of the things that need to be improved. They want to place a halt on the Ark Project until it's been more fully investigated. Make the camps better; more food, better accommodations, introduce proper schools and work. Relax some of the strictures on the No Migrant policy, so that if you marry an Australian, you can apply for residency. That kind of thing."

"Not close the camps altogether? Not give the current refugees citizenship or legal residency?"

Joph's voice was a singsong. "Australia's resources are limited! Australians have a right to an ethical government, but its first priority must always be the welfare of its own people!"

"Bring in the new boss, same as the old boss."

"I think they would be better than what we have currently, but not ideal. Those are the people behind Carl. He doesn't think just telling the truth will help; Tegan did that already and look what it got her."

I snorted. "The incorruptible Carl Hurfest. Who would have guessed he just wanted power?"

"I don't think he'd turn power down," Joph conceded, "but he means it, you know. He thinks things can be better, and he thinks that if he were in charge, he could make it that way."

"You're so nice," I said. "Always thinking the best of people."

She shrugged, looking embarrassed. "Well. Anyway, Hurfest is also backed by the third, more...intense faction. They think we're already at war with an illegal government that lied to its people."

"Lat's faction," I said. It wasn't a guess.

"Well, he joined them, I think. But he really believes in Tegan. To most of them, Tegan's...not exactly a martyr. The first casualty, maybe. A fallen comrade who could be a convenient figurehead."

"She wasn't the first casualty," I said, thinking of those dead children in cryocontainers.

Joph was silent, and I knew she was seeing the same thing.

What would happen if Hurfest's people won and the project was halted? Would those sleepers ever be woken? Not that they'd even figured out how to wake them, yet. From the 'casts, it seemed as if Tegan was still the only successful revival.

And if Lat's people were the violent type...

"I take it these militants were the ones who pushed for using the EMP?" I asked.

Joph leaned her head back and closed her eyes, hand still working at her leg. "I should have known," she said wearily. "They kept saying things like, 'casualties are inevitable,' but I thought it was just hyperbole. I didn't want to see that they meant it."

"How do you talk to these people, anyway?"

"Oh. Online, mostly. It's relatively safe. We're decentralized and anonymous."

"There will be spies," I said.

"Sure. Bethari handles all that, and her security's tight. When she spots a spy, she gives them lots of useless information— she'll even make them work for it a little, so they think it has to be real. But you don't get to know about operations like last night's without personal contact and demonstrating you can be trusted. This, we didn't plan online." Her expression lightened. "Soren tried to join the movement."

I choked. Soren Morgensen had been the worst of the fame-hunters at our school. He'd tried to befriend Tegan when she was famous, but he'd started tormenting her the second she'd made it clear she preferred the company of a dirty thirdie like me to that of a selfish party hound like him. "He did?"

"He *tried.* He somehow failed to realize that everyone who joins Save Tegan actually listened to Tegan's story, and heard just what she thinks of him. Not even the politicals had any use for Soren Morgensen." She leaned over my shoulder to check the time, then pulled a pillbox from her overalls pocket. "Time for my dose."

"Does that hurt often?" I said, nodding at her leg.

Her brown eyes were steady as she looked at me. "All the time."

"I'm—"

"Don't you dare apologize to me. I knew what I was risking. I made my own choices."

I shut my mouth.

"Better." She swallowed her medicine dry and belched with no shame. "Sometimes I wish we could go back to the simple times," she said. "When all I had to do was pretend to be a ditz high on my own supply and make you lots of pills, and all you had to do was pretend to hate everyone and take the pills from your contact in her janitor's closet to pass on. No casualties, no politics, no hard decisions. It was so clearly the right thing to do."

I thought of Digger Jones, and how careful he'd been not to let me know who the next contact up the chain was. People learning too much about the smugglers would probably wish they hadn't. And those little pink pills were bound for the black market. They would be useful for trade, useful for bribery. I knew from the rare news reports about smugglers that a lot of the pills had gotten to their intended destination, but not all of them had. Some of those pills would go to very bad people to be exploited in whatever way best served their ends.

Consequences.

I sighed. "It probably wasn't that simple. There were all sorts of hard decisions we didn't have to make, that's all."

"Bethari thought putting the EMP together would be a simple way to get you back," Joph said. Her tone wasn't nasty.

"Yeah," I said. "All right. I get it." And I did—I understood how Bethari's hope had misled her. I could sympathize with that desire for an easy fix. "But things are never so straightforward, are they?"

"I know," she said, and laid her head on my shoulder. "But just for a minute, let's pretend."

I put my arm around her waist and breathed in the hot, still air. I'd been pretending to make other people happy for so long. Just for a minute, I could sit in the sun and comfort myself with the pretense that everything would be all right soon.

CHAPTER NINE
Semplicemente

Joph and I sat in the garden for a long time. The tree skeletons didn't give us much shelter from the summer sun, but the house wall did, so I didn't have to go in and meekly ask Lat for sunscreen or a hat. I could sit with my friend and watch insects I didn't recognize leap through the dry stalks. A faint smell of smoke was in the air—Australians didn't cook their food over coals or fire anymore, so it had to be a distant bushfire, one of the blazes that sprang up in summer and autumn.

Joph's breathing was deep and even, and I wondered if she'd fallen asleep, but a quick glance told me her eyes were open. She was smiling, dreamy and unconcerned, her pupils huge. Whatever took the pain away apparently had other, more recreational effects. I found myself wondering if she'd share. Asking would have roused me from this pleasant stupor, though, so I kept my mouth shut and watched the insects.

The sound of an electric motor shook me out of my haze. It came from the other side of the house, on what must have been the road there.

The sniper in the trees was gone; I hadn't seen her leave. Now, when she might be useful, she'd decided to take a break?

Joph hauled herself upright. "What?" she said, her voice sluggish.

"Stay here," I hissed. "Hide."

I didn't wait to see if she obeyed. I hugged the house wall and slid around it, counting on the weeds to hide me. I knew that I should go back inside, with all the armed people, but being startled from my reverie had made my blood race. I wanted to move, not cower. I wanted to fight.

The motor stopped. Boots crunched on gravel. I scooped up a stone as big as my fist and held my breath as I sneaked the final few steps, to a point where I could see our noisy visitor.

She was a tall woman, wearing a long-sleeved robe of midnight blue that flowed around her muscular frame. Two holsters swung from the wide belt around her hips; a sonic pistol in one, a bolt-gun in the other. Her tight, dark curls were cut close to her skull. She was shading her eyes with one hand as she looked at the house, so I couldn't see her whole face, but there was a weary set to her mouth.

I knew her.

It was Zaneisha Washington, Tegan's former bodyguard. She'd once held a sonic pistol to my back and made me think it was a weapon that could kill. Tegan had responded by shooting Washington with another sonic pistol, but even stricken with vertigo Washington had fought back. She'd still tried to take us in, before Tegan could tell her story to the world.

My fingers tensed around the stone, and I stared at the side of Washington's head, ready to throw.

"Please don't, Mr. Taalib," she said, without turning her head. "I'm on your side."

A lot of people I didn't like very much had been saying that lately. Nevertheless, I paused, and the front door swung open.

"Zaneisha!" Tegan's voice said. "Lat, it's okay; let me go!"

I tensed, ready to go to her aid, but Tegan apparently didn't need me to get away from Lat. She ran out the door and halted just in front of the tall woman.

I couldn't see Tegan's face, but Washington's normally expressionless face had produced a small smile. "It's good to see you, Tegan," she said.

"You too! Where's Marie?"

"In the car. Sleeping."

Tegan moved forward, and Washington shifted to block her. "She needs the sleep." Her eyes were grave, and I wanted to give Tegan some warning for the bad news I could tell was coming. "Some physical damage was inflicted on her."

"In the escape?" Lat asked professionally.

Washington's lips thinned with distaste. "Before."

Tegan made a sound that squeezed my insides. "Because of me," she said.

"No," Washington said. "She told me it had something to do with her work. Nothing to do with you."

Tegan tilted her head. "Marie wouldn't be involved at all

without me." She squared her shoulders and moved toward the car. Washington, apparently resigned, moved out of the way.

I heard Tegan's sharp inhale and moved forward as she stumbled back. She steadied herself before I could reach her, but she leaned on my shoulder for a brief moment, feeling a lot heavier than her slight frame suggested. I didn't know whether to hold her hand or say something consoling, but her face was closed off, rejecting pity.

Solidarity, though, she would take. I stood there, shoulder to shoulder with her, as Washington reached into the car and gently lifted Tegan's foster mother out.

Dr. Marie Carmen was a short woman, barely taller than Tegan, although she looked even smaller in Washington's substantial arms. Her plain, shabby shirt and long drawstring skirt hung from her thin body and her straight dark hair fell to her shoulders in ragged strands. Clearly, the standards of personal-appearance maintenance that Tegan and I had endured hadn't been applied to the doctor; it was her brain that was valuable to SADU, not her face.

That face was slack, whatever intelligence that normally inhabited it swallowed in the depths of her unconsciousness. *Sleeping* had been a convenient euphemism; Dr. Carmen was clearly dosed to the eyeballs. Even with chemical relaxants, however, there was tension around her tilted eyes, deep lines dug out between her snub nose and full mouth.

I saw no signs of physical damage until Washington shifted her a little higher and I caught a glimpse of the bulky bandaging on her feet. Washington saw my face.

"She didn't need to stand to work," she said grimly.

"I hate them," I snapped, and Tegan nodded fiercely.

Washington merely dipped her chin in acknowledgment. "Get the door," she said, and I held the front door open, then the trapdoor, then the door to the bedroom downstairs that had been set up as an infirmary. The man there made efficient, unsurprised noises and shooed us all back into the hallway, where Lat was waiting.

His handsome, serious face was the very last thing I wanted to see right then. He might have helped Tegan, but he was SADU, he'd been SADU for a long time. Lat had hurt and manipulated people without pause until whatever spark of conscience that remained in him had flared the night Tegan spoke. I thought of Dr. Carmen's bandaged feet and knew that if he made a word of excuse or apology, I was going to try to finish the job I'd made strangling him.

Tegan didn't wait for him to speak. She took a step forward and slapped him hard across the face.

It wasn't a ladylike, delicate blow. She put her shoulder behind it, and Lat's head snapped back. She raised her arm again.

"SADU," she hissed.

"Not anymore," he said, and caught her wrist. "Tegan, stop. It's me."

She twisted free of him, staring intently into his face. Then she made a noise like an angry cat and pushed past him, moving farther down the corridor. I wanted to follow her example—but maybe with a closed fist.

I needed to find a place where I could sit and think and try to get a grip on the rage that kept vibrating through me. I wasn't any use to anyone, much less myself, when I was this furious, and I didn't know what to do about all these impulses toward violence. Impulsive physical action was Tegan's job; mine was observation and strategy, and I needed a clear head for both.

I was so exhausted by being angry all the time. If I couldn't make it stop, perhaps I could put it to use.

But Lat wasn't looking at me.

"Sergeant," he said to Washington.

"Agent."

"Are you ready for a debrief?"

"Yes."

There was a gap where a *sir* should have been, and judging from Lat's brief frown, he heard that deliberate absence, too.

"We should discuss…" he trailed off.

"Phase Two?" Washington said. "Yes."

Lat's eyes flickered toward me, then back to her impassive face. My skin prickled. That was something he hadn't wanted me to hear.

"I'm finding Tegan," I said, needlessly defiant, trying to sound like a sulky teenager. It wasn't difficult. I wandered around the nearest corner, my mind working furiously. If the previously established pattern held true, they'd be having their little conference in the main living room upstairs. I'd need to give them some time to go in and get the preliminaries over, but not so much time that I missed any important information.

Turning the next corner, I nearly ran into Bethari and Joph, who were gathered by the barely ajar door to a room I hadn't seen yet. Through the gap, I could hear a muffled sound that might have been crying.

Bethari looked at me inquiringly.

"What?" I said.

"Aren't you going in?"

"I don't know if she wants me to," I said. It was true, and I meant it to be considerate, but the words came out bitter. Kissing Tegan in the dining room had been so easy, all of the betrayal and lies and pain made distant by the miracle of touch. But those things had still marked me, marked both of us. I was stupid to think that kisses could erase those marks. They could only cover them up.

Bethari waited a beat longer and then shoved past me, not gently. She was a lot stronger than she looked—all that cheerleading meant hidden muscle under her long sleeves and skirts. I had to haul back sharply on the urge to shove her, too.

No, I really shouldn't go in there, not with this violence surging in me. Tegan needed comfort, but I didn't think she would want me to see her being this vulnerable. We'd both been forced to witness the other's degradation and exposed weaknesses—going in now would only bring back those memories for us.

That was what I told myself, anyway. Truthfully, I wasn't certain I could stand seeing Tegan weak, when she'd only just started to show her strength again.

"Tegan, let me help," Bethari said as she went in. I caught a glimpse of a crumpled heap of silver on a bed, and Tegan's teary face, and then Joph slipped in after her ex-girlfriend.

All right, then. When it came to offering comfort, I was a miserable failure.

But I *could* get some information and help her that way.

I retraced my steps and found the trapdoor again. When I set my ear against the metal, it was soundproofed, as I'd suspected. No word of Phase Two filtered through that heavy shielding.

Plan B involved wandering back out to the garden and going for a casual walk around the premises, coincidentally passing any handy windows. Not as subtle, nor as likely to gain much data, but still better than nothing.

I set my hands to the trapdoor and pushed. It was locked.

The worst thing might have been that I wasn't actually surprised.

The physical shock of shoving against that unyielding door translated into a sick, spinning sensation in my head. We were imprisoned again, and the adults were talking upstairs, about Tegan's importance, about the things they were going to do with us.

And not telling those things to us.

I sat on the steps and put my head between my knees until the dizziness passed and my breathing steadied.

Then I went back to Tegan's room, took a deep breath, and knocked once.

"Come in," Tegan said. Her voice was strong and clear. I took it as a good sign and slipped in.

She'd been crying, but there were no tears now. Her mouth was tight and her jaw set; not angry at me, I thought, but at the world in general. I looked past her, at irritated and irritating Bethari, and said, "We need to bug the briefing room upstairs."

Δ ʃ Ω

The girls gave me identical blank looks, and Joph said, "What?"

"I already have," Bethari said, looking curious.

"What?" Joph repeated. "When?"

"Just now," Bethari said. "Shoved the bug into the couch cushions. I haven't turned it on yet. There's more chance they'll pick it up if it's transmitting."

Despite myself, I was impressed. "Who sweeps the compound for surveillance?"

Bethari looked slightly affronted. "I do. This room's clear." Thoughtfully, she added, "But I wouldn't put it past them to have backups in place. Military redundancy."

"We're all on the same side," Joph said uncertainly.

Tegan pressed her lips together. "I'm not on the side of people who think it's okay to have civilian casualties as a side effect."

"Or as a secondary purpose," I said. "Don't look at me like that, Joph; I know you might not want to believe it, but deliberately killing civilians is an act of terrorism. And it's one this movement can use to threaten the government. You're the one who told me about militants backing Hurfest's political crew."

Bethari had pulled her computer out of her pocket and was squinting at the screen, her fingers flicking in neat, efficient motions. "I can start remote transmission, if you think we should risk it now."

"Washington let something slip about a Phase Two. And they've locked the trapdoor."

Tegan looked alert. "Zaneisha said...what did she say?"

I cast my mind back and repeated Lat's and Washington's words.

"Is that exactly right?" Tegan asked.

"Yes," I said, mildly annoyed. I had the family memory—very useful for studying, remembering complicated maps in video-game scenarios, and accurate eavesdropping.

"She was tipping you off," Tegan decided. "Zaneisha doesn't just let things slip. Bethari, go ahead."

Bethari held up one finger and dropped it.

"—proceeded through the gates with no difficulty," Washington was saying. "The SADU ID codes were uncompromised."

I sat on the edge of the bed, listening to the story of Dr. Carmen's rescue and trying to assess Tegan's state of mind without appearing to do so. She looked better like this, intent and indignant. Joph was chewing on a strand of her own hair. I automatically reached out to brush it away from her mouth, and then paused, startled by my own ease in carrying out such a familiar action. Joph let the hair drop and placed her hand over mine in a brief hold.

"In your assessment, when can Phase Two begin?" Lat's voice asked at the end of the report.

"If you still wish Dr. Carmen to provide evidence on the current state of the revival procedure, and thus emphasize the futility of the Ark Project, I suggest waiting for her to heal." Washington's voice was even, but it was interesting that she was repeating details that Hurfest and Lat must surely know already. Perhaps Tegan was right; perhaps Washington really was directing her remarks to us.

"That could depend," Hurfest said thoughtfully. "How photogenic are her injuries?"

Lat made a brief, disgusted sound. Washington was silent.

"The more proof we have of government perfidy the better," Hurfest pointed out. "Abdi and Tegan are just too attractive to be downtrodden. The only visible injuries they have are the ones we gave them, for heaven's sake."

My hand went to the hole in my neck. At the head of the bed, Tegan was touching hers, too.

Washington cleared her throat. "I suggest asking Dr. Carmen if—"

"Yes, of course," Hurfest said. "I'll talk to her. She'll see the logic in it. Lat, how about Tegan?"

"She's traumatized."

I winced.

"Obviously. Is she fit to be a spokeswoman? She's the only thing that makes us freedom-fighting guerrillas instead of terrorist threats. I think a statement should go out as soon as possible, before we use the EMP on that army base."

Joph pressed both hands over her mouth, looking as if she might be sick. Bethari's eyes were wide and anguished. Tegan didn't look sick or ashamed. She was bright with fury, as filled with rage as I was. I wouldn't have been surprised if we'd both burst into flames.

"Sir, I must protest. Civilians will be caught in the dark zone again." Washington's voice was measured, her tone as casual as if she were requesting that he pass the water jug, but there wasn't a hint that she could be moved.

"Protest noted, Sergeant." Hurfest sighed, sounding a lot less arrogant and a lot more exhausted. "I'm not happy about it, either. If we're lucky, Cox will resign quietly after Tegan speaks up. In the ensuing fallout, my people can move, and we'll force a reelection under the Save Tegan banner."

"Do you think he's likely to give in that easily?" Lat asked.

"I've been a political reporter for two decades, Agent. Not a chance. We've got to make a sizable impact on public opinion before his own people give him the shove, hoping to salvage what they can. We're in for a long, dirty struggle."

And Tegan would be his symbol of resistance, for as long as it took.

I glanced at her. From the fury in her eyes, I didn't give much for Hurfest's chances of getting her to cooperate.

"I don't know if Tegan will be willing," Lat was saying doubtfully, and I hated that he knew her that well, that he was thinking my thoughts.

"She'll have to be," Hurfest said bluntly, and my hands clenched. "We don't have a chance without her."

"And if she says no?" Washington asked.

"Then we'll need to persuade her," Hurfest said, his voice heavy.

I felt his words like a blow to my chest, an impact that nearly knocked the breath out of me. Beside me, Tegan was clenching and unclenching her fists, her mobile face alive with fury and fear.

"You can't be serious," Lat said. "She's just spent months being *persuaded* to speak."

"We won't hurt her," Hurfest promised. "It won't come to that. But speaking up really is in Tegan's best interests, and if she can't see that, we need to make her do it anyway. Do you honestly think she'll be safe with this government in power?"

"No," Lat said, sounding more convinced.

"And we unfortunately don't have time for the trauma to fade. We need to take advantage of this confusion as soon as possible. I don't take any pleasure in it, believe me."

I did believe him. Hurfest wasn't someone who enjoyed making others suffer. But he'd clearly do it, if he thought it was for the right reasons.

Someone else came in then to report on flier movement, and the meeting broke up. Bethari turned off the transmission with trembling fingers.

Tegan pulled herself off the bed, moving with deliberate calm. I wasn't fooled. The muscles in her bare arms were tight, her pupils blown out so that her brown eyes looked almost black.

I was so relieved to see her come alive with passion again that I really didn't want to do what would have to come next. But I had to stop her, or she'd endanger herself, and us with her.

"Where are you going?" I asked, pitching my voice at reasonable.

"I am going to hammer on that trapdoor, and then I am telling Hurfest exactly what I think of his plan to use me as a puppet."

"And then what?"

"And then I'm leaving."

"By yourself?"

She squared her shoulders. "You guys can come with me."

"Definitely," Bethari said.

"And Marie? Will you take her, too?"

"Of course."

"Well, that's already a problem, because she's not awake right now, and even if she were, I doubt she could walk. She probably needs surgery, or some kind of assistive technology, before she can even hope to bear her own weight."

Joph nodded. "Hurfest has the medical setup, Tegan."

"You can look after her," Tegan told her.

Joph looked doubtful. "I could try. But I'm a chemist, not a doctor."

"And you're assuming that if you confront him, Hurfest will just let us leave," I pressed. "You heard him; he needs you. If he'll force you to speak, I don't think he'll hesitate to restrain us. Do you *want* to be locked up again?"

Tegan flinched, and, internally, I did, too. But my mother's training wouldn't let that show on my face. "Don't forget all those people with guns; they might look to you as a symbol, but he's the one who commands them. We need to keep our heads down and wait for our chance. And in the meantime, prepare for a quiet escape."

Tegan glared at me. "I can't believe this! You're acting like a robot. Aren't you angry?"

"I want to kill Hurfest for even thinking he could do this to you," I said, with absolute honesty. With the rage subsided, I could see clearly again. "But I can't do that, so I need a Plan B."

"And Plan B is *waiting*?" Bethari asked. "For how long?"

"For as long as it takes us to be sure we've got everything we need," I said. "Which is going to take at least a couple of days. I don't want to walk out of here and get picked up by SADU an hour later. When we're ready, when the opportunity comes, *then* we move. But before that, we have to be patient and pretend we're fine with their plan. We need supplies, and we need transport so that we can move Dr. Carmen. We need whatever medicines and equipment she'll have to use."

"I can work on that," Joph said, looking thoughtful. "Getting medicines, anyway."

"And the EMP," Bethari added. "I'm not leaving it here for Hurfest to use again." She brightened. "I had to test it away from here, or we'd have fried all the electronics in the complex. We could go on another testing expedition and try to lose our escort."

"Good," I said, trying not to sound surprised. Bethari *was* intelligent, I knew that, but I tended to forget that when she went for her first impulses. "We'll refine that a little more, but it's a good starting point." I looked at Tegan, wishing there was a better way to tell her the next part. But if we were to succeed… "Your role is going to be hard," I said.

"I get it," she said. "I'll pretend that I'd be happy to be everyone's speaking doll. Again. You know, ever since I woke up, there's always been someone who wants to use me as a mouthpiece." She didn't say it with complaint. It was just a fact of life: The grass is dying. Sunlight causes cancer. Everyone wants to make the Living Dead Girl their personal spokeswoman.

"But if it helps the refugees…" Bethari said tentatively. "I mean, we don't have to do it with Hurfest, of course, but in your own time, when you're ready."

Tegan shook her head hard, almost violently. "I can't do it anymore, Bethi. Not again. Not for anyone. I start hearing every word I say as if a stranger is talking, as if all the people looking at me are inspecting a statue carved with a permanent happy face. And I'm inside it, trapped under the rock, and I can't scream, and

I'm suffocating." Tegan looked pale, far too pale, and her skin had the waxy sheen of cheese left on the table to sweat.

I was beside her before I'd even thought of moving, guiding her down to the floor with anxious hands. She was rigid with tension, the lean muscles jumping as I helped her sit with her back against the wall. I was peripherally aware of Bethari's concerned face, of Joph rummaging through a bag, but my focus was on Tegan and the long breaths she was forcing in and out, at a deliberate, regular pace.

"What do you need?" I asked.

"I don't know. Just be here."

I sat cross-legged beside her, my shoulder against hers, the long length of my thigh pressed against her leg. I didn't touch her with my hands again. She was so tightly coiled I was afraid she'd explode.

I might have been too hasty in thinking that Tegan had had it easier with Lat on her side. After all, he'd only replaced her former handler after a few months. Before that, she'd been as lost as I was. And I'd forgotten to take her stage fright into account—under SADU's tender care, it seemed that what had been an aversion to public performance had blossomed into a full-blown phobia.

"Do you want me to give you something, Teeg?" Joph asked softly.

"No. I can do this." She took a couple more deep, even breaths, then looked right at me. Her eyes were still red-rimmed, but she wasn't crying. "Abdi. Whatever I tell them, I can't actually handle a 'cast. If they put me in front of a camera, I'll lose it."

"You won't have to. Not ever again," I said, and desperately hoped I could keep my promise. She nodded. "Just pretend that I will. All right. I'll talk to Zaneisha, too."

I hesitated. We *might* be able to trust Washington, but perhaps she was in double cover, a way for Lat and Hurfest to anticipate any resistance on Tegan's part and take steps to counter it.

On the other hand, there were all those people with guns. Washington was a warrior, and we could really use her help if we had to fight our way out. Tegan and Bethari were athletes, and I knew how to point and shoot, but none of us had the expertise that seemed natural to almost every adult I'd seen in this place. "Good idea," I said. "But carefully, all right? Just try to sound her out at first."

"I can do that. And you?"

"I'm going to go sulk at Lat," I said, the idea coming with the words. When we'd been kidnapped by zealots, Tegan had managed to get us some supplies by working in the kitchens. "I'll see if I can guilt him into letting me do something that will give me access to food."

"You could just ask him if you could help out in the kitchen," Tegan said. "You don't need to manipulate *everyone*, you know."

I winced. I'd hoped that Tegan hadn't caught how I'd redirected her first, destructive impulse, but she saw me too clearly. "We should try to be ready to go in forty-eight hours, no more. I think Hurfest's going to push fast."

"Where are we going?" Bethari asked, looking doubtful again.

I turned to her in surprise. Wasn't it obvious? "New Zealand, for a start," I replied. "And then we'll consider our next steps. We're getting out of Australia, and we're not coming back."

CHAPTER TEN
Andante

"Leave Australia," Bethari said. From her tone, you'd think I'd suggested she do something impossible, not take the best possible escape route.

"Yes. New Zealand still takes immigrants, and we can certainly make a case for political asylum."

"We're all *criminals*," Tegan pointed out.

"Activists," I corrected. "Fighting the illegal and immoral actions of a government at war with its people. Don't worry, there'll be lawyers throwing themselves at the chance to represent us. And while they're preventing immediate extradition, we can work out our next steps." I slid a glance at Tegan. "My mother might have some ideas. If we can just get to Djibouti, we'll be safe."

"I'm not yet convinced that we should leave the country," Tegan said, chin raised.

Bethari nodded firmly. "I've lived here my whole life; my family's lived here for eight generations. Do you think I'm going to just *run away*? We have to stay and make things better, not take off and never come back."

My temper flared again. I couldn't shout at Tegan, but Bethari was a far easier target. "I didn't say I didn't want to make things better, but so far your efforts haven't done much except—" I bit back on what I wanted to say, but Joph's warning look hadn't been fast enough. Bethari's cheeks flamed.

"I'm sorry about the EMP," she said. "You don't know how sorry. But we could get in touch with the other Save Tegan people, the ones who are about awareness, not guns and violence."

"Do they have a secure network and a fully prepared hideout?" I demanded. "Because the one thing I can say about Hurfest is that the guy knows how to organize a revolution. That's why you went to him for help, remember?"

"And that was my biggest mistake!" Bethari said, folding her arms. "We need to stay here and help the refugees."

Tegan nodded. "Bethi's right."

"It's not a zero-sum situation," Joph said, her voice unusually firm. "We *can* return, when it's safe to do so. And we can talk about government abuse of refugees and the No Migrant policy from anywhere. Right now, I think Abdi's right. If the headquarters of Save Tegan isn't safe for us, nowhere in Australia is."

Bethari snorted, and Joph turned to her, hand held out. "I'm no happier than you are about leaving the country. And I don't want it to be a permanent change. But for now, we have to go."

"So we get to the coast," I said. "And steal or hire a boat that's seaworthy enough to cross the Tasman."

"The Coast Guard—" Bethari began.

"Don't care about people leaving." My lip curled. "It's people trying to get *into* the country they have a problem with."

"They might care if it's us," Joph said gently. "But it's a good plan. I can't come up with a better alternative. And we don't have a lot of time to discuss our options. Are we agreed?"

Tegan gritted her teeth. "All right. We'll leave, for now."

There was a pointed silence, while Bethari's mouth stayed stubbornly shut. I was so frustrated I could have screamed. Didn't she understand how much trouble we were in? Would it take someone like Diane to make it clear to her how dangerous this country was for us?

But screaming wouldn't help, and logic hadn't been useful. I cast about for something that might motivate Bethari and came up short. I just didn't know enough about her to hit those soft spots.

"I've been praying," Tegan said abruptly. "Quite a lot. Maybe God is guiding us this way, Bethi."

It was all I could do not to gape at her.

Faith was the only thing I'd ever fought with my mother about. She was a tolerant Muslimah, but she believed, as did my siblings, and she wanted me to believe, too. At the very least, she wanted me to pretend; a nonbeliever would have a much harder time getting elected to any post in Djibouti. My father was an atheist, and he supported me. Sometimes it felt as if we were the only two people in the country who didn't waste worship on a myth.

Tegan had been religious. I knew that, but how was she still able to have faith? After all the terrible things people had tried to do to her in the name of their gods, how could she think religion was a way for reasonable people to live their lives? If she

120

believed in a god that could leave her in the hands of SADU, tortured and desperate, how could she be anything but furious at him? She was a smart, ethical person, and she still believed in this stupid fairy tale. It was beyond belief.

And worst of all, Bethari was nodding along with her.

My logic hadn't persuaded Bethari, but Tegan's appeal to faith was going to do it.

Joph caught my eye, a glint of humor in her face, combined with a very real warning. Yes, no matter what I thought of Tegan and Bethari believing in supernatural guidance, now wasn't the time to express my opinions on the subjects of faith, fiction, and the many ways the unscrupulous took advantage of the gullible. Not if it meant they'd agree to take the best course of action.

I felt bad about the manipulation, but if it kept them safe...

"*Fine*," Bethari said at last. "We'll work on getting out of here, and then see about getting out of the country. Is that what you wanted to hear?"

"Great," I said. "Now if you'll excuse me, I have a torturer to trick."

Δ ∫ Ω

The Save Tegan people at the house were quite happy to point me in Lat's direction. I didn't try to get any more information out of them—though I did make sure I had the layout of the underground part of the base firmly in my head before I ventured back upstairs. Lat was in a small room that had probably once been a bedroom, sitting at a map-covered table that took up most of the room.

The rest of the room was dominated by a huge fireplace that would have been outdated a hundred years ago and now assumed the fascination of a museum piece, complete with a heavy poker and brush set. Burning fuel was common enough in my homeland, but the mere suggestion gave eco-righteous Australians the screaming horrors. Even if it was handy for getting rid of incriminating paper evidence.

In a low voice, Lat was discussing something with a white-haired woman. They both shut up as I came in.

I'd neglected to knock.

"Can I talk to you?" I asked.

Lat looked wary, but not alarmed. "Sure. What's wrong, Abdi?"

The older woman slipped discreetly out, murmuring something about *vehicle maintenance*. I ignored her, though it reminded me of another item on my checklist: Find a vehicle that we could steal—at least Bethari ought to be useful for slipping through the car's antitheft codes. Then we needed to find the best route to the coast and kidnap an injured woman. And secure supplies.

"When can I talk to my parents?" I asked.

Lat blinked. "Oh," he said, his face suddenly sympathetic. It was a struggle to keep my own expression from reflecting my distaste. I didn't want his sympathy. "I'm sorry, Abdi. We won't be able to do that yet. Our communication networks are locked down to essential messages only, and anything connecting to Djibouti is going to raise red flags with the people looking for us. If it helps, your parents will know from the news 'casts that you've escaped SADU."

I tamped down the disappointment. I'd known it was a long

shot, and, after all, I wanted him to feel like he owed me. "Really. They think I'm safe?"

"Well, SADU is saying that you and Tegan were kidnapped by a terrorist faction," he admitted. "But they looked like sensible people, your mum and dad. They'll work it out, surely."

I glared at him, not bothering to moderate the bite in my voice. "So they're really worried about me, and I can't get in touch?"

He winced. "As soon as I can safely place a call, I'll let you know," he promised. "Is there anything else I can help you with?"

The warm glow of satisfaction ignited in my stomach. Excellent. Now he was feeling guilty and ready to offer me something in exchange for alleviating that guilt.

Tegan was right—I shouldn't try to manipulate my friends. But Lat was no friend of mine, and I was glad that I was able to twist him so easily.

"Actually, there is. I want something to do, so I can help out."

"Why don't you just relax?" he said. "Get some downtime."

"I got lots of downtime, between torture sessions and being made to perform on cue."

His fingers drummed a tattoo on the maps. Hard copy, which was unusual. But impossible to hack remotely. I wondered if I could steal one of those and decided I probably couldn't. I injected a note of pleading into my voice. "Give me a gun and let me stand a watch, or put me on monitoring communications channels, or...I don't know. Something!"

He looked awkward, doubtless at the thought of me with a weapon in hand or anywhere near a secured communication route. "We have ample operatives for—"

"It doesn't have to be exciting," I begged. "I just want a task that keeps my hands busy, something I can do that helps the cause."

He brightened. "How about kitchen duty?"

I made a face, the picture of impetuous youth restrained. Actually, I was delighted he hadn't started with latrine duty. I'd have had to talk him out of it—and the longer I messed with someone's thought processes, the faster they were likely to realize I was doing it. Instead he'd landed me exactly where I wanted to be.

"I know it doesn't sound glamorous. But an army marches on its stomach. If you could put lunch together, that would be really useful, and we'd all be grateful."

As if I wanted Lat's gratitude. "I suppose that would be all right," I said slowly, trying to sound reluctant but not so much that he'd try to give me another task. "All right." I almost said *thank you*, but the words stuck in my throat, and he wouldn't have believed them from me anyway. Instead, I turned on my heel.

"You don't trust me," he said.

I turned back. "Should I?"

He frowned. "You *can*, but I understand why you don't. You saw me hurt Tegan."

"For things I did," I said automatically. "Because I wasn't good."

There was pity in his eyes. I wanted to poke them out, so I wouldn't have to see it. "No. Abdi, it wasn't your fault Tegan was hurt. It was Diane who ordered it done."

"And you who did it."

He sighed. "Yes."

Fury snarled through my veins. "You didn't have to hurt her. You could have faked it."

"I couldn't. The implant monitored pain responses. Tegan knew why I had to go through with it. She said that made it easier."

"Not for me," I pointed out. "And you said…you said you'd hurt her in new ways. You said you'd make me *watch*."

"Put the poker down," Lat suggested.

I started, as if I were coming out of a dream.

I couldn't even remember going to the fireplace, but I was definitely clutching the heavy poker in my upraised hand, point held low toward Lat. With exaggerated care, I laid it on the table, a thick black line across the maps. Then I stepped back, my hands held out from my sides. "Were you scared? Of savage thirdie me?"

"I could have taken it from you," he said, which I knew was true. "But I'd rather I didn't have to. We're not enemies, Abdi. We would have been once, I have to admit. But I saw Tegan's story. I thought, this is wrong. And I thought of all the wrong things I'd been ordered to do in the years since I joined SADU, and all the wrong things I'd be ordered to do in years to come, and I thought, *I have to help that girl*."

"So you had some sort of epiphany, and now you think we should be friends? That I should just forgive and forget all of those wrong things? You threatened to rape her!"

The word cut through the air like a clean knife.

Lat's lips flattened. "I wouldn't have. Never, even if they'd ordered. It was only a threat."

"Sure. It was only to make me move, get me into position for an escape I didn't even know was coming. Ever since I came to this stupid country people have wanted to make me their puppet. Just like Tegan, but less valuable. They want me to sing for them, run for them, scream for them—" I bit back the rest and swallowed it.

"I'm not saying you have to forgive me," Lat said after a moment.

"Good. I don't. Tegan's the one who believes in absolution, not me."

"We don't have to be friends, either. But we should be allies. We want the same things."

We want the same girl, I thought. But I didn't dare say it. I could tell all my feelings were off-kilter—too strong, too raw, suspicion and rage coming too easily to me. Tegan was clearly more than a symbol to Lat, but I couldn't be sure exactly how he felt about her. He was at least ten years older than she was— maybe he saw her as a little sister in need of protection and care. Or maybe he saw her as something else. And I didn't know how much Tegan liked him back. Maybe she'd found comfort in his presence; maybe that comfort had turned into something more. If she'd found some kind of solace in our imprisonment, should I blame her?

I probably shouldn't, but hot with jealousy, I knew I would.

"Allies, then," Lat said, as if it were all settled. He held out his hand.

I had a mission. I couldn't compromise it. I took his hand and shook it, palm pressed against palm. We released the grip together, and I resolutely did not wipe his touch off on my pants.

"Did Diane hurt you?" he asked, apparently apropos of nothing.

I stared at him. "You saw she did." He'd seen me sobbing on the floor, begging for forgiveness, saying anything I thought might make her stop.

"I meant…hurt you."

Diane's hands, brushing my skin; Diane's whisper in my ear. *Be a good boy, Abdi. Don't make me punish you.*

"I don't know what you mean," I lied, and went downstairs to find the kitchen.

Δ ∫ Ω

The problem was that I didn't really know how to cook. Somewhere in the back of my mind, the task had been relegated to a category labeled "Servant's work; probably easy enough." This was shameful thinking—the same sort of stupidity that had people automatically labeling me a barbaric thirdie—but realizing the flaw in my logic didn't help me put a recipe together.

When Tegan found me in the industrial-sized kitchen, I was swearing at a potato in French, which was my favorite language for curses. Something about the way *merde* spat out of my mouth was very satisfying.

Tegan looked at the chunky peelings in the sink and at the few potatoes I'd managed to rid of their skin, mostly by slicing off large portions of flesh with it. The potatoes in the pot were much smaller than they'd started out.

"You couldn't find a potato peeler?" she asked.

I scowled at the knife I'd been using. There was a specific tool for potato peeling? Why hadn't it been labeled?

Tegan rooted through a drawer and passed me a small, white-handled thing with a double blade. Then she casually slid a knife into her dress. She'd borrowed an outfit from Bethari, something long and flowing with lots of convenient folds.

"Beans in the pantry," I said quietly, and watched, impressed, as she loaded herself with various useful staples and walked out again, looking perfectly calm. Just visiting her friend in the kitchen, not stealing supplies for a cross-Tasman journey, not a bit.

I got to work with the peeler and barely escaped scraping the skin off my thumb. How did people do this every day? I should definitely be more respectful of cooks.

A harassed-looking man stuck his head in the door and performed a double take. "But…Uh, hi, are you…?"

"Lat said I could make lunch," I said, making no attempt to be friendly.

"Your help would be very—"

"By myself."

His eyes flickered over the sad potato remnants. "Are you sure you don't want a hand?"

"Call Lat," I said, and turned my back on him. The man withdrew for a brief and predictable conversation. I caught the frustration in the man's voice as Lat presumably told him to let me have my way and to stop bothering him with trivialities, and I wasn't surprised when he looked back in to anxiously inform me that if I needed help, all I had to do was ask.

Left alone, I turned the potatoes into chunks and then eyed the onions. I was almost certain that you were supposed to peel them, then chop them, not the other way around. Tegan turned up again midway through the chopping and grabbed my wrists before I could rub my stinging eyes.

"Rinse, don't rub," she said, sending me to the sink. By the time I turned around again, blinking furiously, she'd transformed my uneven onion chunks into fine, even pieces, her knife a blur in her practiced hand.

"You're good at that," I said.

"My mum was a chef, remember?"

I did. And there would have been no servants in her house. I'd been pampered.

Sometimes, when I was really honest with myself, I had to acknowledge that some of my resentment at the way Australians treated me was that at home I'd been the wealthy, important one, not the strange, poor relation to be pitied. The change in status had been hard to take.

"I was making vegetable curry," I said. I'd grown up on curries, so I'd reasoned that at least I'd be able to taste if I was doing it wrong. And I'd seen my Australian host father make them. It seemed the method was to chop the ingredients into pieces and boil them together until they became thick. Add seasoning to taste, and eat with your starch of choice, which was going to be rice. It seemed fairly easy.

"That works. Go and see if there're some canned tomatoes in the pantry. We'll want cumin, cayenne pepper, turmeric if they've got any. Salt."

Maybe not so easy. I rummaged things up for her, and after being sent back twice—"Cumin, not coriander. Oh, and see if there are any dried chilies"—I leaned against the bench as she mixed spices and threw them into a huge pan with a lot of oil. The domesticity was unfamiliar to me but reassuring all the same. She tipped the onions in and stirred, while a warm, fragrant smell swelled to fill the room. Not a lot of ventilation down here, but I couldn't find myself caring much. In fact, it would be a bonus if Lat's room, wherever that was, got extra stinky.

"Carl found me," she said quietly. "I told him that I wanted a couple of days to get my head together but that I'd be glad to do a 'cast then. I think that works with whatever schedule he's got for that army-base attack."

"Good."

"And I talked to Zaneisha, but I really can't tell which way she'd jump. She's so restrained."

I nodded. "Then we won't take the risk. We'll plan to leave without her."

"Anything else you need from me?"

"Not right now."

She sighed. "Figures. People don't want me to *do*. They just want me to *be*. And sometimes I think they're right."

"How do you mean?"

"I look at my friends, and I don't know why you bother. Joph's a chemist. Bethi's a journalist hacker. You speak four languages *and* wrap people around your finger at will *and* sing like an angel. Compared with that, what can I do?"

I stared at the fragrant pot. "I can't imagine."

The joke didn't go over well. She twisted to scowl at me.

Her self-pity might be justified, but it was annoying. I scowled back. "You discovered a human-rights abuse scandal that had been kept secret for months, jumped over rooftops to put down a hostile military response, escaped imprisonment by religious freaks, and then gave up everything to expose the Australian government to the world. That people didn't capitalize on that the way we'd hoped isn't your fault. You *did* plenty, Tegan."

"And where did that get us?" she said, dropping her gaze.

"Here," I said. "And eventually, home to Djibouti."

"Your home," she said. "My home doesn't exist anymore."

The quiet desolation in her voice was much worse than the self-pity. I wrapped one arm around her, careful not to impede the movement of her wooden spoon as she shifted the onions about. "You can come with me, if you like," I said tentatively. "Make a new life."

Tegan bit her lip. "It's just…if I can't stay here, I think I'd like to come with you. I mean it." She tilted her head up at me, her eyes solemn and sincere, and my heart turned over in my chest.

"But," I prompted.

Tegan broke eye contact. "But I don't know what Marie wants. I need to talk to her first."

I nodded, trying not to look as wounded as I felt. Of course she'd do anything for Dr. Carmen, just as I'd do anything for my mother. "Take your time." I had to resist the urge to make stronger arguments, to get her to see things my way. I could do it, maybe, but it wouldn't be right. If she came with me, I wanted it to be her decision.

"I'll think about it. I promise. But I've been trying so hard to make a new life *here*. Or I was trying, at any rate." She shook her head. "'We shall not all sleep, but we shall all be changed.'"

It sounded like a quote. "What's that from?"

"The Bible. Saint Paul talking about the end of the world. 'The trumpet will sound, and the dead will be raised imperishable, and we shall be changed.'"

The Bible. Ugh. "You're perishable," I said, and poked her in the side.

She didn't react to this joke, either. "But changed. And maybe not changed enough to cope with this world. I thought it would be better, Abdi. I thought the future was going to be so much better than *this*."

I'd thought so, too. I'd been working my whole life so I could make it happen. That was what my mother's games were designed to do, after all: put me in a position where I could make positive change.

I held her a little closer, unsure of what else I could do and disturbed by the note of despair in her voice. She seemed to be feeling something similar to what I had before our rescue, but where escape had improved my outlook on life, it seemed to have damaged hers. Or maybe it was that she'd been given an opportunity to hope, that she'd been told that soon she could stop being a political mouthpiece…and then her rescuers had made clear that they expected her to keep talking. The new players were on the opposite side, but they still wanted her to be a pawn.

Tegan was strong, but everyone had limits.

There was a furtive knock at the door, and Tegan stiffened, moving away from me before the intruder came in. "What is it, Lat?" she asked, her tone ordinary.

"Dr. Carmen's still asleep, but the doctor says she can have visitors now," he said, glancing at me and then back at her.

"Marie!" Tegan thrust the spoon into my hand. "Put the potatoes in, add the tomatoes, throw in eight cups of water, and simmer until the potatoes are done."

She slipped past Lat without another word for me, or even a significant look. He watched her go, smiling slightly, and then came closer to where I stood by the pot, spoon gripped tightly. "How's it going?" he asked. "Smells good."

"Yeah."

"It's pretty hot up there," he tried. "Bushfires to the west. They're readying evacuation orders."

I remembered the smell of smoke in the garden. "That sounds serious," I said.

"It's probably not a big deal. We just need to keep an eye out, in case the wind changes."

I cocked my head at that. "This place isn't fireproof?"

Lat looked encouraged by the fact of our conversation. "Well, there are protective measures in place. It's really not something you need to worry about. We had three fire warnings in the summer, and nothing came of them. The only issue is that if the fire does reach here and the cottage collapses, rescue services coming afterward might find the complex underneath."

"Right. Not so secret a secret location, then."

His lips flattened at my tone. "When's lunch going to be ready?"

I turned back to the pan. "Soon," I said, and hoped I was right.

Δ ∫ Ω

I was wrong, but thanks to Tegan's cooking prowess, the trickle of people who moved into the kitchen to fill their bowls didn't seem to mind waiting. Most of them thanked me, the harassed-looking man from earlier doing so with justified, if insulting, surprise. Nobody seemed worried about the fires Lat had mentioned; they gathered in small groups to have focused, but not particularly tense, conversations about whatever they were working on for the next stage. I tried to eavesdrop without making it look obvious but stopped the second time a conversation topic shifted in midphrase. Wherever Hurfest and Lat had found these people, they were well practiced at keeping secrets.

Which was probably just as well, given that we were all fugitives. But it was frustrating.

I thought about getting a curry bowl of my own, but the girls hadn't turned up yet. Instead, I casually grabbed a few cans of preserved fruit and wandered out, hoping to find them. It would be nice to eat with Tegan. We needed a chance to have a normal conversation.

Tegan and Bethari's room was empty, but Joph was sitting on the bed in our room, checking the contents of a little red bag. "Got plenty of painkillers," she said.

I held up the cans I'd taken. "Got plenty of... what are these, peaches?"

"Nectarines."

"Those. Where's Tegan?"

"Still in the infirmary with Marie, I think. And Bethari's upstairs working on the EMP, making a lot of noise about how she's going to make it smaller for next time."

I hadn't asked about Bethari, mostly because I was just happy she wasn't here. But it was hard to get that kind of neglect past Joph, who was as observant as she was good-tempered.

"Did you want to get lunch?" I said instead. "Tegan mostly made it, so it's good."

She rolled off the bed. "Let's go."

Δ ∫ Ω

The second I stepped into the kitchen area, I stopped moving. Tegan was back from the infirmary. She was sitting at one of the mismatched tables with Lat and a couple of bowls of curry.

And she was laughing.

It was her real laugh, the one she'd given me earlier, but now it was for Lat, not me, and he was gazing at her with an expression I'd felt on my own face. And she was grinning up at him, seeming just as pleased with his company as she had been with mine. In a second, she'd be climbing onto the table and kissing *him*.

"Hey," Joph said, and laid a hand on my arm.

My jaw was clenched so tightly it was actually painful. I forced it to relax. "I'm okay."

Lat caught sight of me and looked momentarily uncertain, and the movement prompted Tegan to look over her shoulder.

"Abdi!" she called, raising her hand. "Sit here!"

I turned abruptly and sat at the nearest table. Joph eyed me uncertainly. Then she sighed and put her tray down beside me. Tegan's face dropped. I ignored the stab of guilt her hurt look

135

gave me and started chewing. Somehow, the curry didn't taste as good as it had before.

"Are you sure about this?" Joph asked quietly.

"I'm not sharing a meal with that man," I said, viciously tearing at a hunk of bread with my teeth.

She dipped her own bread in the curry. "You called him a torturer, before."

"He is," I said. "He and Diane—my handler. They tortured us both."

It felt good to say it. The immense pressure inside my skull eased a little. Joph had stopped eating.

"You didn't know?" I asked. She'd taken the implant out; surely she'd known what it could do.

"I knew. I just hoped…" She shook her head. "I hoped Lat had protected you a little, that's all."

"Hah. No. Not him. He might have protected *Tegan*. He gave *her* hope. Not me." I hadn't known I was this bitter. "I know she couldn't tell me about the escape," I amended. "I would have told Diane anything if I thought it would make the pain stop. Every time, I promised her all sorts of things, if she would just stop hurting me."

Joph swallowed hard.

"Sorry," I said, abashed.

"No," she said, her voice soft, but certain. "I'm listening. If you want to talk about it, I'm here."

"Diane—" I began, and then stopped. There were some things I couldn't tell even Joph. But I could tell her a lot of it. "The first five days, Diane wouldn't let me sleep," I said. "That doesn't sound so bad, but by the second day I was seeing flashing lights out of the corner of my eyes. By the third, I was exhausted. It felt like there was sand in my brain, like heavy stones were weighing down my body. I craved sleep more than anything. Then Diane told me she'd let me sleep if I apologized to her for telling lies about the government." I shuddered, hard, and couldn't stop. Joph carefully laid her hands over mine, a warm pressure that took some of the chill out of my body.

"I thought, I'm going to break eventually, so why not get it out of the way? I told her I was sorry. She said she didn't believe me. I apologized over and over again, until I began to mean it, until I really *was* sorry. Then she patted my head and told me that she believed me now, but unfortunately Tegan hadn't apologized yet. I could sleep when she did. Tegan didn't give in until the fifth day. Forty-two hours after I did. I know that, because Diane told me."

Joph's eyes were wet, but they were steady on mine. And I didn't think I could stop now, not unless she begged me to.

"I was so ashamed," I told her. "Tegan had lasted so much longer before she broke, because she's stronger than me. But at the same time, I was so *angry* with her. Why couldn't she just let us sleep? She'd have to give in at some point, so why *didn't* she; why did she have to be so stubborn; why was she torturing me like this?"

"It was Diane who was torturing you," Joph said.

"I know. I know that. But when you're in it, you can't think like that; you can't be fair. All you know is that your whole body is screaming for sleep and the one person who you thought was on your side is the person who's keeping the torture going." I let out a long breath. "But she gave in. And we slept. And when we woke up, they'd inserted the implants."

My hand went to the hole at the back of my neck. It hurt, but it was a pain I welcomed, a signal that the real agony was finally over. "It got worse then," I said, and felt a pang of guilt at Joph's flinch. "I can stop; you don't have to hear all this."

Joph shook her head. "Tell me."

I did. She sat there, while the others left, while Tegan followed Lat out without looking at me, and she listened the whole time.

"I'm sorry they did that to you," she said when I was done. "You're a good person, and none of it was your fault."

I nearly burst into tears. I gripped her hands instead, trying to tell her with that hold how much I liked her. Joph squeezed back. "I'm always on your side," she told me. "And Tegan's and Bethari's. We're a team."

"Us against the world, is it?" I said.

"Us against anyone who gets in our way," she said, more fiercely than I thought Joph could say anything. "Lat and Carl Hurfest included." She stood up. "Come on, you need to get that dressing on your neck changed. Let's go to the infirmary."

Where Tegan was likely sitting with her foster mother. If she wasn't hanging out somewhere with *Lat*.

I made a face. But Joph was standing up, and when she left, I went with her.

Δ ∫ Ω

Lat wasn't there, but Tegan was, sitting beside the bed in which the silent, shrunken figure of Dr. Carmen was sleeping. Tegan didn't say anything to me, but her eyes were red around the edges, and I was immediately sorry for my previous ill-humor. I hoped Joph wouldn't repeat anything I'd said; I was almost positive she wouldn't, but I should have extracted a promise.

The infirmary physician was a tall, efficient man with a shock of blond hair he kept tied back in a long ponytail. "This is going to sting a bit," he warned, so I had time to grit my teeth before the dressing came off.

He hadn't lied. When he pulled out the padding packed in the hole, it caught on some of the microwires still in my system. I expressed my feelings about this in a few short French phrases.

"Sorry," he said, and finished securing the new dressing. He dropped the old one in a biobin and headed for a little set of drawers. "Let me get you something for that."

Beside me, Joph stiffened, and I remembered the painkillers she'd stashed in her red bag. When the physician turned around, he was frowning. "I'm running low on Guthritenax. Do you have any, Ms. Montgomery?"

Joph hesitated.

"Is that anything like Lebeaumitol?" I asked. "Joph's got plenty of that. It worked great on me before."

"I'd prefer...oh, well, that should be fine. A half dose only." He turned back to his drawer, rearranging the contents. "I wish people wouldn't come in and take whatever they wanted," he muttered. "It's so hard to keep an accurate count."

I risked a glance at Joph. She looked hideously, obviously

guilty, a red flush spreading over her face. The instant he turned around, he'd know where those missing supplies had gone, and after that it was anyone's guess as to whether he blew it off as Joph being weird or mentioned it to Hurfest or Lat and stopped our escape before it began.

I shot a look across the room to Tegan, and she picked up the hint without a pause. "Dr. Beaumont," she said, lurching to her feet. "Marie just moved! I think she's waking up!"

The physician immediately refocused on his patient, and in the intervening moments, I pointed Joph to the door. She escaped into the hall, where her blushes would lack context and so look much less suspicious.

I should have followed her. But I'd liked it, that moment where Tegan and I had been working as a team, where we'd clicked back into being able to tell each other's intentions and needs without words. I hovered by the door instead.

Dr. Beaumont explained patiently and sympathetically that Marie wasn't waking up yet, that Tegan must have just noticed an involuntary muscular twitch. She looked convincingly sad about that. "Have you had lunch yet?" she asked him. "There's curry in the kitchen. It's good."

It wasn't a very subtle hint. The doctor gave both of us an amused, tolerant look that itched under my skin. I could have slapped him; did he think we were going to canoodle in the infirmary? In front of a sick woman?

But he left, asking Tegan to fetch him if Marie actually did wake, and Tegan got to her feet.

"So," she started, her voice low and dangerous. "What was that about?"

I didn't pretend I didn't know what she meant. I hit back. "I didn't want to interrupt. You seemed to be having so much fun with Lat."

She flushed. "He helped us," she said hotly. "Without him, we'd *both* still be there. Did you and Joph have a nice chat?"

"Not really," I snapped. "Mostly I was talking about how I'd been tortured, with the collusion of your *boyfriend*."

"He's not my...why can't you talk to *me* about that stuff? We both went through it, Abdi! You want me to move to another country with you, but you don't want to have a conversation about the horrible experiences we shared?"

"*We* didn't share all of it!" I shouted. It nearly came out then, the thing I'd managed to hide even from Joph, but I reined my temper back. "I mean...you knew we were going to be rescued! You knew there was an exit clause, but *I didn't*. I have never been so alone, and I thought it would never end. Unless I ended it myself, and I nearly *did*."

I stopped, appalled. Tegan looked equally shocked. She was so strong. She would never have thought about the escape route I'd contemplated. I backed away from her, terrified that I was going to cry. My mother would have been ashamed that I was so out of control.

"I really think we need to talk about this stuff," she said. She didn't sound angry anymore, but tentative, almost pitying.

I couldn't look at her. I could only send glances around the room as if the answer were written on the walls or upon a shelf. "We do," I said. "But it has to be later, Tegan. I can't do this now; I need to concentrate on getting us out of here and finding somewhere safe. I don't have time to fall apart." My restless gaze landed on the face of Dr. Carmen.

Her eyes were open.

I didn't know for how long she'd been watching. But her eyes were intelligent and thoughtful, and she looked at me as if she were measuring every grain of goodness in my soul—and found the weight lacking.

"Tegan," I said, and pointed.

Tegan's face transformed—joy and relief and guilt splashed across it, shining from her huge eyes. "Marie," she said, gasping, and then wrapped her arms around her foster mother's neck, embracing her as gently as a cobweb. I might as well have vanished.

"I'll tell the doctor," I said awkwardly, and got out of that room as fast as I could. There were too many feelings in there— hers and mine, too hot and twisted up. They pressed against the walls and couldn't escape.

Δ ∫ Ω

From the expression on Joph's face as I walked into our bedroom, I must have looked fairly terrible. I braced myself for another heavy conversation, but she jumped off the bed and pulled her red bag out of one of the chests of drawers.

"Your neck must be really hurting!" she exclaimed, yanking the bag open.

"Yes," I said, relieved. It was true, actually—the sting from the dressing change was definitely still there, and I was becoming more and more aware of the low throb of the cut itself. But if that pain could stand in to disguise my turbulent feelings about things I didn't want to discuss, then so much the better.

Joph selected two bottles from the nine or ten in the bag and shook out some pills, taking a couple of green ones for herself. "The white ones are immunoboosters—take them all. And the green ones will help with the pain."

I swallowed them dry, without hesitation, and ten minutes later was very pleased that I had. As well as numbing the pain, the green pills had done something wonderful to my brain chemistry. I didn't really care about my neck or about anything else that was bothering me. It was the first time I'd been almost worry-free in what felt like years, and the freedom was incredible.

"When they caught us, I thought they were going to prosecute you," I said sometime later, sprawling loose-limbed on the bed. "You made all that medicine for me."

"They did. But I'm rich," Joph said, and waved her hand around. "I got lots of lawyers. And they'd shot me, too. It's hard to put a rich ween in jail when you've shattered her femur. My parents paid off the pharmaceutical company, the police broke down the lab, and I told them everything I knew about the smuggling operation. For my cooperation, I got a suspended sentence."

"Everything you knew," I said, and giggled. "You knew less than me!"

"That's why it was such a great deal," she said, lolling against my shoulder. "Then I promised to be good."

143

"You liar."

"You bet. But my parents preferred that to all the drama of a trial."

"How are they going to feel about you helping us? Running off?"

Joph was quiet for a long time. I watched the dust mites drift through the warm air. "Annoyed, mostly," she said. "Disappointed, maybe."

I'd never met Joph's parents. They were distant figures, proud of their daughter's brilliance insofar as it reflected on them, but otherwise too busy with their own concerns to spare much interest for their daughter.

"You can come home with me," I suggested. "My parents would like you."

She yawned and curled up. "You've already got sisters."

"I could have another."

"That sounds nice," she said sleepily, and I let my eyes drift closed. There was a scent of smoke in the air—those bushfires to the west Lat had talked about.

I wanted to dream of home. Instead, I dreamed of Diane and woke up fighting.

"You're fine!" someone said. "Abdi. You're here. You're safe."

It was Tegan. I was gripping her wrist, fingers digging into the soft flesh. My hand sprang away. Beside me, Joph was sleeping, unmoved by Tegan's presence.

Tegan brushed my forehead with her warm fingertips. "Come with me," she said. "The wind has changed."

CHAPTER ELEVEN
Con Fuoco

When I staggered out into the hall, my head still fuzzy with the drug aftereffects, people were milling around in confusion. Some were fully dressed; others were in sleepwear, apparently unsure as to whether this was an emergency evacuation or just a notice to be extra alert. I wasn't certain myself and followed Tegan as she darted into the bedroom she shared with Bethari.

"Wind's changed," she said.

Bethari sat up, registered there was a man in the room, and dove over the side of the bed, reappearing with a scarf hastily tied around her hair. I didn't think this was a time for modesty rules, but whatever. "The fires are heading this way?" she asked.

"I don't know," Tegan said. "I think we should check. But if they are…"

Then there might be an opportunity for us to escape. Even an orderly evacuation would have a certain amount of chaos.

I met Tegan's eyes and nodded. "Can you girls get Dr. Carmen ready to go? I'll check out what's happening upstairs, then get Joph."

Tegan rummaged under the bed and pulled out a black bag, presumably full of food. "No problem. Come on, Bethi."

Bethari pulled on her shoes and hefted another bag over her shoulder.

"The EMP," she said suddenly.

"Is it here?" I asked.

"Kept in one of the vehicles. Um, big blue one, six-seater. I can get the control unit."

"Then that's our ride," I said, and headed upstairs to scout out the landscape. There, air smelled of smoke. The closer I got to the trapdoor hatch, the stronger the stench became, until I had to fight the urge to cough just to get the stink out of my nostrils.

The central room was crowded with people tensely watching Hurfest and Lat discuss whether an evacuation was warranted. I could see no lights outside, and the full moon's glow was sullen red, hazy behind the smoke. Lat slept in his underwear, I noted, sour at the gleam of red light on his muscled chest.

Both he and Hurfest seemed as if they were coming to an agreement to hide and wait out the fires when Washington brushed by me. She stood poised in the front door, looking at the sky and holding her hand up to test the wind. When she came back in, the red glow was behind her, her face in shadow. But her voice was clear, cutting through the murmurs of the men. "We have to go."

"I've got people hiking up the hill to see if they can get a better view from the ridge," Lat said.

Washington shook her head. "Call them back. This house is indefensible; there's too much dry growth and no water. If the trapdoor caves, we might not even be safe underneath."

"These walls won't burn," Lat protested.

"Oxygen will," she told him. "And the smoke will get in. If we can't breathe, we're just as dead. We have to follow the plan and get to the evacuation sites. Reconvene at the northwest base."

Hurfest grimaced. "Is this really necessary? Aren't we being a bit alarmist?"

"You two aren't from bushfire states," she said, which was news to me. As far as I knew, the whole of Australia regularly burst into flame. She tilted her head at the man who'd tried to take over lunch preparation. He was looking even more harassed. "Ask Ewing."

"It's bad," he confirmed. "Some of the communities to the west have been forcibly evacuated in convoys. They don't bring in the army unless it's serious."

Washington suddenly cocked her head and lifted her hand. I wasn't sure what we were listening for until I heard a dull roaring sound, like a car on a distant road. "We have to go—now," she said.

Hurfest gave in. "Evacuate," he said crisply, and the room exploded into tightly planned movement; most people headed down the stairs, giving up their personal computers for destruction before they went. Before I could duck down the stairs again, Hurfest spotted me at the back of the room and oiled through the crowd to get me. "Abdi, you and the girls are with Lat and me," he said in a low voice. "We're the Bendigo group. Go and fetch them. I'll be preparing the vehicle." That was both good and bad news—less chance of an immediate escape, but if he was keeping all his assets close by, the EMP would probably be going with us.

But—

"Tegan won't leave without Dr. Carmen," I said.

"She'll be evacuated with the group going to Huntly."

"Tegan will want her with us," I said, and accompanied the statement with a conspiratorial roll of my eyes. *Tegan, right? Such a pain. But what can you do?*

He grimaced.

"I'll get her," Washington said quietly, and we went down the stairs together. She broke off to go into the infirmary. I caught a glimpse of Bethari and Tegan bent over the sickbed before I took off around the corner for my own bedroom.

Joph was sitting in the middle of the bed, clutching her red medicine bag.

"Why is there so much noise?" she asked.

"The fire's come too close. We have to go; come on."

"Go where?" she said, without moving. "I like fires. We're not allowed to have them, though. Air pollution."

Joph must have taken her pain meds while I was upstairs, and a high dose at that. She wasn't worried about the fire; she wasn't worried about anything. And that meant she wasn't going to run on my word. We didn't have time for explanations. I pulled her arm over my shoulder and yanked her up, steadying her waist with my other arm. We took a few stumbling steps that way, but her legs were like sacks stuffed with wool, and when she tried to move faster and put more weight on her left leg, it gave out entirely.

I scooped her into my arms, red bag and all, and ran through the halls, which were mostly empty of people now. My arms and thighs strained under Joph's weight as I lumbered upstairs.

"Ow," she protested, as her elbow whacked against the edge of the hole in the floor.

"Sorry," I gasped. I saw the white-haired woman in the map room, industriously stuffing maps into the fire set there. Ridiculous, to burn that evidence when a major disaster was bearing down on us. The burning smell was even stronger, and the air in the house was thick with haze.

Outside, people were piling into vehicles and taking off quickly. A larger blue car was pulled up by the door, with Tegan and Washington carefully laying out Dr. Carmen on the backseat. Bethari was looking in the trunk, under the guise of dumping her bag in. She looked up as I came forward and pointed significantly, and I breathed a little easier, even with my long-legged burden. We had the EMP at hand.

Tegan helped me get Joph into the middle seat, pulling while I pushed; it was easier when Bethari climbed in the front seat and started telling Joph to move, because Joph actually made an effort when her ex-girlfriend delivered orders.

Lat was in the driver's seat, drumming his fingers against the wheel. "Get in with us, Sergeant," he said abruptly. "Your group's gone."

Washington closed the door on Dr. Carmen and came around to the front, moving Bethari into the jump seat in the middle. Hurfest squeezed in beside me, the doors slammed, and Lat guided the car around two in the driveway and hit the dirt road running. I caught one glimpse over Hurfest's shoulder of the stone house that had been our all-too-temporary refuge. Then it was gone, swallowed by a curve in the road.

With four of us in the middle seat, it was a tight squeeze, and I regretted the new breadth of my shoulders. Washington twisted around from the front and handed out strips of toweling that had been dampened. I didn't know what to do with them until I saw Tegan wrap hers around her mouth and nose.

Smoke inhalation, I realized, and made sure Joph's cloth was on tight. Bethari had merely wet one end of her headscarf and pulled it over her face as she messed with the car computer, and I conceded, privately, that the hijab could be useful after all.

Through the car windows, I could see little black dots floating down through the air. They looked like the snow I'd seen on 'casts if snow were black, and for a moment I was confused. Then one flared red and died, and I realized they were embers and ash. We went up a long hill, and I twisted in my seat, ignoring Hurfest's grumble.

From this height, I could see what the landscape had obscured before. Behind us, maybe three or four kilometers back, was the fire. It stretched out for miles, an uneven and roiling mass of black smoke, with red and orange flashes of light at the base. The embers were soaring ahead, borne by the savage wind, and even as I watched I saw them smolder in dry brush, setting more of the land alight.

The smoke swept over the patched green roof of the stone house and swallowed it whole. Washington had been right; if anything, we should have left earlier. As it was, we were racing the fire, and the fire was winning. I didn't think much of the chances of the people who'd left after us.

I turned around again. "It's coming," I said, my voice shrill in my own ears.

Lat didn't waste time responding. His eyes were narrowed, and he was coaxing more out of the electric motor than it should have been able to give him. Bethari had set up the car's computer to bounce through several proxies instead of revealing our location to anyone who cared to look. She gave him terse status updates from the satellite footage, guiding him through the twisty country roads.

Tegan reached over Joph's lap and took my hand in hers. She was staring straight ahead, the strong bones of her clear features muffled in her damp towel, but I could see her lips moving underneath it. She was praying.

It was harder to get angry about her beliefs now.

The car jerked violently as Lat swung the wheel and pulled us off the road onto a field baked dry. I saw why as we bumped over the lumpy dirt—a stand of eucalyptus trees by the side of the road had caught fire, sparked by a floating ember, and one of those trees had fallen across the road, blocking the path. The turn and the uneven ground cost us speed. Lat muttered something in a language I didn't recognize and turned back to the road.

The noise was tremendous, louder than a train, louder than the engine of the jet I'd flown in to Australia. My family was wealthy compared with almost everyone else in Djibouti, but not wealthy enough for air travel; it had been the first time I'd ever been in the air. Probably the last, too. I brought Tegan's hand to my face and pressed my cheek against her palm. My eyes were stinging from smoke irritation, and every breath I sucked in seemed drier. I was sweating, but my exposed skin was dry, the heat sucking the moisture away as soon as it touched the surface.

Half an hour to Bendigo by road. Half an hour to safety, if Bendigo was safe. How long had we been driving? Even at the speeds Lat was pushing out of the car, how long did we have to go?

Through the driver's windshield, I saw red light flare ahead. Another fire across the road. But this time there was no handy field to the side. Lat cursed viciously and shouted, "Get down!"

His voice cracked on the words. I had time to grab Joph's head and force it down, time to feel Hurfest hurl his body on top of mine, and then, somehow, Lat forced the car to go even faster. Something struck the undercarriage and scraped hideous sounds out of the road. The engine whirred. I could smell the stench of burning hair, as the heat sizzled at my arms.

This is it, I thought, oddly calm, and then whatever branch or rock had blocked us gave way, and we leaped through the flames.

CHAPTER TWELVE
Poco a poco

We made it to Bendigo.

"No one's fighting for their houses," Tegan said, as we drove through the empty outskirts of the town. She sounded puzzled.

"In your time, they could use water to soak the roofs," Washington told her. "Now all the available water is for the fire brigade. Everyone else gathers in a clear space and hopes that the wind will change to spare their homes."

The population had gathered on the local rugby grounds, on the east side of the town. Once, people had played on genuine grass, but as the droughts went on and the rivers dried up, they'd had to lay down a synthetic substitute instead. It was fireproof, which, as far as I was concerned, made it several grades better than the real thing.

Tegan and I kept our cloth masks on, just in case, but the police officers and volunteer fire-brigade members waving people into the grounds had much more important things on their minds than looking out for a pair of famous runaways. "Any injured?" one woman with a flashlight asked. "Smoke inhalation, second- or third-degree burns?"

"Only minor scorching," Lat promised.

I winced and hoped she wouldn't take too close a look at the blanket thrown over the woman lying in the backseat. Dr. Carmen was conscious, but keeping very quiet. Her injuries would demand medical attention immediately, and other, much less welcome attention would follow swiftly afterward.

"Then you might need to wait. Emergency cases go to the white tent if it gets worse, all right?" The woman pointed out a spare patch of ground near one set of goalposts and told us where to pick up some water. If she bothered to think about us at all, she probably took us for vacationers who'd chosen a bad place for a break.

We stayed in the car, but opened all the doors to get what cross breeze we could. "I'll get the water," Washington said, and strode off to the field next door, where volunteers were handing out big bottles, guarded by armed police. No one wanted water riots tonight.

"Hurfest, how's the arm?" Lat asked.

Carl Hurfest had been the only one injured as we burst through the flames. He'd flung himself over Joph, Tegan, and me—whether to try to protect us, or just because he was slow to get down, I didn't know, and wasn't sure if I cared. The burn on his right arm looked like a bad case of sunburn— darker than the surrounding skin and starting to wrinkle around the edges. He inspected it with a detached air and then shrugged. "If you fetch me a fork, I could see how cooked journalist tastes."

Bethari giggled and then crushed the sound with both hands. "I'm sorry," she gasped. "I just…out of all the people trying to get us, I never thought we'd have to worry about the *weather*." She laughed again, her voice high and climbing.

"This is a deadly land," Lat said, which he probably meant to be a sobering reminder. Instead, it sounded pretentious. Hurfest and Joph started giggling, too, and I was hard put not to join them. Tegan ducked her head to hide a smile.

Lat stared at us as if we were all infinitely confusing and then shook his head. "I'm going to steal someone's computer and check in with the other groups," he said. "Hurfest, Bethari, you're with me. You four stay here."

He vanished into the night, seemingly unaware that he was still wearing only sleep shorts. Bethari rolled her eyes and followed him.

"You four stay here," Tegan said in a deep growl, and I did laugh then, Joph joining in until we had laughed most of the terror out. It was all right for Lat and Washington—they were warriors, trained to face death and recover swiftly. We civilian folk needed a few moments to adjust to the aftermath of deadly peril.

"As if I could walk," Dr. Carmen said, flipping the blanket off her face and sitting up. "Phew." It was the first time I'd heard her voice in person; it was a pleasant contralto. I bet she could sing.

"Are you feeling all right?" Tegan asked anxiously.

"I'm fine. Let me see the medical supplies?"

I fetched the bag from the trunk and deposited it politely on her lap. She poked through, making pleased noises, and commended Joph on her insight. "I think I've got everything I'll need here." She fished out a blue bottle and tossed it to Joph. "I believe these are yours."

"More painkillers?" I asked.

"My antiandrogens," Joph said.

I knew that Joph had…what was the polite phrase? Been born with a male body? But she was so solidly a girl in my head that it was always weird to be reminded of it. Whatever my face did, Joph smiled peaceably at me and dry-swallowed a pill without ceremony.

"Thank you, Abdi," the doctor said. Her eyes measured me again, flickering to Tegan and then back to my face. Her introduction to me had been my fighting with Tegan in the infirmary. What else did she know? Had Hurfest—or Lat—told her what I'd been doing with her foster daughter on that table?

And how would she react to my wanting to take Tegan to Djibouti?

My best bet was a consistent demonstration that I was a nice, polite young man. Fortunately, I really was young, and mostly polite. Nice was a little harder to fake.

"You're welcome, Dr. Carmen," I replied, and took the proffered bag.

"Call me Marie," she said. "Tegan told me your plan. It sounds practical." That measuring look was still there, though.

"If they'd left Bethari here, we could go now," Tegan said.

I didn't bother remarking that we could go without Bethari, since she wanted to stay in Australia so badly. Tempting, but the suggestion would only start a fight. And I really didn't want to leave her to Lat's mercy when he discovered us vanished.

Besides, we needed to know where to go first.

"Do you have any suggestions for somewhere we could hide, Marie?" I asked.

"No, I don't remember everything I told them, but it would be safer not to depend on me as a source of safety."

I winced. "Joph?"

"The compound was the only place I knew."

"Tegan?" I said, without much hope. All the places she'd known—if they still existed after a hundred years—would be in the city, and we needed to head for the coast.

She shook her head. "Sorry. I haven't really had time to find hidey-holes."

"Bethari's contacts," I thought out loud. "Are they all Save Tegan contacts, too, or can she approach a couple of people who are largely unconnected?"

"You'd have to ask her," Joph said doubtfully.

Tegan grinned at me. "Look at your brain, ticking away. You'll figure something out. Just as well, the details are your specialty, not mine."

I laughed, probably more than the joke deserved. "Well, while Bethari's gone, I might as well scope out the camping ground."

"But Lat told us to stay here," Tegan said.

My good humor vanished as abruptly as if she'd popped a balloon with a pin. "I heard him," I said, and walked away.

The atmosphere in the grounds was heightened but not particularly grim. There hadn't been any confirmed deaths this evening, and most of the inhabitants of Bendigo were only at the refuge as a precaution. Unless the wind started blowing northeast, their town would survive the blaze. The prevailing mood seemed to be hopeful; people felt that so far this summer, they'd gotten off lucky, and the weather might continue to be kind.

I kept my mouth shut, marveling at the capability of people to accept anything as normal. In Tegan's time, such enormous, life-threatening bushfires had been rare but increasing in severity. Now they came often, even after the official end of summer. It probably hadn't been a good idea for Hurfest to plan a revolution for the tail end of the fire season.

Unless he wanted army resources tied up in rescue efforts and government infrastructure overloaded with relief requests.

Then it was probably a very good idea indeed.

I shook my head as if I could dislodge my reluctant admiration for the man's planning. I didn't want to be impressed by Carl Hurfest. But it *was* politically pragmatic thinking, the sort my mother had raised me to consider. There was room for idealism in her world—and Hurfest's, obviously—but it had to be carried out in a practical manner.

I gnawed at my lip. My mother was nothing like Carl Hurfest, not really. She'd taught me to think this way so that I could survive in the maze of political machinations. Hurfest was using pragmatism at the cost of innocent lives.

But I couldn't shake the notion that she might admire his methods, too.

The medical tents were surrounded by the densest concentration of people, functioning as a social hub as much as a treatment center. Volunteers sorted through people efficiently, triaging the injured and moving their supporters aside. I drifted through the mass and listened, keeping my face hidden behind my towel. I didn't look unusual; with the scent of smoke still poisoning the air, most people were in masks or something like them. And I needed to get some sort of a handle on how successful Hurfest's planned coup was likely to be with Australia's citizens.

Unfortunately, all anyone seemed to want to talk about was the fires. I was just about to break my cover of silence and ask a few leading questions out of sheer impatience, when my ear caught a word guaranteed to make me pay attention.

"—think about the *Resolution*?" I heard. I sat down on the grass and turned slightly, trying to observe without being noticed myself.

The speaker was a tall man with a long beard, his hair caught up in a turban. "Personally, I think it's a bunch of bullshit," he said importantly. "All those public funds tied up in a fool's mission."

"They're not using public funds anymore," a woman in a pink dress said mildly. His wife, maybe. "It's all private donations now."

"People with the money to waste on starship donations could find better things to do with that money," Long Beard insisted.

"It is their money, though," Pink Dress told him. "Did you see they've decided on the planet? Keolanui D. One huge continent, plenty of fresh water, plenty of native flora, but no large animal life."

"A proper mickey operation, if you ask me. How can they get a starship to Keolaney whatever if they can't even hold on to their, what do you call 'em, youth ambassadors?"

"Those poor children," Pink Dress sighed. "Kidnapped by terrorists; they must be so scared. Tegan's had enough to deal with."

I tensed, then forced my shoulders down. Just a typical Australian boy, bored by the need to leave his home for the day.

"It's the refugee children I feel sorry for," another man broke in, pushing his fair hair away from his face. "Some of them were born in those camps. Can you imagine? The chance to get on board the *Resolution* must be such a relief."

I chewed on my tongue so that I wouldn't break into the conversation, to tell Blondie exactly what I thought of the *Resolution*'s cryocargo.

"I wouldn't bring children into the world if I lived in such circumstances," Long Beard declared.

"Their parents might not have had much choice," Pink Dress pointed out.

"Well, that's exactly the problem! Why wasn't government funding going to better birth control? How come honest Australians get hit with tax increases for having more than two kids, but these thirdies can have as many as they like on the public dollar?"

Blondie was looking grim. "Are you in favor of forced sterilization, then?" he asked sternly.

By his face, Long Beard hadn't thought that far ahead. "I'm just saying something should be done, that's all."

Blondie opened his hands. "The *Resolution* is something. Opening up off-world colonies will free up Earth's resources and reduce population strain—"

"For billions of dollars! We could be fixing the planet for that. Doing something about these bloody fires."

"Anything that could make a substantive difference should have started decades ago," Pink Dress said. "You know that, Sanab; you've read my thesis."

"You want to go to this new planet, then?" Long Beard demanded. "Good luck; they won't let you on the boat. It's refugees and rich drongles only, and good riddance to both of them. Leave Australia to the real Australians, that's what I say."

"Sanab!"

"Scrap this," Blondie said, and stalked off.

"What's his problem?"

"His mother was a refugee, from the American fundamentalist wars. I know I've told you that before!"

"Oh, crap, I forgot. I'm sorry."

"You don't owe me the apology. It's his face you broke."

"He just gets so self-righteous! Why couldn't the money go to developing crops or trying to get some of the water out of Europa? That would be a good use of off-world technology. Then we might actually have room for these refugees. Some of them, anyway. The ones that'll actually put in an honest day's work for an honest dollar—"

"Go and find him," Pink Dress interrupted. "And for goodness' sake, don't mention *that*."

"All right. I love you."

"I love you, too."

They kissed, and Long Beard left. Pink Dress lifted an eyebrow at me, and I realized that in my absorption in the argument, I'd abandoned all pretense of not listening. I turned away, feeling heat flare in my cheeks. *Go away*, I chanted silently. *I'm just a rude kid; don't bother with me; go away go away go away.*

There was a rustle, and then Pink Dress sat beside me. "That looks sore," she said.

My hand flew to the back of my neck. I'd almost forgotten the wound there, though the implant had been cut out barely twenty-four hours before. "It's all right. I got cut, that's all. In the fire."

Her other eyebrow rose. "Not a local, are you?"

"I'm on vacation," I said. "From New Zealand."

"Ah. Don't pay any attention to Sanab. He's got a good heart."

A good heart didn't count for much when your bad mouth was spewing lies about thirdies, but I didn't want to draw any more attention to myself. I nodded.

"I hope this isn't rude, but you look familiar," Pink Dress said.

"People say that all the time," I said, hand creeping up to adjust my towel mask. "They think I look like Dominic from *Talented Australia*."

"Oh! He's the juggler, right?"

"Yes. I don't see it myself."

"No," Pink Dress said, scrutinizing my face. "You don't look much like him, when you look close."

Long Beard and Blondie were coming back, amicable again. "Oh, there are your friends," I said.

"Nice to meet you…" Pink Dress said, and left a space for my name.

"Soren," I said, and shook her hand.

"I'm Eliza, Soren. Nice to meet you. Stay safe." She greeted her friends, then, and I left as soon after that as I could, feeling an itch between my shoulder blades.

Without turning around, I knew Eliza was watching me go.

CHAPTER THIRTEEN
Divisi

Tegan looked happy to see me return. Lat, his face set in hard lines, did not.

"I gave you a specific order," he hissed, hauling me into the car by my arm. "I said, 'stay here.'"

"Did you forget you don't give me orders anymore?" I focused on his shark eyes and was a little surprised to see him flinch. "We're allies now. *Allies* don't issue orders, Lat."

"Abdi's right," Tegan said, and the rush of victory was sweet. She gave me a water bottle and wiped her sweaty hand on her loose pants. "So it went okay?"

That was the perfect opportunity to tell them that Pink Dress had paid more attention to me than might have been ideal, but I didn't want to give in to Lat that easily. I tugged down my mask and took a long drink instead. I'd only meant to buy myself time before I talked, but as soon as the water hit my parched throat I couldn't stop drinking. It was the best thing I'd ever tasted. By the time I emptied the bottle and redamped my mask with another, Lat was looking awkward.

"I'm sorry for what I said," he said. "I'm not really used to a less...top-down command hierarchy."

After that, I couldn't confess. Besides, Pink Dress had only been curious, not suspicious. What was she going to do, tell someone she'd seen a kid that looked vaguely like a boy in one of the interminable talent shows every moderately peaceful country pumped out like sewage?

I told the others what I'd heard and left out Pink Dress's conversation with me afterward. It was probably fine.

Hurfest looked gloomy at my report. "We do have popular support," he told Tegan. "A lot of it."

Bethari folded her arms. "But there are still plenty of people who think the No Migrant policy is the best approach to a refugee crisis. And that the *Resolution* is the best they can hope for—that they're *lucky* to be cryofrozen and shipped as slave labor and toil for who knows how long far away from the homelands to which they can never return and—"

"We know," I said.

"I'm just *saying*. Maybe if the Save Tegan political wing had concentrated more on raising awareness and less on cozying up with power-crazy military dissidents—"

"Hey," Washington said mildly.

"—then we'd have *overwhelming* popular support, and we wouldn't need to resort to using a weapon that killed innocent people!"

Bethari collapsed back against her seat, lip trembling, and

shrugged off Joph's comforting hand on her shoulder. Marie and Tegan looked as if they wanted to comfort her, too, but weren't sure how.

This wasn't the Bethari I was used to—journalist and activist, self-righteously demonstrating that she was more politically pure than you. She was genuinely upset, about the EMP, and about the choices Save Tegan had made. And about the prospect of leaving Australia, a homeland to which she could maybe never return.

I should be nicer to her, I thought, and immediately tried to unthink it. I didn't want to have sympathy for Bethari, who was annoying in her best moments and infuriating in her worst. At school, I'd been able to hide my irritation, leverage her political inclinations to get some protection from her against people like Soren Morgensen. Now that my emotions were so raw, though, it was harder to treat her with the proper distance, as someone who was useful to me and pointless beside that.

My mother's third rule for political success was *empathy*— not to be mistaken for sympathy. You had to watch the other party, work out what they wanted and why they wanted it— what motivations drove them. And then formulate your strategy so that you could give them—or seem to give them—what they wanted by accomplishing your own goals.

For the first time, I wondered if applying those rules to my personal relationships was really ethical.

Questioning my mother's methods felt wrong, like I'd bitten into something tasty only to find rotten meat inside. But trying to see from someone else's perspective surely couldn't be wrong. Empathy was *good*.

So how would I feel if I'd made a weapon that I'd never intended to be used, that was supposed to function only as a threat. How would I feel if it *had* been used? How would I feel if that weapon had saved my friend but killed fellow citizens of the country I loved? Wouldn't I want to stay and make amends? Wouldn't I think that leaving was a betrayal, of my country and of the deaths that I'd inadvertently caused?

I did feel sympathy for Bethari, and I had to acknowledge it. Unfortunately, she couldn't get what she wanted. But I could try to be nicer to her.

It was a few hours before dawn until any of us got back to sleep. Joph took one of her pills and passed out facedown on the pretend grass, curled up beside Bethari, who had apparently recovered from her bout of grief to happily poke at her purloined computer. I wasn't sure I believed her seeming good humor—her hands shook as she stabbed at the screen, and Joph had watched her carefully until the pain became too much.

Washington catnapped sitting against a tire, opening her dark eyes every time there was a louder-than-usual noise. Marie lay down in the backseat and appeared to rest. The rest of us stayed awake, silent. Lat sat between Tegan and me. I couldn't tell if he'd done it on purpose.

A moan shivered through the campsite, a sort of collective shudder. Lat was on his feet at once, Washington on hers straight after.

I sat up. "What—"

"Shhh." Washington licked a grimy finger and held it up. "Wind change."

All over the rugby grounds, lights were going on as people woke up and shook their families and computers to life. Hurfest was hurrying back to us, water bottle in hand.

Bethari was pulling up satellite images on her computer, sneaking into the footage of news crews. "They say it's at the outskirts of the town," she reported. In the pale light of the pre-dawn, I could make out part of the sky that was darker than the rest. That sullen red glow suddenly fired underneath it.

Fear gripped my belly. "Should we run?"

Washington shook her head. "This is the safest place to be."

Firefighters were spraying the grounds. A fine mist landed on my bare shoulders, and I took comfort in that, though it did little more than dampen the soot smeared all over me.

A massive detonation rolled through the uneasy atmosphere, so loud that it shook the ground under us. The black smoke flashed orange and yellow and white, a giant column of flame flaring through it before dying away. The air was suddenly heavy with the stink of burning petrol, an oily, acrid stench that easily penetrated my mask. I gagged.

"What was that?" Joph asked.

"Diesel storage," Lat guessed.

It made sense—those farmers who were still trying to get crops out of this land would rely on diesel for their heavy machinery, not the rechargeable batteries that powered light, everyday vehicles. But it wasn't a good sign.

We waited. We didn't have any choice. While the fire brigade fought the flames, we could do nothing but huddle together and hope.

When dawn came, we were still alive.

But half of Bendigo was a smoldering ruin.

Δ ∫ Ω

In the morning, word came that the roads to the south were cleared. A few people, against the advice of the police, were already starting to leave—either to stay with family and friends somewhere else, or to find out what damage the fires had done to their homes. Apparently, the new base of operations of Save Tegan was in the North, so Hurfest and Lat were waiting for the way to be declared safe before they took us there.

I, of course, had other plans. We had the car, we had the supplies, we had the EMP, and we had a couple of computers that Bethari had managed to smuggle out of the underground complex. We just needed to be left alone with them for long enough to make our escape. I racked my brain for an excuse to get Washington, Lat, and Hurfest all gone at the same time— preferably far enough away that they wouldn't see our direction as we went.

But they seemed content to stay at the car throughout that long day. Once, Washington went to get more water, and Dr. Carmen suggested that Lat and Hurfest check in with the disparate groups again. Hurfest patronizingly explained that excess communication increased the chance of being traced and didn't move an inch. Once, Lat strolled off to see if he could increase our weapons cache, and I was sure that Tegan and Bethari and I could have overwhelmed the unarmed Hurfest between us. But

169

not without drawing attention to ourselves. And we certainly couldn't defeat Washington, who was armed and might have been a match for us even if she weren't.

As the day drifted on, in smoke and sweat, the strain between Hurfest's intentions and our secret plans began to grow.

I was practiced at concealing my true feelings, and Joph wore her serenity like a mask. Even Tegan had gotten better at lying. Not as good at it as I was, but she could keep quiet and nod along every time Hurfest talked about her exciting new role as speaker for the Save Tegan movement. But Bethari was jittery, constantly tweaking her clothes or twitching her fingers. I hoped that could be accounted for by her anger over the EMP, a subject both Lat and Hurfest walked very carefully around.

There was no credible reason for Marie's behavior when Hurfest asked about her research.

"No," she said. "I don't want to talk about it."

Hurfest looked patient, an expression that was becoming more and more strained as the day wore on. "We don't need the medical details; anything you can tell us about the progress of the revival project would be very helpful. So far, Tegan's the only survivor. If she's likely to remain so for some time, we retain a lot of leverage. Just an indication of how long it will be until more people can be safely revived—"

"You have all my records of my work until I was imprisoned," Marie said. "Anything I did after that was done under duress and is thus unethical medical research. I won't be telling you—or anyone—anything about it."

"But how do we make it clear to people how terrible this research was unless—"

"This conversation is over," Marie snapped.

Her voice was too loud. I saw people in other groups looking over. Hurfest noticed, too, and shrugged theatrically before turning away, acting as if he no longer cared. The spectators went back to their own concerns—just another couple having a brief argument after a stressful event. But only an idiot would believe Marie didn't have something to hide, and Hurfest wasn't stupid. He'd keep pushing her to reveal what she knew.

I had a certain amount of curiosity myself.

I was annoyed, though; Marie's outright defiance wasn't in our wait-and-see escape plan. I could see Hurfest's suspicions rise, and Lat, who was paranoid by profession, had clearly worked out something was wrong. He didn't say anything, but he sent Washington on all the necessary errands after that. He and Hurfest stuck near the car.

Which, as it turned out, was fortunate. Because if they hadn't, I would never have heard what I did next.

That afternoon, the girls sacked out in and around the car, catching up on the sleep they'd lost during the night. I'd planned to follow suit, but after Marie's outburst, I thought that one of us should stay awake and alert for any changes. I was lying near the edge of "our" territory, pretending to nap while Hurfest and Lat conferred, when a brief exclamation from Lat made me listen up.

He sounded excited. Given the circumstances, it was an out-of-place emotion, especially on Lat, who tended to go from dour to stern, with the occasional detour into grim. I kept my eyes shut but listened harder.

"...best opportunity we might have," he was saying. "Are you sure?"

"I've got it from three different sources," Hurfest said. "President Cox should be here tomorrow."

"And your sources can let us know his exact arrival time?"

Hurfest laughed. "They won't need to. His office will let the media know well in advance, and that's public information. There's no point in touring a disaster zone to offer consolation to the devastated if the world doesn't see you do it."

"That's it, then. I'll have my people carry out the operation. Yours can move in the government the minute we do."

"Can we keep the children hidden around here for so long? Or should we move them?"

Children, I thought scornfully. But what did they mean by *the operation?*

"It's a risk," Lat conceded. "But there are risks in moving, too, and there's a lot of confusion here—four more weens without ID or possessions aren't going to stand out that much. There are measures we can take to make them less recognizable. And it means Tegan will be in place when we strike."

My blood chilled at the word. *Strike.*

If Hurfest and Lat were planning a presidential assassination for tomorrow, and Tegan was an essential part of it, then we either had to talk them out of it or get out of the grounds tonight. Otherwise they'd throw her in front of the camera as soon as it was done.

I'd promised Tegan she'd never have to perform again. If I wanted to keep that promise, I had to let her know what I'd heard.

In my shock, I must have made some sound or movement, because Lat's head shifted. "Abdi?"

I'd closed my eyes again the minute I saw the movement, but I could hear him walking toward me.

"Abdi, I know you're awake."

Fine. I abandoned the pretense and sat up. "How will you strike?" I asked, sitting up on the plastic grass.

Lat blinked at me. "How much did you hear?"

I rolled my eyes at him. "You said, 'ready to strike.' At the president, presumably. How exactly will you strike?"

Hurfest looked politely blank, but Lat's face flickered with guilt.

"You're going to use the EMP," I said flatly, my voice concealing the racing of my heart. "So you're planning an assassination?"

"An overthrow," Hurfest said. "And one as peaceful as possible. Abdi, President Cox is the man ultimately responsible for what was done to you. SADU reports directly to him—"

"I don't care about him," I snapped, and glanced around at the crowded grounds. "It's everyone else! Haven't the people here suffered enough? Can't you do this without the EMP?"

Lat shook his head. "No. We need it to control communications in and out of the dead zone. The media will gather to hear the president. We'll take down the guards and use the EMP to blow the tech in the area. We'll be ready to bring new

173

equipment in for the journalists, and then Tegan can talk to them and explain why this is necessary."

"She doesn't want to do that," I said. "You'll have to find another way." I rolled to my knees and headed to the car, where Tegan was sitting up, roused by the sound of her name.

"They're planning to assassinate the president," I said, fast and quiet. "Here, tomorrow. They want you to do the talking."

I saw the knowledge hit home, and then she was on her feet as Lat and Hurfest came striding up behind me.

"I won't do it," she said to them. Her cheeks were flushed and her eyes bright, and she looked beautiful. Beautiful, and furious.

Lat turned to her. "Tegan, I promise, this will limit the inevitable collateral damage. I can't promise there won't be civilian casualties, but it's the best way to remove this president."

"Remove who?" Joph said, sitting up. "What's going on?"

Lat's tone had been soft and conciliatory, but Hurfest went for arrogant—always a mistake with Tegan Oglietti.

"I thought Joph and Abdi would understand, Tegan, even if you didn't," he said. "Politicians have to be practical."

"My mum wouldn't do that," Joph protested, but knowledge of some of my mother's practical measures saved me the bother of disagreement. You didn't get to be part of parliament in a small country surrounded by much larger political bodies without making compromises between the right thing to do and the most expedient choice. If Joph's mother had never made the hard decisions, it was only because she'd never had to.

"This is the kind of decision you can't make unilaterally, Carl," Marie said crisply.

"We have to move fast!" he protested. "This is the best chance we're ever going to get. Lat agrees from a military perspective. I agree from a political perspective—"

"Well, here's the humanitarian perspective," Marie said. "It's not happening. Furthermore, I'm Tegan's guardian, and you do not have my permission to use my ward in this way."

"You don't have my permission, either," Tegan said. "If you were wondering."

"Tegan, there are more important things at stake," Hurfest said.

Tegan's voice sharpened. "I've heard that before."

"Shut *up*, Carl," Lat said, and turned back to Tegan. "Cox has to die, Tegan." His voice was soft. "This government has to change. It's the only way you'll be safe."

"Safe! Did you forget how I died the first time?"

Lat blinked. "You were shot."

"I was shot by a sniper who was aiming at the Prime Minister, Lat! How are you planning to take down the guards? That won't be bloodless. Using the EMP will start fires here, in this tinderbox. There will be cross fire; there will be chaos. I've *been* a civilian casualty. I've been *inevitable collateral damage*. And now you want to use me to justify a plan that will do the same to others? No. I won't let you."

Lat looked slightly desperate. "Cox won't let you go, Tegan! He and his cronies will want you back, and if they can't have that, they'll want revenge. If you just speak up, you can make the coup legitimate, make the changeover smooth. If you don't want to talk again afterward, you won't have to."

Hurfest stiffened at that, but Lat kept going. "Tegan, I've thought about it a lot. This is the best way to avoid repercussions, so that you can make a new life. One without fear." He was so sincere, and, despite myself, I felt his reasoning tug at me. He was an experienced operative, after all, and Cox really was a threat. If Tegan could be kept safe…

But Tegan would never willingly sacrifice others for her safety. She turned to me, ignoring Lat. "We're leaving. Right now."

Oh, great. So much for a careful, sneaking getaway. But now wasn't the time for dissension in our ranks.

"You got it," I said. "Bethari, wake up."

"I'm up."

"Secure the EMP."

"On it." She'd slept in her headscarf this time, and she righted her clothes with precise, controlled gestures as she moved to the back of the car.

Lat's hands were working, muscles in his jaw jumping. I kept a wary eye on him as I grabbed supplies. Food, a knife. Too bad that Washington had all our empty water bottles; they would have come in very handy.

"That's enough," Hurfest said crisply. "Honest opposition is one thing, but walking away is quite another matter. Do you really think that four teenagers and an injured woman, whom the forces of a powerful government are hunting, are going to get as far as whatever imagined safe destination you've thought of at random? Do you even *have* a destination in mind?"

"You should stay here," Lat said, taking a step toward Tegan.

His eyes were trained on hers. "Tegan, we can talk about it. We can come up with a better plan."

"You promised that last time," I said. "But you came up with this one and slotted Tegan into it, without even asking. Because you knew that if you asked, she'd say no."

"I thought I could trust you," Tegan said. I wasn't sure if she'd even heard me. Her hands were trembling as she met Lat's gaze. "I thought you were my friend. That's what I told myself, when you hurt me. He has to. He's your friend."

"Tegan," he said heavily. "I'm sorry. But for your own safety, I can't let you leave like this. Carl's right. You have to stay."

My whole body tightened. Tegan, Bethari, and I might be able to take Lat down, if we moved fast and moved together. Hurfest wasn't a physical man; he probably wouldn't interfere. The fighting would draw attention. We'd need an explanation. Perhaps forcing some of Joph's pain meds into Lat would make him docile enough to go along with whatever we told anyone nosy. I glanced at Tegan, and she nodded slightly. The hand at her waist, no longer trembling, extended three fingers. She tucked in the first. Two—

"What's happening here?" Washington asked.

I froze, defeat sour in my mouth.

In her right hand, she held a bag, heavy with our refilled water bottles. In her left, she carried a sonic pistol, concealed from the rest of the rugby grounds by her body.

It was pointed at me.

Then, with a smooth pivot of her hips, it was pointed at Lat.

"Tegan?" Washington said. "You want to get out of here?"

"Yes," Tegan said, the word bursting out of her. "Zaneisha, I don't want to be a puppet anymore. I can't do it, and Carl said he would *make* me and—"

"And they're planning to assassinate the president when he visits this site," I said. "It's going to be a war zone."

Washington's eyes flickered. "All right. Let's go."

Marie, to my surprise, frowned.

Lat looked stunned, but Hurfest had adopted a sneer. "Sergeant, I thought I could depend on you to see sense."

"I do," she said.

"Sergeant," Lat said, inching closer to her. "I just want to—"

"Stay still," she said, keeping her weapon aimed on him. "You're right. They're not likely to make it alone. So I'll escort them. And you will do…whatever you do. But my parents escaped one civil war, Lat. I don't plan to participate in another."

"This won't go down that way," Hurfest said. "It'll be a peaceful process."

"A peaceful coup? Whatever you want to believe, Hurfest. Bethari, Joph, get in the car. Abdi, take the wheel."

I slid into the driver's seat, staring doubtfully at the controls. My mother's driver had given me a few lessons, but those were in a much nicer car, and I wasn't sure what processes would be manual instead of automatic. I'd have been a lot happier if the car were a ship.

Bethari climbed into the passenger seat and settled a black box the size of a clenched fist in her lap.

"Is that the EMP?" It looked far too small to be responsible for so much damage.

"The control unit; the actual EMP is in the trunk." She peered over my shoulder. "The start is the one with the lightning symbol," she said helpfully.

"I knew that," I said, annoyed. I just wasn't positive where the brakes were.

"I'll lay out a course for Crib Point," she said, and started playing with the car computer.

I started to snap something about not giving away our plans in front of the enemy and then stopped. Bethari was too smart for that kind of mistake, and even if she weren't, I was trying to be nicer to her.

Outside, Zaneisha was having a conversation with Lat that appeared to be conducted entirely in minute adjustments of their facial muscles. Her sonic pistol was still in her hand, and though it would attract too much attention to our departure, part of me hoped she'd shoot him with it. The sonic wave would rupture his eardrums, disturb his equilibrium. Let Lat be the one who was unsteady and uncertain, let he be the one who tasted vomit on his tongue and felt his feet go out from under him, the way I'd suffered so many times.

Instead, Zaneisha tucked the pistol into her skirt pocket and backed toward us. This would be the time for Lat to move, but he stared in the back window, eyes pleading. I wanted to see if Tegan was looking back at him but forced myself to start the car moving forward as Zaneisha got in.

"Bethari, are we really going to Crib Point?" she asked.

"No," Bethari said. "I'm not stupid. But maybe Lat and Carl will send people to look for us there."

"Maybe," Zaneisha said. "They're not stupid, either."

As I negotiated our route through the still-crowded rugby grounds, my attention was focused on the people around us, alert to the possibility of an escaping toddler running right under the wheels. That was probably the only reason I spotted Pink Dress—Eliza—talking to a police officer, her face thoughtful as she gazed around the grounds.

"Oh no."

"What?" Zaneisha asked.

"That woman in the pink dress. Do you see her?"

"Yes," Zaneisha said, almost immediately, which meant that she'd taken barely a second to find the woman in a huge space filled with over four thousand people. If I'd been less terrified and guilty, I might have had time to be impressed.

"I think she knows who I am. And she's talking to the police."

"What do we do?" Tegan asked.

"We drive," Zaneisha said, the calm of her voice barely wavering. "And as soon as we're out of the grounds, I take the wheel. And while I put as much distance between us and these people as possible, Abdi will tell us why he thinks that woman might know him and why he failed to mention this before."

CHAPTER FOURTEEN
Furioso

I spotted the flier first.

I'd been banished to the backseat while we drove to Wilsons Promontory, where my evil, deceiving ways couldn't offend Zaneisha's tender sensibilities. Marie took up most of the space, sitting sideways with her legs laid out along the seat, but there was enough room if I crammed myself against the side window, which is how I saw the flier crest the scrubby treetops.

The sleek gray shape slid through the air as deftly as a dolphin did through the water. Like a dolphin, it was fitted exactly to its environment, so as to use as little fuel as possible.

"Flier," I reported. "On the left."

Zaneisha kept driving at the same unexceptionable speed, five kilometers over the limit—just like every other car on the road. "Bethari?" she said crisply.

"Standard patrol patterns," Bethari reported, scowling

ferociously at her computer. "I could try to intercept their transmissions?"

"No. Too risky."

"Is that it there?" Tegan asked, peering out through the back window. The windows were opaque to people looking in, but we could see out easily enough, through a thin gray haze.

"Yes. You hadn't seen a flier before?" Marie asked.

"No. The plane we used on tour was more like the ones from my time."

"Fliers aren't really planes," Bethari said. "They're like… flying robots. They have surveillance equipment and sometimes weapons. They're controlled by people, but there's no one actually inside."

"Drones," Tegan said. "Got it. We had those in my time. Yours are probably more fancy."

"What was it like back then?" I asked. "To have so many planes in the sky?"

"Noisy," Tegan said thoughtfully. "But kind of nice. I'd hear the roar, and look up, and think about those people. Where they were going, where they'd come from. What their stories were."

"Very kooshy," Joph murmured.

"My grandfather lived in London when he was a boy, near their big airport," I said. "I forget the name."

"Heathrow," Tegan said, smiling. She was always pleased when she knew something we didn't, since she was so far behind on so many things.

"He said that over a thousand planes had landed and taken

off from the airport there every day." I couldn't quite keep the tinge of horror out of my voice. So much fuel.

"That would be too noisy for me," Tegan conceded.

"Have we stopped being angry at Abdi?" Joph asked hopefully.

"No," Zaneisha said.

"No, but we're thinking about it," Tegan countered. "He could sing, if he wanted to. That might make us think harder." For a moment, she almost looked shy, which was so impossible I immediately put it out of my mind.

I hadn't sung for nearly three days now. I missed it, like a deep ache in my bones. I'd gotten my student visa on the strength of my singing, but in order to smuggle medicines effectively, I'd had to avoid singing, so that I could avoid publicity. After my capture, SADU had made me sing, had made my performance an imperative, not a choice. I hated them for that, but the singing itself—that I loved.

There was no one to notice me now, no one I had to perform for but these five women, my friends.

Well. Two friends, one friend-of-friends, one sort-of-mother-of-a-friend, and one not-really-friend who was armed to the teeth.

What would they like? Well, that was easy.

I got two lines into "The Ballad of John and Yoko" before I looked at Tegan to judge my performance and realized my mistake.

Tegan had gone absolutely still. Her eyes looked like bruises in the dead white of her face, and her hands were clenched together so tightly I knew it had to hurt. I stopped immediately, the last word hanging in the air.

"Why'd you stop?" Bethari asked, twisting. "...Oh."

"No Beatles," Tegan said, in a voice as sharp and lifeless as an obsidian shard.

Thick gray despair rushed through my veins and settled solidly in my stomach. I struggled for breath, for control, against the urge to scream. This wasn't about me; it was about Tegan. I couldn't lose it now.

But I so desperately wanted to kill Diane. Shoot her, stab her, or, better yet, strangle her with my own two hands. I wanted to squeeze the life out of the woman who had made the Beatles a reminder of torture and captivity for Tegan, who had loved their music more than anyone I'd ever met.

The Beatles had meant hope to Tegan, once. Now they meant pain.

Tegan was still staring straight ahead, her breath coming in little pants.

"Marie, can we give her something?" Joph said. "Tegan, what can I do? What do you need?" Her hands fluttered with her distress.

"Give her space," Marie said. "You're here, Tegan. You're in a car. We're driving to a cove on Wilsons Promontory. I'm here and Bethari and Joph and Zaneisha and Abdi. Can you breathe with me? In, and out." She demonstrated, her voice rising and falling. "In, and out. Breathe with me. That's it, very good. In, and out."

Tegan's chest rose and fell, her breath easing from those tight bursts of air. She closed her eyes, and her hands loosened a little, no longer bone-crackingly tight.

"Oh, that's wonderful; you're doing so well," Marie told her.

"How do you say it? You say *awesome*. You're doing awesome, Tegan. Just breathe. In, and out. In, and—"

"I know how to breathe," she said, and tossed her head. The motion didn't conceal that she was swallowing hard, but there was some pink in her cheeks now. "Abdi, are you all right?"

Joph was biting her lips. Bethari was darting looks at Tegan and at me, and I realized Tegan must have told her something about the torture. I waited to feel angry about that, but the rage didn't come. Instead I was relieved—while I hadn't been able to talk to Tegan about it, at least she'd had *someone* to listen.

"I'm fine. I'm so sorry," I said. "I didn't think. I should have *thought*."

"It's okay." She laughed, a little shakily. "It's almost nice to see you do something without thinking about it. Sing me something else?"

Joph exhaled and leaned against the headrest. "We should get you therapy when we get to New Zealand," she said, her voice limp with relief.

"Ugh," Tegan said. "No, thank you. I got enough therapy for a lifetime when I woke up. I hated it, all those people picking at my head. It was so gross."

I was almost used to Tegan dropping her past-timer slang into conversation now. *Gross* meant bad, disgusting. "I could use some therapy when I get home," I said. "My brother probably knows someone."

Tegan opened her eyes. "Your brother? You mean...when you said you were going back to Djibouti, you meant right away?"

"Well, obviously we have to get to New Zealand first, and

then find a ship bound for the Horn, or one going to a port where I could find one. But Djibouti City's a shipping hub. It shouldn't take too long to find a suitable vessel." I sounded apologetic, and that was wrong. I'd wanted to go home for eighteen months, almost since the second I'd set foot in Australia. I didn't want to feel guilty about my need to return there.

Bethari, of course, was frowning at me. "You're not going to help the Save Tegan campaign from New Zealand? Or whatever we call it, once we get organized again?"

"They don't want *me*," I said, managing not to sound annoyed at her assumption. "You didn't call it the Save Abdi campaign, did you?"

"But you don't have Tegan's problem with public speaking, and you'd be a valuable spokesperson for—"

"Haven't I given *enough*?" I demanded. My voice was too harsh, too loud. "Let me rest; let me go *home*!"

"How much is enough when—"

"Shhh, Bethari," Tegan said. Her cheeks were flushing. "I'm sorry, Abdi. I didn't think about it. I should have. Of course you want to see your family as soon as you can."

I did feel guilty. Tegan had been right back in the complex—she didn't have a home anymore. She'd had Melbourne, but now Melbourne, past and present, was lost to her. Her family was long gone—her father before she'd died, her mother and brother afterward. Her first boyfriend had married the love of his life and died old and happy.

And I would be leaving, as soon as I could, and if she meant what she'd said in the underground camp, Joph would come, too.

And I hoped Tegan would come with us.

In the kitchen, she'd said she'd like to come.

No, my memory for conversations wouldn't let me get away with that. She'd said, "I *think* I'd like to come." But she hadn't known I meant to go so soon, and she'd worried about Marie, who was watching me with hooded eyes and not saying a single word.

Maybe Tegan and I weren't meant to be happy together. Maybe there would always be those gaps between us—time and culture and belief. Maybe there were supposed to be oceans between us, too.

How could I hope that the feelings I had, confused and shadowed as they were, were reason enough to ask her to go so far? I couldn't promise that I could give her anything—safety, freedom, or love.

And even if I could, how could I expect her to want those things from me?

Bethari was pointedly playing with her computer. I wasn't fooled that she'd given up on getting me to speak to her, though—Bethari wasn't the sort of person to let an argument go. I sat back and tried to avoid looking at anyone.

Δ ∫ Ω

The next time we passed a rest stop, Zaneisha pulled over and parked under the bright yellow sign promising FREE CAFFEINE!! I could have used a jolt, but the pill dispensary attached to the sign looked unpromising. Either animals or less fastidious humans had gotten dirt all over it, and the dispensation slot cover had been wrenched off.

"We need to discuss the presidential assassination attempt," Zaneisha said, twisting in her seat so she could measure us all with the same level gaze.

"But there won't be an attempt," Bethari said, patting the control unit in her lap and looking smug.

Over her, Tegan said, "Would they really try without the EMP?"

Bethari lost the smug expression.

"It's a definite possibility," Zaneisha said. "Less chance of an ideal outcome, but no battle plan survives contact with the enemy. Lat might well recommend an attack, hoping to use overwhelming force in place of an equipment advantage. The risk may be judged worth the potential gain."

It would if Hurfest had anything to do with it. He was pushing for speed, hoping to ride the momentum of a swift political change.

"Well? We know that there's the strong possibility that the president will be attacked if he visits Bendigo, as planned. What will we do with that knowledge?" Zaneisha's tone didn't give away any clues on her own preferences.

"We should warn him," Joph said.

I shrugged. "Let him die."

Joph stared at me. "You don't mean that."

"Oh, I really do," I said. But I also remembered the people packed into the rugby grounds. I could see how it would play out very clearly. They'd all gather to meet the president, and the assassins would hide among them. What would happen to the people when the attack began? I sank into my seat. "I don't want anyone else getting hurt, though."

"They will be, if the president is attacked," Marie said softly.

"We should warn him," Tegan agreed. She looked about as unenthused as I did. "But if we do that, then we have to let Lat know."

Zaneisha nodded. "I was about to advise that. Once warned, the president may set a trap for those attempting the attack."

I focused on Bethari. "Can you set a call so that we can talk to Cox without it being traced?"

She hesitated. "Talk, yes. Video, probably not. It's too much data, makes it more difficult to—"

"Set it up," I said, and then amended with "Please."

Bethari sniffed, to indicate what she thought of my belated courtesy, but flipped her computer open. It took several minutes of muttered commands and squiggly finger gestures before she was ready.

"Who's going to do the talking?" she said.

I looked expectantly at Zaneisha. She caught my eye. "I'm driving. Dr. Carmen?"

"I'd rather not." There was an odd note in Marie's voice, as if she were trying very hard to control herself.

"Abdi," Tegan said, sounding very definite. "You'll be great." Joph was nodding in agreement. Bethari looked dubious but didn't say anything—besides she'd be too busy with her computer.

Neither Marie nor Zaneisha objected. I took a deep breath and hoped my nervousness didn't show. "All right," I said, with the confidence I didn't feel, and signaled Bethari to start the call.

A woman answered. Her voice was nicely modulated, with an Australian standard accent. If she was surprised that there was no visual component to my call, it didn't show in her tone. "Hello, president's office, Charlene speaking, how can I help?"

"Hello, Charlene. This is Abdi Taalib. I will speak to the president now."

There was a brief pause, while the woman on the other end of the line doubtless gestured at her colleagues and set a half-dozen tracking programs in motion. Bethari, grinning viciously, was waving at her computer as if she were conducting an orchestra. For now, at least, we had little to fear there.

"I'm afraid President Cox is in a meeting, Mr. Taalib. May I ask what this matter concerns?"

"It concerns whether he will be assassinated, Charlene. If he is not speaking to me within ten seconds, he will regret it for the rest of his life. Which will be short."

"I'll see if he's available! Please hold the line!"

I waited, counting down while Tegan chewed her knuckles and Bethari watched her screen. My nervousness had transmuted to confidence, energy zinging around my body. I knew how this was going to go. At nine seconds, just as I'd expected, I got a response.

"What's this about?" a man demanded.

It was certainly him—that smooth voice, as luxurious as melted chocolate, was unmistakable.

"Mr. President," I said. "Good evening."

"Good evening, Abdi. I don't appreciate threats."

"I don't appreciate being tortured for six months. We all have to put up with these little inconveniences."

There was a split-second hesitation, so brief I nearly missed it, and then he said, "I'm afraid I have no idea what you're talking about."

Unseen, I bared my teeth. That tiny pause had told me everything I needed to know.

Cox went on: "I can assure you that any irregularities in your treatment will be investigated, Abdi, by the proper authorities. Would you like to have me connect you to them?"

"Oh, no. That was merely an aside. I regret to have troubled you with it."

Nathan Cox's voice became fatherly, almost cloying in its concern. "Are you all right, Abdi? Your parents are very concerned; you gave them quite a scare. Is Tegan with you?"

He was trying to control and redirect the conversation away from the topic he most certainly didn't want to be questioned about. He must suspect that we were recording, of course—he'd have to be stupid to think that we weren't.

I thought this man was many things but stupid wasn't one of them.

Bethari was making a rolling motion with her wrist. I cut to the substance of the call.

"Don't go to Bendigo tomorrow," I said.

"Are you threatening me, Abdi?"

"Warning you," I growled.

There was a pause while he processed that, then the voice came back, smoother than ever. "I *see*. Your concern for my well-being does you great credit, young man."

"I don't care about *you*."

He chuckled. "The feeling is not mutual, I must say. Look, Abdi, can't we work this out? You and Tegan must be lonely, scared—"

"Oh, we're doing much better now."

"As you say. Tell me, is Bethari Miyahputri there? Incredible, really—once we went looking for people talking about EMP devices, we found so much discussion. We've been having some lovely chats with the most talkative people."

Bethari's contacts—so much for trying to use them to find a safe hiding place or a boat.

Bethari made a choked noise. Zaneisha frowned and pointed back at the screen.

"Her mother had to be brought in for questioning by SADU, of course. Captain Miyahputri misses her daughter very much, and it's so difficult to be sure what she might have known about Bethari's less legal activities."

"She didn't know anything!" Bethari broke in. "Leave her alone!"

Shut up, I mouthed.

"Ah, she is there. Bethari, I do regret the necessity of keeping such a fine officer detained, but perhaps if you came and redeemed her in person—"

Zaneisha grabbed the computer from Bethari's hand and cut the feed.

"That is an awful man," Marie said. "What a horrible, horrible man. I'm so sorry I voted for him."

"Bethi?" Joph asked. She reached forward, but her ex-girlfriend pulled away.

"Do you want to call Lat now, Tegan?" Bethari asked, her voice strained.

"Um, in a second," Tegan said cautiously. "Bethi, are you okay?"

"I'm fine," she said, her breath hitching. It was an obvious lie, and I felt her pain twist at me. Brave, mouthy Bethari, beaten down by the government's cruelty. To save her mother, she'd have to give herself up.

"We could try for some safe-conduct guarantees," I offered. "SADU probably isn't that keen on us spreading stories of torture around." I took a deep breath. I didn't want to be a spokesperson, but if it had been my mother in danger... "I could record what happened to me and Tegan. When you hand yourself over, you can give them copies of the recordings, and let them know that if we don't get regular proof of life, we'll release them." I frowned. "I don't think we can leverage that into much more, though. It's the kind of thing they'll be able to discredit too easily."

All three girls looked at me as if I'd grown another head.

Tegan and Joph would hate to be separated from Bethari, especially after Tegan had only just been reunited with her friend. It was going to be hard on all of them, and they probably weren't ready to start the planning. "Do you want me to start looking at options for a hostage-exchange site?" I asked. "Probably somewhere on the coast."

Bethari stared at me. "Do you think I'm going to exchange myself for my mother?" she asked hoarsely.

I blinked. "You're not?"

I didn't mean to sound quite so horrified. It just hadn't occurred to me that she'd make any other choice. But the second I said it, I saw Tegan's eyes flash and realized the depth of my mistake.

"You *ass*," she said. "She risked her life to save you! We just escaped from SADU and their mercy, and you want to hand Bethari over to them?"

"I don't *want* to. I just thought that she'd...I was trying to help!"

"Help?" Tegan said, her voice filled with disbelief.

"Well, excuse me for having a little family feeling," I snapped.

"It's not the torture," Bethari said. "I mean, I'd hate it, but you heard Cox—he wants me because I know how to put together the EMP. I can't risk that knowledge getting to this government. And *I* need to be available to help the new movement."

I wasn't imagining the emphasis on the *I*.

"Oh, I see," I said. "You have to leave your mother in SADU hands because *I'm* selfish enough to want to lay eyes on mine."

"This is a really important cause," Bethari said shortly. "We can't all run away at the first sign of trouble."

Joph looked alarmed. "We're all tired and stressed," she said. "Bethari's just had terrible news. Let's all—"

I ignored her. "Excuse me, but I would hardly characterize escaping a brutal regime as *running away*," I told Bethari, and looked significantly at her headscarf. "Besides, isn't filial loyalty one of the principles of your religion? Not that you don't pick and choose."

"Shut up, Abdi," Tegan said.

"You stay out of this," I snapped.

Marie gave me a sharp look. "Young man, if you can't—"

Bethari spoke over her. "Pick and choose, do I?" Her eyes were glittering, her cheeks suffused with blood.

I knew where Bethari Miyahputri's buttons were now. Faith, family, and the internal pressure that drove her to always do the right thing. And I was angry enough that I could press every one of them. "Oh, it's fine to wear a hijab and kiss some girls," I mimicked, my voice unnaturally high. "I can leave my mother to rot because *I'm* so important to the cause." I dropped into my normal register. "I mean, I don't care; do what you like! But at least don't be hypocritical about it."

"Don't you dare tell me how to practice my faith!"

"Don't you tell me how to live my life! You as good as told me that going home was cowardly."

"I didn't say that!" she shouted. "But, hey, now that you've brought it up, it sure is! We've all risked a lot to get you out, my *mother* is in *jail*, and you just want to run? There are larger issues at stake!"

"My family is not a small issue!" Ifrah, who was confident and forthright; Halim, who could fix any broken machine; Sahra, who listened to my music collection and wanted me to play my favorites again and again for her. And my mother and father, who had talked to me every week when they had to know every word out of my mouth was a lie. I had to return to them as soon as possible. Anything else would be a betrayal, a further pain to inflict on them with my foolish choices.

"I'm not saying that family isn't important, but if you'd just think about those poor refugees—"

My brain ignited. "Oh, I can't manage that much thinking. I'm just a stupid thirdie. Please, firster, ma'am, tell me what I should do to help out them other unfortunate thirdie scrappers—"

"Be quiet," Zaneisha said. She didn't speak very loudly, but her voice resonated through the car.

"But he—"

"She said—"

Zaneisha slammed her hand against the steering wheel. "Shut up!"

We obeyed. For the first time since the shouting had begun, I glanced at Tegan, who had her face turned toward the window, her shoulders set. Marie's hand was pressed to her mouth. Joph was looking at Bethari and me wide-eyed, as if she'd never seen us before.

For a moment, I saw myself through her eyes, and I didn't like the image at all.

"I have a limited tolerance for adolescent squabbling, and you've both exceeded it," Zaneisha said, her voice measured. "If you cannot speak civilly to each other, don't. If you can, now would be a good time to apologize."

Bethari's cheeks were still flaming, but this time with embarrassment, not rage. I met her eyes, glanced away, and made myself look again. "Sorry," I muttered.

"Me too," she said.

"Well, it's a start," Zaneisha said after a moment, and started the car. "Don't do it again. I need to concentrate."

"We still need to get a message to Lat," Tegan said, ten minutes down the road.

I scowled. I mean, she was right, but did she have to sound so concerned?

Zaneisha didn't miss a beat. "A text version will do. Bethari, I'll dictate. Send the message to one of the dead drops."

She composed the message in brisk militaryspeak but signed off "Washington." No rank. The army would have stripped her of it, declared her a deserter, or perhaps even a traitor.

I looked at Bethari, hunched over her computer screen and resolutely not making eye contact with anyone.

I didn't feel much like conversation myself. I leaned back and closed my eyes, going over the incident in my head. Slowly, in the strained, cramped atmosphere of the car, I eventually figured out that I hadn't actually been shouting at Bethari.

Well, my resentment at her telling me to think about the poor refugees was genuine. But the bits about Islam hadn't been about Bethari, but about growing up a nonbeliever in a country where most people believed as easily as they breathed. Tegan's religion didn't bother me quite as much, because Catholicism, ridiculous as it was, wasn't the religion I'd had to resist for most of my life. And I'd been angry at the suggestion that I should delay going home in order to help the Save Tegan movement, because at least part of me wondered if I should. If I really was a good person, wouldn't I offer to dance on the string, for at least a few more months? Wouldn't I chalk up the pain I'd cause my family against the pain I could save others from suffering, and make the decision to stay?

Perhaps Bethari had reacted badly to my assumption that she'd trade herself in for her mother's freedom because she thought that a good daughter would do just that—regardless of her own safety or the higher cause she served.

We'd been yelling at ourselves, not each other.

It was disconcerting to recognize that I might have more in common with Bethari Miyahputri than I'd thought.

But what I didn't have was her impulsiveness. Her tendency to act without thinking, to make sacrifices without blinking— that was something I hated. And almost envied. If I'd ever had that ability, it had been trained out of me from the time I was four. Now I calculated every move before I made it and pushed people to the places I needed them when it came time for plans to become action.

I was beginning to wonder if my mother had known exactly what her training would do to me.

Tegan was rubbing the dressing at the back of her neck. "This hurts," she said.

"I can change it when we stop," Marie told her.

"Yes, please," Tegan said, which meant that her neck really did hurt. Tegan loved Marie, but she wasn't a big fan of medicine or health care in general—considering all the interest doctors had taken in her revived body and brain, it made perfect sense to me. She took one of the pills Joph gave her and washed it down with a whole bottle of water. She was sweating again, even in the temperature-controlled car. The world had been so much cooler in her time; it was odd to think how hot this mild autumn must be to her.

I looked away from her and toward the windshield. Zaneisha was watching me in her mirror, her dark eyes as expressionless as ever. I couldn't tell if she was sympathetic to our situation or planning my imminent demise.

"I must swap the battery," she said, a sentence so removed from my state of mind that it took a moment to work out that it wasn't some elaborate code. The car battery needed to be swapped for one that was fully charged. Normally a battery would go all day, to be recharged all night, but this one had been at the rugby grounds—not plugged into a home electricity supply.

"There's a swap station about two kilometers up the road, just before the entrance to the promontory proper," Bethari said, busy with her computer. "It accepts credit, eco-credits, cash—must be old—and direct transfer. How many hidden accounts do you have left, Joph?"

"Oh, all the real ones," Joph said. "I think we can assume SADU froze all the decoys, but that leaves forty-six million dollars, all up."

Tegan startled, and then shook her head at my glance. "I always forget about inflation," she explained. "That's about... three million, in my day. Which is still...wow, Joph."

"You knew I was rich."

"I didn't know you were a millionaire!"

"Wise investments," Joph said, unruffled. "A trust from my grandmother. My parents limited my allowance when they found out about the drug smuggling, but I'd already put most of my savings in a hidden account. I just moved it out and around before they could find that one. I'm not as good as Bethi when it comes to covering up my online activities, but I'm not a complete slouch."

"I thought you had to sell more recreational drugs to get money for the equipment you needed," I said.

She frowned. "Yes, Tegan said that in her 'cast. But I didn't. I sold the breathers so people would believe my ditzy act."

I'd just assumed otherwise. In her own quiet way, Joph tended to show you how stupid assumptions could be.

"Problem," Zaneisha said, and the car slowed down as the recharge station came into view. It wasn't the automated one I'd been expecting, but a real station, with food and drink and a counter attendant.

A witness.

"Do we keep driving?" I asked.

"No." Zaneisha's head jerked decisively. Still two hundred meters or so from the station, she parked on the shoulder of the road, long grass scraping the belly of the car. Trees with black, deeply furrowed trunks provided cover, a few spindly red flowers still holding on among the olive-green leaves.

"Stay here," Zaneisha said, and checked her weapons belt before she got out of the car and pried the battery free. She kept to the trees as she went, the battery balanced awkwardly on one hip. It would have been easier to carry it in both arms, but her free hand held a bolt-gun, hidden by her side. We watched as the strong figure became smaller. A few cars passed, but none stopped.

In the late evening light, the station looked less welcoming, more menacing. Without speaking, we exchanged glances as Zaneisha vanished inside.

"Um," Marie said. "I don't want to sound alarmist, but just in case, maybe we should get out of the car?"

"More cover in here," Tegan said, but her face was intent. "Abdi, the weapons bag is under the backseat."

I bent, careful not to brush against Marie's feet, and pulled out the long black bag. It looked innocuous enough, but when I unfolded it I had to clamp down hard on my reaction to all the weapons carefully strapped into place. Auto-rifles, bolt-guns, something in complicated pieces that might have been an anti-flier shooter—the sonic pistols in their braces at the top looked harmless in that array.

"Do you want something now?" I asked Tegan, trying to make it a polite inquiry.

She grimaced. "Not yet. I'm probably just being paranoid. Zaneisha wouldn't have gone if she thought we were actually in danger."

I'd forgotten that Tegan hated guns. But she'd pick one up if she had to.

"Nothing on the channels," Bethari said, and then yelped. "Oh no. Oh no!"

"What is it?" Joph asked, but I didn't need clarification.

Rising from the trees like a huge gray wasp, the flier swooped over the station.

CHAPTER FIFTEEN
Tutte le corde

"God protect us," Tegan said, and grabbed for the weapons bag.

"It's a *flier*," I said, clutching the bag against my chest. "You can't get a flier with hand weapons! You'd be dead before you took a step."

"They won't kill *me*!" Tegan said. "I'm the Living Dead Girl, the only successful revival! They won't—"

"No," Marie said.

"Marie, I have to; we can't leave Zaneisha to face it alone!"

"I mean, no, you're not the only successful revival." Marie's face was pale, far too pale. "There are two others now. At least two. The process works."

The silence in the car lasted an infinite moment. "Why didn't you tell us?" Tegan said.

"I couldn't," Marie said. "I don't know if we can trust Zaneisha."

"Can't trust—"

"Why do you think that?" I asked over Tegan's half-articulated protest. "Do you have any evidence?"

"Just a feeling. She's been army all her life. Maybe she's still with the government. Or maybe she's reporting on us back to Hurfest." Marie's eyes were haunted. I couldn't tell if it was paranoia or justified suspicion—we'd both been betrayed too often to trust easily anymore.

"She's in danger right *now*," Tegan said, and grabbed for the bag again. "Abdi, we can talk about this later! Let me go!"

"If they have other revivals, they don't need you!" I shouted back. "Just think for a second!"

"The flier can't kill us if it's not working," Bethari said, in a voice that was far too calm. She'd dropped her computer and picked up the EMP control unit. "We need to bring it down."

There were cars on the road, all traveling at speeds that might kill when their internal computers cut out. Bethari's hands were shaking, but she was opening the red box and reaching inside, and my lunge forward wasn't going to be fast enough to stop her flipping the switch—

The flier exploded.

It was so loud that I thought my eardrums had burst, so bright that white spots hung in front of my eyes. I closed my eyes and ignored the enormous shudder of something heavy hitting the ground, counting three silent seconds, before I opened them again. The flier body had fallen among the scrubby trees, where it was spitting and roaring, the burning fuel stench strong.

"I didn't think the EMP could do that," Joph said.

"It didn't," Bethari said, sounding equally stunned. "I mean, I didn't. I didn't turn it on."

"That wasn't you?" I asked—foolishly, since cars were

already pulling to a halt, bystanders already getting out to gather uselessly round the flier's funeral pyre. "Then it was someone else. Lat's people, maybe, or a third party. We have to leave right now." My head was already spinning through likely scenarios and plans for the next minute, hour, week.

Tegan opened her car door and ran toward the station.

"Oh no," Bethari said, and scrambled out after her, the EMP box still in her hand.

"Tegan, wait!" Marie cried.

I was already moving, but Tegan with a head start could be hard to catch. I passed Bethari but got to the station just in time to see Tegan drop low and crawl through the front entrance. Joph had the sense to stay with Marie in the car, and Bethari jogged up behind me.

"Teeg!" Bethari whisper-shouted, but Tegan gave no sign of hearing her. "Shoot! We can go around the back. Give me something."

The weapons bag was still in my hand. I pulled out sonic pistols for Bethari and myself and hesitated a moment before I stuffed a bolt-gun into the back of my pants. Safety on.

My hands were shaking. I was furious—with Tegan's recklessness, with my own cowardice. I was gripped in a bone-deep terror I couldn't even put words around. There was a kind of wailing at the back of my head, a low, drawn-out cry of *nono-nonono*. I couldn't go back. I couldn't let Diane take me.

But I couldn't let her take Tegan, either.

Bethari's computer made short work of the back door's electronic lock, and we snuck through the employees' break room, which was suspiciously empty of bags, computers, and other things you'd expect from someone who'd actually turned up to work that day. It had been a trap, and we'd sprung it—perhaps all the swap stations were being monitored by fliers? No, too many resources needed, even with Cox's approval. And they hadn't pinpointed us exactly, or we'd already be in custody. They'd narrowed down the area and planted people at various stations we *might* use and then had fliers on standby to…

Bethari put the EMP control box down by the door and went to her stomach, wriggling through the open door into the main shop. I joined her, trying to keep my sonic pistol clear of the floor. I wasn't good at instant action. I liked to plan things out, assess the circumstances, and this was clearly a moment with no time for that. I'd do better to follow the girls' leads.

There was a man behind the counter, wearing a black SADU uniform. His chest had been blown out. Bethari visibly steeled herself before she crawled through the pool of congealing blood and very carefully poked her head around the edge of the counter. She stiffened, ducked back, and beckoned me to join her.

Zaneisha was on her knees, hands locked behind her head. Her back was toward me, but I could read her tension in its stiffness—and little wonder. She was surrounded by three silent men, all big and well armed, and two of them were holding weapons on her. They weren't wearing Australian uniforms, but worn jeans and heavy jackets. And they all looked African—unusual for Australia, where things tended to be both more white and more mixed up. The whole tableau was completely incongruous to the surroundings, where brightly colored stands of food and drink fought with one another for your attention and a video loop of a popular sportswoman promised that the energy pills that sponsored her would improve your performance and make you more attractive to whoever your preferred partners were.

I couldn't see Tegan anywhere.

The front door opened and another man came in, cradling a bolt-rifle and shaking his heavy bald head. "The car is empty," he reported. "Marks in the brush."

Joph must have gotten Marie out, I thought, and only then realized that the man hadn't been speaking English.

He'd said it in Somali.

The man he'd reported to made a gesture of impatience so familiar that it tugged directly at my heart. That was how my father and uncles talked among one another, with their hands saying almost as much as their voices. "Who are you?" he asked Zaneisha, in accented English. It was a stronger version of *my* accent.

She didn't speak.

"Where is Abdi Taalib?" he asked. "Are you Australian military? Why did he shoot at you, if so?" He gestured negligently toward the counter and presumably the dead man there.

No reply.

The big man shook his head. "You are brave," he said in English, and then, in Somali, "We have no time. Shoot her."

"No!" I shouted, and moved forward. I got three steps into the room before the stupidity of my action caught up with me. Three of the four men had swung their weapons around, and my own bolt-gun was stuck in my waistband. A sonic pistol wasn't going to do anything. But the leader's gun stayed down. He was smiling at me, closed lips curving warmly. "Abdi. Good. Your mother sent us. We've come to take you home."

He said it in Somali, and Zaneisha clearly didn't understand. But she saw an opportunity and moved, hands swift and precise as she elbowed one of the men in the face, relieved him of his gun, and aimed it at the leader's face. He stood calm and assured, but the other men were reacting, and the man on the ground was getting to his feet with an expression that promised revenge.

"Don't hurt her," I said in English, hoping that they all understood. One of the men looked puzzled, but another muttered a translation—in what I thought was Portuguese. This was going to get confusing fast.

"She is with you?" the leader asked, this time in English.

"Yes," I said, in lieu of the complicated explanation that actually described the complex relationship between Zaneisha Washington and me. "He says they're from my mother, Zaneisha."

Zaneisha—and her gun—didn't waver. "I assume you have some credentials to support that," she said.

"Yes." He slid one hand toward the breast pocket of his dusty coat, moving with a sort of slow fluidity that echoed Zaneisha's own motions. They made a matching pair, really, both tall and broad and dark-skinned, with short military-style haircuts and that deadly efficiency in every gesture. But Zaneisha was Australian and incomprehensible to me in some fundamental ways. Every word out of this man's mouth sounded like home. Hope was pounding at my limbs like a hammer.

He pulled out a necklace.

It was a red-enameled pendant on a gaudy, fake gold chain, mimicking the shape of a flame. Poorly made and cheap-looking, utterly worthless on grounds of aesthetics or value.

But it was infinitely precious to me, and as I involuntarily reached for it, Zaneisha must have seen something in my face that made her own features relax and her gun arm lower.

"It's my mother's necklace," I said, my voice struggling. "I gave it to her, Zaneisha. No thief would take it; only she would remember that."

"She said you were nine years old," the man said, smiling wryly. "That you gave it to her as an apology gift."

I'd said something hurtful. I didn't remember what, but I could remember my mother's face closing up like a flower at night before she turned away, deliberately putting her back to me. I'd been sorry, so sorry that I'd run to the old souk to find something to make it up to her. At the time, the pendant had looked perfect.

My mother had sent these men to rescue me. I was finally going home.

Δ ∫ Ω

Behind me, Bethari stood up, very slowly, hands raised above her head. She'd left the sonic pistol behind, but the men still swiveled to inspect her before their leader signaled them to stand down.

"How did you find us?" she asked.

The leader shrugged at the wreckage outside. "We followed them."

"You hacked military communications?"

"Not me personally, but yes." He looked at me. "This isn't the girl."

"What?"

"The one who got you kidnapped, and imprisoned after."

"No. Tegan did that. I mean, she didn't exactly…"

"I saw her story. All very well to tell the truth, but not so smart to do it with no thought for the consequences." He shook his head. "That medicine-smuggling operation did good work. It had to be shut down when that girl spoke, governments suddenly having to notice things they had managed not to see before. A shame."

Bethari looked indignant, but I knew he was right. I'd told Tegan she could talk about the operation as a way to underline the unfair first-world practices that made it necessary. But the practices continued, and in the meantime, people were dying. Consequences.

"I'm Tegan Oglietti," Tegan said, coming into view from around a shelf.

"Our perimeter observation needs work," the leader said in Somali. His voice was calm, but two of the men flinched—not the bald one, who looked amused.

"Were you with one of the medicine-smuggling teams?" I asked.

He laughed. "Me? No. I am a retrieval specialist."

"A mercenary," I said, trying not to sound judgmental.

I don't think I entirely succeeded, but he took no apparent offense. "Yes, if you like. I am paid to do this work, to find people and bring them places."

He didn't need to tell me that he didn't always bring people places they wanted to go. But my mother had hired him; I had to have faith in her choices, faith in her. Or maybe just faith in her desperation.

It was almost nice to be the important target, the one people were after. These men saw Tegan as the extraneous one, not me.

"How did my family pay for you?" I asked.

It was a rude question, and the men around us looked askance at me. The leader's eyes narrowed. "We haven't been properly introduced."

"I'm sorry," I said. I'd been raised to respect my elders, but eighteen months in Melbourne had eroded my manners. "Please, forgive me. May I know your names?"

He nodded. "I'm Hanad. This is Ashenafi and Thulani. Eduardo is over there." The bald man.

That was an interesting mix. *Hanad* was a Somali name, and *Ashenafi* was Amharic—both names from my part of the world. I wasn't sure about *Thulani*, but it might be Xhosa, which meant the south, and the Portuguese probably meant Eduardo was from Angola or Mozambique. They were different shades and builds, too, from Hanad's dark muscularity to Thulani's light wiriness. An odd group, maybe, but they all had that air of physical competency that I associated with Lat and Zaneisha. And Diane.

And Tegan, too. She was standing with her hip cocked, but there was a tension in her arms that I didn't trust.

Hanad focused on me again. "Come, Abdi."

"Come where?" I said cautiously.

"We have a boat moored off the coast."

Tegan's eyes narrowed.

"I can't.... It's not just me. There are six of us." I tried to say it firmly, but knew I'd misstepped when Hanad frowned.

"I was hired to retrieve you. Not these Australians."

"We don't have to take them all the way," I said. "Just to another boat they can use, one strong enough to get them to New Zealand."

"No. Too risky. Come."

My brief burst of satisfaction at being the person in demand had faded. It seemed that the position gave you fewer choices, not more. I was trying to decide how much resistance might be met with violence, how much I could endanger the others in my quest to help them, when Bethari made an alarmed noise.

"Actually," she said, "I think the risk would come in heading out to sea." She flipped her computer over to show them, as Thulani's beeped an alarm.

"Three fliers on the coast," he reported. "One of them heading this way."

Hanad said something nasty in Somali about fish-eating Australians, and then nodded at me. "All right. We go inland, to a safe house there."

"You don't know the territory," Zaneisha said.

"You do," Hanad said. "I'll hire you as guide. Two hundred thousand Australian."

"My fee is that all the members of our party go with us."

"Ridiculous!"

"One of them is the girl who made the pills for the medicine smugglers," I said quickly.

Hanad looked interested. "Joph Montgomery?" He spread

his hands. "All right. I can see you Australians are as stubborn as your flies. We go together. But I am not taking this many strangers to our Melbourne safe house. We'll use one of yours."

"Ours are jeopardized," Zaneisha said, and didn't mention that it was because we'd split away from the rest of the movement.

Hanad's eyes narrowed. There was going to be a limit to how far we could push him, and I suspected we were coming very near it.

We needed someplace that would be safe, private, preferably invisible to fliers, which meant underground, and—wait.

"Underground," I said. "Tegan, that urban exploration you used to do. Would any of those tunnels be suitable?"

Tegan's eyes gleamed. "Yes! The old drains wouldn't have changed."

"To Melbourne, then," Hanad conceded. "Very well, let's go."

"One second," Bethari said, and went behind the counter, into the employee break room again. There was a brief silence, a strangled shriek, and the strident clatter of metal being banged about. Zaneisha vaulted the counter, Tegan right behind her, but they both stopped dead when Bethari came back in, negligently carrying the twisted remnants of the EMP control unit.

"*Now* we can go," she said, and sauntered out the front door.

Δ ∫ Ω

Tegan obviously wanted to ask Marie about the *other* successful revivals—but we weren't going to do so in front of Hanad and Ashenafi, much less Zaneisha, whom Marie was still treating with suspicion. The men traveled with us, wide shoulders crushing me between them, while Zaneisha drove. Bethari and Joph had transferred to the men's car, to go with Eduardo and Thulani. Both groups were hostages to the other's good behavior, depending on everybody to keep faith.

It was a neat compromise, and I was pleased that I'd arranged it so quickly. But I wished we could talk to Marie.

Instead, when I could, I snuck glances at her in the rearview mirror. She was stretched out on the backseat, taking short breaths through her tight mouth. Joph's red medical bag was sitting on her stomach, but Marie hadn't taken anything, preferring to keep pain and sharp wits, rather than exchange them for more comforting woolly-headedness.

Actually, as far as I could remember, she'd chosen either total oblivion or no real pain relief ever since she'd been rescued. No in-between relaxed state where she might be tongue-loosened and vulnerable to inquiries about what research she'd done in captivity; she'd repulsed Hurfest's questions with a prickly vehemence I'd attributed to personal dislike. In retrospect, it was very interesting.

Ashenafi seemed to be content with silence, occupying himself with his computer. Hanad, however, asked questions. Zaneisha answered and countered with her own. It was hard to tell who was getting the most out of the competition for information, but a competition it certainly was.

"So you have no reliable contacts left in the city," Hanad said at last, and sat back, looking disgruntled but not surprised. "And you, Abdi?"

"Me?"

"Who are your contacts?"

"I don't have any," I said, confused. "I only knew one man in the smuggling ring, Digger Jones. But that wasn't his real name, and I don't know where he is." I hoped he was either lying low or out of Australia; the medicine smuggling had been beneath SADU's notice, but the ordinary police might have been able to make something out of even the fuzzy and inaccurate details I'd given Tegan permission to talk about in her 'cast.

"Your ordinary contacts. Your mother said you had a host father."

"Him? He's useless." Reese Chang was clueless, not malicious, but no great addition to the species. Oddly, it was he who'd introduced me to Tegan. I'd been doing an assignment in my room when he'd knocked on my door. "Would you like to see history made?" he asked in the special voice that meant he was pleased that he could give the thirdie boy a treat.

I'd seen history made many times before, watching my mother usher in new law in the National Assembly. She'd been one of the driving speakers in favor of cutting our ties with the French military. But that was Djibouti history, thirdie history, and of no interest to Reese. I had to humor him, so I let him order the house computer to show me the video of a terrified girl, shying away from the crowding press. She was bald, dressed in a flimsy medical tunic, and bleeding from scrapes on her arm and bare feet. She looked small and delicate and weak. But her dark eyes were huge and observant in her bare white face, and even as her body flinched from the bumblecams, her gaze was direct.

For a moment, it seemed as if she were looking directly at me.

A camera trick, of course. Everyone watching that 'cast—and there were millions of them at the time, and billions later—saw the same thing. But it had caught my attention. I'd thought, *That girl is beautiful.*

In the car, from the front seat, Tegan caught my eye in the mirror. "What?"

"Nothing."

"Well, what about the local Somalis?" Hanad persisted.

I shifted uncomfortably. It wasn't an unreasonable question; Melbourne had a sizable Somali population. Thanks to the No Migrant policy, they were all at least a generation removed from Mogadishu or Toulouse or Minneapolis or any of the other places they might have come from. But they were my people. We shared some of our long history, some mutual understanding of our food and language and heritage.

I'd avoided them deliberately.

"I didn't want to risk them finding out about the smuggling. In case I was caught." Or in case they'd given me away.

Hanad looked at me for a long time. "You should learn how to trust," he said at last.

This struck me as particularly ridiculous advice from an acknowledged mercenary and kidnapper, but I kept my peace. I wouldn't be trusting Hanad. But I could trust my mother, who'd sent him.

The atmosphere grew less tense as we got closer to the city, and the traffic became more dense. Even with Australia's rigid and extortionate taxes on car ownership, not everyone was willing or able to take public transportation, and it was easier to lose ourselves in ten thousand vehicles than in a few hundred. In fact, the danger was that we'd lose the other car in our convoy, but Thulani was a good driver and tailed us with ease.

It was nearly full dark by the time we arrived. The suburb Tegan directed us to had once been a town that had sprawled until the city and the town met. Along that uneasy border was a quiet, weed-strewn wasteland, where old factories that hadn't been upgraded to the most recent air-pollution standards had been abandoned. There was a onetime estuary that had dried out and, overlooking it, several government apartment blocks in the traditional gray. The inhabitants had made an effort with bright curtains and hardy, drought-resistant flowers on the balconies, but it was hard to disguise the grim air of that institutional architecture, especially in the harsh lighting that limned the buildings at night.

We parked by the head of the estuary, where a huge concrete grill was set into the hillside. "Those buildings weren't there before," Tegan said, eyeing the apartments with suspicion.

"Are you sure the tunnels will be?" Hanad asked. Again, a reasonable question. I had the feeling that Hanad prided himself on his reason.

Unfortunately, so did I. I didn't want there to be so many similarities between this man and me. It made me doubt myself, and doubt was dangerous.

"They were built to last a couple of centuries. Melbourne doesn't really get earthquakes, and definitely no volcanic activity."

"Superstorm erosion?" Zaneisha suggested.

"Maybe. Which reminds me. The first bit of the way is vulnerable to flash flooding. Alex and I didn't go into tunnels in the rain, because we weren't freaking stupid, but a couple of guys she knew did, and one of them nearly drowned just a few meters from the exit. If a storm starts, we have to stay put. The central chamber's huge, with a lot of high ground. Our feet might get wet there, but trying to get out would be much worse." She looked sternly at the men, making sure that they were taking in all of my Somali translation. Thulani's English was just conversational, and Eduardo barely spoke any—about as much as I did Portuguese. They all looked appropriately impressed.

I was, too. It was one thing to know urban exploration had been something Tegan had done in the old days and quite another to see her put those skills into action.

We grabbed necessary supplies without a lot of discussion, and while the cars were driven away, to be parked inconspicuously, Hanad and Zaneisha rolled out a field stretcher for Marie. She watched, silent and bright-eyed.

"Are you sure you don't want anything?" Joph asked, picking up her medicine bag. "You're going to get jolted around a lot."

"I'm fine," Marie said tensely. "Let's save the pills for when we need them."

Joph's bag was packed with pills and breathers and pain-relieving gels. There was no need to hoard them. I exchanged a significant look with Tegan, and she adjusted her computer in the band about her wrist. "Lights on," she told it, and slipped between the massive concrete slats, leading us into the earth.

CHAPTER SIXTEEN
Con sordino

The journey back to Melbourne had been mildly uncomfortable. The tunnels were much worse.

They were made of curbed slabs of white-gray concrete, powdery with age, but still stolidly strong. They weren't smoothed off prettily—the walls had never been intended for public viewing—and I stumbled more than once on irregularities in the flooring. I'd expected damp. Instead, it was dusty dry, but the air smelled musty, and patches of lichen and moss grew in the cracks of the rough concrete. We were doubtless breathing in countless spores; I was glad I was still on the immunoboosters given to me after the implant had been removed.

Tegan and Bethari could walk upright for the entire route, but the rest of us had to stoop most of the way, with Zaneisha and Hanad nearly bent double in some of the lower stretches. The worst moment was when they had to take Marie off her stretcher for a tight bend, so they could collapse it. While she was dangling from Zaneisha's arms, one of Marie's bandaged feet brushed the concrete. I was standing right behind her in the bottleneck, crouching so that I could straighten my aching neck, and in the wash of my computer's light, I distinctly saw in her face the agonized moment that her foot made contact. Her eyes showed whites all round the iris, her mouth opening on a silent scream before she bit it down, glancing at Zaneisha with well-concealed fear.

I recognized that pain, and the immediate fear that followed.

My anger, which had been absent in the presence of so many interesting new problems, roared back to life, and my paranoia with it. Maybe Marie could be forgiven for not telling us about the apparent success of the revival program. If she feared Zaneisha as a potential traitor in our midst, I'd do well to pay attention. What evidence did we have for Zaneisha's apparent change of heart, from one of Lat's loyal lieutenants to our stalwart defender? An interest in Tegan's well-being, a willingness to go into danger—these were circumstantial proof at best.

True, Zaneisha had been the one to suggest warning the president, so that innocents wouldn't be hurt if Lat tried to attack even without the EMP. But one of us would have thought of it eventually; I should have thought of it sooner. Perhaps she'd taken my slowness as an opportunity to put herself beyond suspicion.

I reached behind me, for Joph's cold hand. "How are you?" I whispered.

"Kooshy-keen," she whispered back cheerily. Joph hadn't scorned the aid of painkillers. She wasn't in the obliviating state of a full dose, but she walked easily, only wincing as we covered a couple of the rougher patches.

We piled together at another bottleneck, and I felt restlessness stir about us. Ten people, lined up like ants marching back to the hive. But unlike ants, people weren't suited to pushing through tunnels. For the first time, I felt the weight of the rock and soil above me, vast and suffocating.

"Almost there," Tegan's voice said, clear and confident. I felt obscurely better. The rock was still there, but Tegan's matter-of-fact competence made it lighter.

She was right. It was only a few minutes before we came to the central chamber.

It was huge, a vast space hewn out of the rock like one of the mountaintop churches I'd seen in Eritrea. As I swept my computer's light over the walls, I could see that some of them had the rough grain of natural stone. The hollowing out of this place had been only partially at human hands; the rest of the cave had been here well before. As Tegan had promised, the floor was uneven, with plenty of spots raised over the high-water marks that stained the walls. A few metal ladders bolted to the rock even led to smaller tunnels.

Hanad put his hands on his hips and surveyed the area with vast satisfaction. "Good," he proclaimed, as if he'd discovered the spot himself. "Set up camp."

I rolled my eyes and went to help Zaneisha get Marie more comfortable.

My hopes of getting a quiet moment to talk with Marie were swiftly foiled. Zaneisha and Eduardo, who apparently performed any medical duties for Hanad's men, changed the dressing on her feet. I caught a glimpse of raw red tissue heaping into scar formation and turned away, feeling ill. It was one thing to know that Marie's torture had involved more permanent physical effects than those meted out to Tegan and me, and quite another to see the results written on her body.

Tegan didn't even try to insert herself into the process. She had a hushed conversation with Joph and Bethari—probably warning them not to bring up Marie's revelation about the two new revivals in front of the men—then followed Hanad's directions in laying out memory-fabric bedrolls.

I went over to assist.

"These are weird," she said abruptly, shaking out a bedroll. The fabric snapped into its prescribed position, automatically filling with air. I tested the flex on one and was satisfied with the firmness.

"It's just a flexible carbon polymer...." I began.

"I know. I looked it up." She sighed. "Sometimes I think I'm getting along okay in the future, and sometimes I just need a second to process it. Computers you can scrunch up or stretch wide, tattoos that blink patterns of light..." She held out her arms. "Surgery that can bring dead girls to life."

"Self-heating food containers?" I offered, unpacking a pile of them.

"Those, we had."

History was a subject I'd thought I excelled at. Meeting Tegan Oglietti had made it clear how many gaps there were in my knowledge.

"Speaking of food," said the living historical monument beside me, "who's in charge of dinner?"

"You are," I said firmly.

She grinned at me. "Trick question. You've got to learn to cook."

"Teach me, wise one."

Tegan gave me a small package. "Place your fingers on one side of the tab, and your thumb on the other," she said solemnly. "Now, in one swift movement, tear."

I performed the motion with equal seriousness. Tegan poured in half a cup of water and made me stir it with the wooden spoon attached to the side.

"Wait five minutes, then consume," she told me. "Ta-da! You are a master chef!"

I laughed and held the package cupped in my hands, giving the chemical pouch at the bottom time to warm the soup through.

"This is pretty good," Bethari said, between mouthfuls. "What's in it?"

The Arabic lettering on the ingredients label mentioned chicken stock. Bethari had eaten most of her portion already. It would only make her sick and sad if I told her. "Lentils," I said. "Various spices."

Tegan, whose chef-raised taste buds doubtless recognized the flavor, shot me a grateful smile that warmed me far more than the soup did.

Marie, who was laboriously eating her own portion of soup, noticed the exchange, and I received a glare that should have stripped off my skin. I frowned back. What the heck was her problem? Other than the fact I existed, and liked her foster daughter, and wanted to take her to another country on the far side of two oceans—okay. Marie had some incentive to glare.

But I wished she'd just come out with it. There were a number of plays I could make in this situation, but all of them required her to make the first move.

Guiltily, I realized that thought was probably yet another instance of what Tegan called "acting like a robot." I *had* to get a grip and stop manipulating people close to me.

After eating, most of us got some sleep on the memory-fabric bedrolls that smoothed out the rough cavern floor. They weren't entirely comfortable, but I was exhausted. It was with real reluctance that I swam to the surface of a dream to find Tegan shaking my shoulder, her hand warm on my shoulder, her eyes bright.

"Come with me?" she said quietly. "I want to explore one of the smaller tunnels. There should be another room in there—not this big, but enough space for a second hideaway."

Anyone capable of finding us here would definitely not be put off by having to go a little deeper into the ground, but Tegan's arched eyebrows said she knew that, too.

"Sure," I whispered back, and followed her to the foot of one of the ladders, carefully picking my way around the occupied bedrolls. Zaneisha was sitting by the entrance to the cave, her bolt-gun ready in her lap, but everyone else was asleep—or seemed to be.

Hanad opened one eye from where he was sitting propped up against the wall, then closed it again. He didn't have to say anything. If I'd somehow taken this opportunity to have Tegan guide me out through a secret exit, the others would suffer for it. As it was, when I clambered up the sturdy ladder, I wasn't thinking of escape. Only of Tegan, and privacy, and how much of it we might claim for ourselves.

"Is there really another room in here?" I whispered. I was bent over worse than before. I didn't mind this time, not with my eyes fixed on the view. There was being polite and not staring, and there was being invited to follow a girl I was on kissing terms with while she bent down and groped her way through ancient drains.

There was laughter in her voice. "I think so. Alex and I only tried the small tunnels once. I know it's in *one* of them." She made a satisfied noise. "Here we are. Room for two."

There was, just. I sat beside her, moved a rock from an uncomfortable place, and relaxed. It felt as if it had been a very long time since I'd let my shoulders stop hoisting themselves toward my ears.

"Does this remind you of old times?" I said.

"Definitely. Tunnels weren't really my thing, but Alex loved them."

Alex, a woman long dead. Tegan's best friend, long ago.

I thought again of the weight above me and made myself concentrate on Tegan's warmth, the firm muscle of her thigh pressed against mine. "Why tunnels?"

"She liked exploring hidden things. She had a set of abusive foster parents, and it took a while before anyone realized. She kept running away, and there'd be an investigation, and they'd lie like champions and be so concerned about their poor, disturbed girl who they loved like a daughter....And when their secrets were finally all out in the open, and everyone could see what disgusting people they were, her life got better. She didn't trust secrets, or governments, or, I don't know, *politeness*. She'd have liked you."

"Really? But my mother is—was—in government. And I lie all the time. I've kept a lot of secrets."

"No, you care about people. You keep secrets *for* them, not from them."

It seemed a fine distinction to me, but if Tegan was happy with it, I wasn't going to argue. "Speaking of secrets," I began.

"Marie and the two new revivals. Yes."

"Do *you* think we can trust Zaneisha?" I asked.

"I want to," Tegan said. "We don't have any proof either way."

"No. But we should be careful." I considered her. "How do you feel about it?"

"About there being two more people like me? I was never really the only one, you know. I saw one guy, right after I woke up. He seemed maybe twenty-one or twenty-two, superhealthy body, no obvious injuries or anything. He looked alive. I mean, he was. He was breathing on his own, and his eyes were open. But he didn't see me. He wasn't taking anything in." Tegan shook her head. "It felt like he wasn't there."

"Marie said you weren't the only *successful* revival anymore," I remembered.

"Yeah. I guess they counted him as unsuccessful. So these two new people must be conscious." She sighed. "I'm not sure how I feel. Strange, I guess. Sort of relieved that I'm not such a freak, and sorry that they'll have to adjust like I did, and worried about what this means for the Ark Project. That was the final missing piece. Now Cox can definitely carry off what he's been planning. More and more people are going to rush to be frozen, so they can buy a place on the *Resolution*."

"I'm surprised he hasn't announced it yet," I said. "He must be waiting for the right moment. We've got to talk to Marie."

"Yeah. When we can." She showed no signs of moving, though, and I was happy to sit there with her and rest.

"Can I ask you a question?" she said.

"Of course."

"Why *didn't* you tell us about the lady in the pink dress? The one who recognized you at the rugby grounds?"

I hadn't offered an explanation, because there really hadn't been any excuse for endangering everyone. I'd just apologized and shut up. But Tegan was asking in the spirit of inquiry, I decided, not to needle me. "Because of Lat," I said honestly. "He told me not to go, and he would have been so happy to hear that I might have made a mistake."

Tegan shuffled round to look at me straight on. "How come you hate him so much?"

I gaped at her. "Because he tortured you."

"He had to," Tegan said. "He didn't do it for fun."

"Not like Diane," I said. "She loved it."

Tegan shuddered. "How could anyone be like that?"

"I don't know. But does it matter that she liked it and he didn't? The results were the same—pain, for both of us."

"It matters to me. Before he came and told me there was hope…Abdi, I think I was going to lose myself. I was so close to giving in for real. I almost became what they wanted me to be." Her face scrunched up. "I hated you a little bit, every time you resisted, even though I should have been pleased, because—"

"I understand," I said. I might have been the only one who could. I'd hated her, too, and hated being made to hate her and… it was awful, what they'd done to us. I could only think around the edges of it, and I was beginning to see that it would take a long, long time to heal.

And she was right. We needed to talk about it. I needed to talk about it with her. I couldn't do it all at once, but I could make a start.

"At the very beginning," I said, "when they made us stay awake, and you didn't give in until the fifth day—I hated you so much, then."

She blinked at me. "You mean the third day."

"What?"

"I gave in on the third day. I went to my knees and begged. I swore I was sorry, so, so sorry, that I would never ever be bad again, and they finally decided I was sincere. I was, at the time. I would have promised anything if they'd just let me sleep. And then they told me you hadn't apologized yet, and I'd have to wait until you did. And you didn't until the fifth day—"

"I broke on the third day, too," I said. "They told me *you* held out."

We looked at each other, and then Tegan began to laugh. It wasn't funny in the least, but I couldn't help joining in, letting the sound leach some of the poison out. With every second, I felt a little lighter, a little less rotten on the insides.

"You know," I said, after we'd subsided, "our first mistake might have been believing people who were trying to hurt us."

"Including Lat, you mean," Tegan said, her voice regaining some edge.

We always had to come back to *Lat*. "Yes. You ask why I hate him. Well, I can't understand why you don't."

"I can't describe it to you, how I felt when he said he'd help us." Tegan's voice cracked. "I didn't believe him. I was afraid to hope. But he showed me I could trust him." She summoned a smile, a small, trembling thing. "And we could. He got us out. I'll always be grateful."

"He threatened to rape you," I said, more bluntly than I should have. But I couldn't bear that Tegan be deceived by someone she thought was a knight in shining armor. And maybe I couldn't bear that she keep talking about him like that. "When I wouldn't go out on stage that last time"—had it really been only three nights ago?—"he told me that he'd do it. That he'd make me watch that, too. He said you might *like* it."

Tegan exhaled slowly. "I'm sorry he said that to you," she said quietly. "I was never threatened with sexual violence. Not once, not by Lat, or by my first handler, or anyone. No one—they did other things, you saw them, but never…"

"Good," I said, and meant it.

"Can I hold your hand?" she asked.

228

"Always," I said, and went further by putting my arm around her shoulders. "Sorry about the smell."

"We all reek of smoke," Tegan said, and kissed my cheek. I wanted more than that. I turned to catch her mouth with mine, but she pulled back. "Wait. I just want to…did Diane…"

Be a good boy, Abdi. Don't make me punish you.

"I don't want to talk about that," I said, suddenly in a fever of longing. I slid my hands up her sides, feeling heated flesh against my own.

She was breathing faster now, her pupils dilating in the dim light. "You don't have to," she whispered. "But are you sure…"

I wasn't sure about anything. But my body was very sure about what it wanted, with whom, and when.

We did smell, of burning things and the acrid sweat of panic. Tegan's hair, when I brushed it aside to kiss her collarbones, smelled strongly of smoke. I didn't care; I buried my face in the soft, dark cloud of it and breathed in deep. I could lose myself this way, give in to the rush of desire and pour fear and confusion into heat and joy. Tegan wriggled in my arms, and I leaned back, pulling her on top, where I could stroke down her thighs as she straddled me.

"Hey," Tegan murmured, braced above me on her elbows, her lips tantalizingly out of reach, her eyes gleaming in the dim light. "We should think about…"

For once, I didn't want to think; I wanted relief from thoughts. I reached up to bring her mouth down to mine, my hands skating up her arms, around the back of her neck—

"Ow!" she cried, and scrambled off and back.

I'd stroked right over the implant-removal wound.

"I'm sorry," I said, sitting up fast. "Tegan, I'm sorry; are you all right?"

"It hurts," she said, gasping. "Ugh, I feel sick; it really hurts."

"Let me see?"

There were tears standing in her eyes, but she turned, and I tugged down the high cowl-neck of her tunic. The skin around the dressing looked tight and red, and when I lightly brushed my fingers on the edges, I felt the heat of her skin.

Not the warmth of a hot day. This was a sick heat. I felt the back of my own neck. There was pain when I pressed on it, but not when I only brushed over the injury, and there was no heat radiating from the site.

"I think you have an infection," I said. "But you took the immunoboosters, right?"

"Of course. The last ones right before we got to that swap station."

"You might need a top-up. And we should change the dressing. Maybe I should take a look?" I tugged at the edge of the false skin, but she jerked away.

"Don't!"

"That hurts?"

She laughed breathlessly. "Uh, yeah."

I laid the back of my hand against her forehead. "Do you feel feverish? Your skin is really warm."

"I'm thirsty. And hot, but I'm always hot now. And I have a headache."

"Anything else?"

"Actually," she said slowly, "I was hoping it would go away, but I have been feeling a bit dizzy. On and off. For a couple of hours."

I scrambled to my feet, no longer in the mood for kissing. "We're going straight back to the others," I said. "Marie needs to do something about this right away."

"Okay," she said docilely, which alarmed me most of all. Tegan was a lot of things, but not docile.

I watched her as we walked back, and not in the same way I had on our trip to the small room. Her breathing was audible, little huffing pants, and twice she stumbled and braced herself with a hand against the tunnel wall. Had she been hiding how unwell she felt before, or had I just not noticed? I itched to help her, but there was nothing I could do until we had space. When the light from the big cave appeared ahead, I breathed a little easier.

And too soon.

Tegan turned around and groped for the ladder rungs with her feet. I saw her face clearly as she descended—one rung, then two, then a small, chilling pause. She looked puzzled, as if she wasn't sure what she was supposed to do next. Her eyes drifted closed.

I lunged forward, heedless of the scrape of my back against the tunnel roof, but I was too late.

Dreamily, Tegan fell.

CHAPTER
SEVENTEEN
Sotto

Tegan had jumped off buildings and landed safely. She'd crawled through roofs and launched herself over rails onto narrow steps, balanced sure-footed on pipes an inch thick, and flung herself over wire fences three times her height.

She must have had bad falls and injuries as she learned and stretched her limits. She must have damaged her small, strong body many times before. But I'd never seen her do it. To me, she'd always been startlingly physically competent—aware of her body and what it could accomplish in the same practiced way that I knew how to use my voice.

As she lay on the dirty cave floor, crumpled at the foot of the ladder, I felt as if the world had shaken around me.

And I was breathtakingly, uselessly, shamefully furious with her.

Marie was sitting by Tegan with Eduardo, doing things with Joph's medical bag and a kit Eduardo had unearthed. The rest of us had been firmly told to move back, but Joph and Bethari and I were clustered close by, with Zaneisha hovering behind us. Only Joph's hand on my arm had made me go that far, as stiff and slow as if I were made of stone.

"Abdi?" Tegan was calling, her voice plaintive. "Abdi?"

Marie looked up and nodded, and I came forward. Tegan was flushed red, her skin drenched in sweat as she lay flat on her back. Her pupils were blown wide, so that her already dark eyes seemed almost black.

"Abdi," she said, as I knelt by her head. "I fell."

"Yes," I said, glancing helplessly at Marie.

"Just be here," she advised. "There's no spinal injury, so we can turn her over and take a look at that wound. We gave her something for the pain, but it's not going to block everything."

"But it's okay," Tegan said. "Because you're going home, yay! Yay for you, I mean. Sad for me." She coughed, then winced. "Ow."

"You have a cracked rib," Marie told her. "Try not to agitate it."

"Did you tell me that before? My head really hurts." Tegan squinted at me. "You're so pretty."

Marie gave me a tight look.

"Joph, isn't he pretty? Don't you just want to lick him?"

Joph managed a smile that came nowhere near the calm beauty of her usual expression. "I don't want to lick men, remember?"

"Oh, yeah! Zaneisha! Do you want to lick him?"

"I don't want to lick anyone, Tegan."

"Bethari? You like boys, too!"

233

"Uh, no. No offense," she added to me.

"None taken," I replied.

"Well, I want to lick him," Tegan declared, and beamed at me.

Eduardo didn't look up from where he was laying out a stretcher, but I saw his shoulders shake silently. Laughter, at a time like this? I could have murdered him.

Except he was a ruthless and experienced killer. I was a soft, pampered boy, and he'd put me flat on my face in a second.

"It's going to be fine," I said.

She waved one arm, and I caught her hand to keep it still. "I don't know. I feel pretty bad."

"I'm sorry," I said, my voice rough. Joph's eyes were tight with anxiety as she looked at me, Tegan's other hand grasped in hers.

Marie took Tegan by the hips and nodded at Eduardo, who braced himself by her shoulders. "We're turning you on your side now, Tegan. You might want to scream, but that'll hurt your ribs, so don't. Abdi, move back." I let go of Tegan's hand and retreated to crouch by Joph.

"Should I bite on something?" she asked brightly. "In past-timer movies—I mean, past-timer movies about the past—they used to—" She broke off as, acting on some hidden signal, they turned her onto one side. I couldn't see her face. She made a funny, choked sound, almost a whine. But she didn't scream.

"All right," Marie muttered, and carefully plucked away the dressing over Tegan's wound.

Tegan screamed then. Her body jerked, hard, before it went terrifyingly limp.

"Oh no," Joph breathed, and grabbed my arm as if she thought I would rush forward. But I couldn't move, frozen by the sight of Tegan's neck.

Whitish-yellow pus was oozing out of the wound in thick curds, and the air was heavy with a sickly smell of rotting meat. Livid red marks radiated from the cut site. And worst of all, as Marie quickly mopped away the pus, I could see movement in the depths of the injury.

The implant wires were alive within her, jerking to some hellish beat as they danced in Tegan's body.

"But she's on immunoboosters!" Joph said.

"They both are," Marie said. "How are you feeling, Abdi?"

"I'm fine."

"No fever, no aches and pains?"

"No, nothing."

"Tell me what they are saying," Eduardo said in Somali as he handed Marie a diagnostic tool. I didn't know what it was. My brother would have, and I wanted him here, to take care of Tegan. All I could do was translate, so I squared my shoulders and did that, my tongue awkward in my mouth.

Eduardo looked at Marie, then carefully pushed the edge of the wound and watched the pus swell, his eyes thoughtful. "And she was on immunoboosters. Has she ever had the measles?" he asked.

"Yes," Marie replied after my translation. "As a child, before she could be vaccinated. Ask him if he thinks it's a—" she said something incomprehensible. I wasn't even sure if it was English.

"I don't understand that term," I said. All I could do was translate, and I couldn't even do that right.

The lines on Marie's forehead were so deep they looked as if they'd been engraved. "Sorry, medical jargon. Ask Eduardo if it's a, um…time-delayed reaction between the remnants of the measles and the boosters."

Eduardo nodded. "This happened to my cousin. He had measles, then many years later a cut on his leg. The cut would have healed, but his wife made him take the immunoboosters the firster doctor recommended." His eyes were sad. "The measles virus interacted with the boosters. It looked like this."

I translated, numb. "Can you fix it?" I asked.

"I can try. Ask what they did for his cousin," Marie said quietly. I think she knew as well as I did that Eduardo's story had no happy ending.

"We prayed," Eduardo replied. "You can pray, too. Perhaps God will listen to you."

Joph was silent, her face almost as white as Tegan's.

Marie was loading a hypospray with something from a clear bottle.

"This will make her more comfortable," she explained in response to my look.

I felt my face stiffen. "That's what you say about people who are going to die. Tegan won't die."

Marie's face was serious, professional, only hints of the pain she must be feeling around her eyes. "Abdi, I'll do the best I can for her, but you need to be aware that she's in serious danger.

This is an unusual reaction, and I need specialist drugs that we don't have with us."

"We could give ourselves up to the authorities," Bethari said.

Hanad looked up at that. "Not you," he said, pointing in my direction. "You come with me."

"Well, maybe just Tegan, then," Bethari said, thinking out loud. "We could drop her off at a hospital. I mean…they'll have to heal her."

I shook my head. "SADU would take her back. She said she'd rather die than go back."

"That's just a phrase," Bethari said. "Abdi, come on."

"Not for us," I told her. I was so calm. Why was I so calm? "Hanad, I need to hire your crew. You do retrieval operations. We'll retrieve the drugs Dr. Carmen needs. My family will pay."

Hanad shook his head. "I'm sorry for your friend, Abdi, but I don't take these risks for nothing. And your parents cannot pay more. They had to sell their house to fund your own retrieval."

I tasted metal in my mouth. The house. No, the terra-cotta-colored house on Siesta Road couldn't be gone. It all had to be there, waiting for me: the flat, sun-baked roof; the white balcony, with its wide, graceful arches; my father's courtyard garden; the little fountain my sister Ifrah had given my mother for her fiftieth birthday; the row of shoes outside the back door. I'd been dreaming of that house for over a year.

"I have money," Joph said. There was color coming back into her face.

"A girl's dress allowance isn't going to cover—"

"I have forty-six million Australian dollars," Joph said, as if Hanad hadn't interrupted. "Get us those medicines, and you can have it all."

Δ ʃ Ω

Hanad was very efficient. In less than three hours I was sitting in an ambulance parked in an alley behind a Melbourne medical clinic, watching Tegan fade.

I wasn't sure I wanted to pry too much into how Thulani had managed to acquire an ambulance with no notice and no alarm. But Marie had insisted on a sterile environment for the actual operation, and the ambulance's air-scrubbers provided that. After the rough trip here, it seemed better for Tegan to have the comfort of a float-bed. I knew it couldn't mean much to her, but it made me feel better.

It was hot in the ambulance, and the little whirry blood chiller that kept Tegan's temperature below brain-melting was going fast. Even with the fever under control, the infection was still raging through her body. Marie had a few less popular immunoboosters with her in Joph's red bag, but she was reluctant to use them until the last resort. I thought we were nearing that now, but I wasn't the doctor.

In the meantime, it was the blood chiller and IV bags to replace the fluid she was sweating out.

I was feeling very friendless, with Tegan unconscious and Joph left behind, guarded by Eduardo. Bethari had insisted upon coming, which Hanad had agreed to with surprising ease—at least until I saw Joph's worried glance and realized that Bethari was functioning as a hostage for Joph's continued goodwill, even if the operation went wrong and Marie and I were hurt or killed. I wondered if Bethari had figured out that was the only reason they'd brought her along.

At first I'd been happy they'd stuck Bethari with Thulani in the getaway car we'd transfer to after the theft. On the one hand, she couldn't bother me anymore with her "just take Tegan to the authorities" argument. But on the other, even Bethari might have been some comfort, under the circumstances.

Hanad and Zaneisha were going over the plan again, while Ashenafi set up the surveillance equipment and slid into the clinic's security feeds as smoothly as Bethari would have, making sure they wouldn't record anything that could identify the thieves. I'd envisaged a quick smash-and-grab, but Hanad had advised subterfuge. "No need to let your pursuers know you are in Melbourne," he'd said. "Not when they are looking much farther away. Better that they not know anything has been taken until it is too late."

Now he squinted at maps. "In the front door, to the dispensary. You are positive there is no pharmacist there, Dr. Carmen?"

"Not at 2 a.m., not unless they've changed procedures a great deal in the past two years. Doctors have to get their own medication at night. Or send nurses for it."

"So, we take what we need and proceed out the back door. An invisible theft. Very simple. If there is a pharmacist, or we are discovered by security personnel, we can take care of them."

"Nonlethally," Zaneisha said, checking her sonic pistol before concealing it under her stolen medical uniform. She looked as comfortable in those clothes as she did in her ordinary long robes.

"Of course. I have no desire to kill anyone on Australian soil. Your justice system is notoriously harsh toward outsiders."

"Didn't you shoot the SADU agent at the swap station?" I asked.

"That was me," Zaneisha said.

"Oh."

"If it helps, the agent was definitely trying to shoot me, too." She looked at Hanad, a little curious. "You did order your men to kill *me*, you know."

Hanad's lips quirked. "I had a feeling we were being watched. I thought threatening you might flush these little mousebirds out of the bushes."

"So you wouldn't have done it if we hadn't come out?" I asked.

"Oh, I probably would. Isolated location, an obviously trained yet suspiciously alone soldier not in uniform; a quick grave would have removed a knotty problem. I am a practical man, Abdi. That is why your mother came to me."

I felt something burn under my ribs. "She'd never have done it if she didn't have to."

"She didn't have to. She could have let you rot. She chose me instead." He shrugged. "People will do many things to protect their children."

"They certainly will," Marie said. She was sitting up on the other float-bed. Getting her out of the tunnel had been just as difficult as getting her in, especially with Tegan to be carried as well. But as Marie had pointed out, she was the only one who could swiftly identify the drugs she needed and then get them into Tegan as quickly and safely as possible. "Abdi, you'll be fine. Just remember, if the blood-chiller dial goes to red—"

"Push to green. Yes, ma'am."

"We won't be long," Zaneisha promised.

Hanad handed me a small device that looked like a very stripped-down computer. "Two-way coms, you understand? Hold it and talk, release it and hear us. We normally have Eduardo as a watchman, but this will take all of us on the ground. You'll be our eyes. We go in the front door and out the back."

He pointed at one of the screens. "This has the best view of our exit point. If anyone seems to be blocking that point, tell me. Understood?"

I thought he was humoring me. It was almost kind, trying to give me something to do that wasn't staring at Tegan and wondering how much time she had left. "Yes."

"And as soon as we go through the back door, start the engine. We will be fifteen minutes—perhaps twenty, if we meet opposition."

"I understand."

"Good. Let's go," Hanad told Ashenafi, in Somali. I began to translate for Zaneisha and Marie, but there was no need—Marie lay down, Ashenafi and Hanad stood at either end of the float-bed to direct it, and Zaneisha marched in front. They all had bio masks, with the "medical personnel" wearing conspicuous and entirely fake IDs that should get them past the front desk.

And I was alone with Tegan, limp and sweaty in the back of the ambulance.

We'd been like this once before, when we'd been tranquilized and kidnapped by the Inheritors of the Earth. Tegan had been unconscious far longer than I was on our sea journey. I'd sat there in the bottom of that boat, wondering if she might never wake up, and feeling as helpless as I did now.

She had woken, that time. I held her shoulders while she threw up what seemed like every meal she'd ever eaten and then sang to her while we drifted into the real, undrugged sleep we so sorely needed. It had been easier, somehow, with just the two of us, united against a known enemy. We'd had a clear mission, too: to escape and broadcast the proof of military conspiracy.

Well, we'd succeeded. And what had changed? The government had claimed it was only trying to protect the cryofacilities and starship against terrorist attack, the military had blamed unethical practices on rogue elements, and the Ark Project had continued under government control, with civilian funding. There were probably more people willing to protest and speak up, more people who had been driven from complacency by what Tegan and I had done—the Save Tegan campaign. But we hadn't reached the people in power. We hadn't changed anything in Australia's horrendous refugee policies. At the most, we'd won a few hearts and minds. And that was something.

But it wasn't enough.

I could see why Lat and Hurfest had wanted to take decisive action to force change. I almost wanted them to go through with it. But I'd studied history. Violent revolt and military coups might remove corrupt aristocrats and politicians—and replace them with corrupt rebels and soldiers. Some of those takeovers resulted in positive, long-lasting change for the people they allegedly fought for. But many of them didn't. Civil war was horrible, and adding more displaced people to the world wouldn't help the refugees who saw Australia as a possible source of safety.

What I wanted was for Australians to take care of their own house. I wanted them to remove their government or embarrass it into resigning, to demand and receive a full investigation into the Ark Project, to refuse to vote for anyone who didn't support immediately suspending the No Migrant policy.

In my part of the world, we didn't need firsters coming over to save us; we had plenty of our own people who could do that. We needed firsters to get out of our way.

Tegan gasped, rolled her head, and murmured in her fevered sleep.

"Okay," I said softly. "No Beatles." I put the two-way coms down on the bed beside her and thought about it.

In the end, I sang to Tegan something I'd sung that time on the boat, when she'd been sick and confused and we didn't know what the future might bring. It was an old Somali lullaby my older sister had used to soothe me when I was little. Ifrah was so smart, so caring. She'd been thinking about getting married when I left. I wondered if she'd found a man worthy of her.

The last soft syllables echoed in the ambulance, and I smoothed back Tegan's hair from her sweaty forehead.

"I liked that," Lat said as he came through the back door, sonic pistol trained on me. I jumped to my feet, placing myself between Tegan's bed and the door.

Then, and only then, I remembered and reached for the coms.

But Lat was much faster than I was, and my stupid first instinct had put me out of position. If only I'd grabbed the coms first, instead of that useless gesture of protecting Tegan. He saw my movement, took one swift step, and knocked me across the narrow aisle onto the other bed. The coms he picked up with a gloved hand.

My ear throbbed from the blow, but I scrambled to my feet.

Lat was barely looking at me. Face anguished, he was staring at Tegan. "My god," he said. "What have you done?"

I felt so incredibly stupid. Marie was right. Zaneisha must have been on their side all along.

Δ ∫ Ω

"She has an infection," I said, while Lat reached out to brush at Tegan's hair, a disquieting echo of my own earlier gesture. "Don't touch her!" I snapped, and he turned to face me.

Lat looked unwell himself—his skin was greasy and his hair in lank strands around his face. Wherever he'd been hiding evidently hadn't included a shower. His shark eyes were narrow and dead, and he looked very, very dangerous. "We're taking her inside," he said.

"She doesn't want that," I said.

"She's not conscious. She doesn't get to decide."

244

My temper snarled again. "She decided before she became unconscious. You don't get to change her mind for her."

He ignored that, of course. "What happened?"

"It's an infection," I repeated. "From the implant. But we're getting the medicine. She'll be fine."

He groaned. "Abdi, I don't know how you talked Sergeant Washington into this, but you'd better call her back now."

Talked her into it?

He offered me the coms device, and I took it, my mind working furiously.

"Lat, you don't understand," I began.

"Lat's there?" Zaneisha's voice said, clear and calm in the ambulance.

"As if you didn't know," I snarled. "I can't believe you. He wants to take Tegan into the hospital! How could you do that to her, Zaneisha?"

"What?" Lat said.

"I didn't tell him anything," Zaneisha said sharply. "Lat, listen. Dr. Carmen is with me. She's confident she can heal Tegan with the right drugs and equipment."

"Washington, she's dying! We've got no options here. I'll leave Abdi outside—you can pick him up and take him wherever you're going next."

Zaneisha didn't say anything. I had to keep him talking, give them enough time to come back and overpower him.

"How did you find us?" I asked. If it hadn't been Zaneisha...

"Tracker in Joph's medicine bag. We had to get back to the others to activate it, but once we did—Hurfest decided it was

245

too dangerous to retrieve you from the middle of Melbourne. I came anyway." He was tapping his sonic pistol against his thigh, apparently unconscious of the motion. Then he squared his shoulders and stepped forward.

Toward Tegan.

"Wait!" I said.

Zaneisha's voice cut in again. "Give us five more minutes, Lat. We warned you about the president's visit being canceled so you wouldn't get caught. You owe me one, soldier."

"Sorry," Lat said. "Priorities."

I dropped the coms and threw myself at him. He wasn't expecting it, and so I got one good strike at his neck before his arms came up and he easily blocked the next blow. I found myself twisting through the air, my striking arm turned against me as he used it as a pivot to smash me against the wall. "I do not have time for this," he growled, while my head swam and I wondered if I was going to throw up. "Stay down, or I will put you down, do you hear me?"

"This is familiar," I said. My face was crushed against the wall and the metallic taste of my own blood was sharp in my mouth. "I knew you hadn't changed."

He let me go as if I were poison.

"I have to save her," he said. "All the things I've done, Abdi—I've done some terrible things. I have to do something to balance that out. I have to save Tegan."

"That's not how it works," I said, so frustrated my skin itched. I couldn't hit him. I couldn't shoot him. I couldn't stop him. All I could do was talk, and talk was getting me nowhere.

"There's no balance, Lat! There are the good things you do and the bad things you do, and they exist at the same time. They don't cancel each other out. You can't buy forgiveness!"

But he'd gone somewhere I couldn't reach, a nightmare place inside his head, where whatever demons he'd summoned with his own misdeeds clawed at his memories. It wasn't enough that Marie was on her way; it wasn't enough that she could probably fix Tegan herself. Driven by his demons, Lat needed to be the one who saved her. "Even if she dies," he said slowly. "She died once before, after all. If she's in the hospital, they can freeze her."

My blood went cold.

"You can't put her in cryostasis again," I said. "She hated it. You can't…"

"This world's not good enough for Tegan. Later, maybe, it'll be better."

"This world isn't good enough for any of us," I snapped back. "I don't know what you think Tegan is, Lat, but she's not perfect! She's not some ideal. She's a real person who's brave and reckless and funny and stubborn, and she doesn't want this!"

"She doesn't know what she wants," he said.

Appealing to Tegan's ability to make her own choices clearly wasn't going to help. Maybe an appeal to self-preservation would work.

"You betrayed SADU. They'll kill you."

"I know."

All right, that was no good, either. "How do you know they can even bring her back again?"

He wasn't listening. I wasn't sure if I was there for him. His world seemed narrowed down to his awful grief, and his even more horrifying hope, and the dying girl on the bed. I braced myself, ready to attack again, knowing that I'd be as effective as a grouper taking a nibble at a shark.

"I'll keep you safe, Tegan," Lat said. "I promise." He reached out to touch her hand.

And his head blew apart in a mess of blood and bone and thick, wet chunks of brain.

Diane stepped into the ambulance, her bolt-gun steady in her hands. She was smiling at the ruin of Lat's face as his body folded onto Tegan's bed. Her eyes were bright and sharp; her smile glittered like broken glass.

"Hello, Abdi," she said. "It's so nice to see you again."

CHAPTER EIGHTEEN
Tenuto

I was too scared to move.

I wanted to. If I could have run at that moment, I would have. I would have left Tegan there, left Zaneisha and Marie, left my self-respect and good intentions and everything else behind, if only I could have run away from Diane, too.

But I couldn't run, and it was Diane; I was far too frightened to fight her.

That was *bad*. I'd be *punished*.

"Leave us alone," I croaked, and even that was almost too much effort. My vision was swimming. I was afraid I was going to pass out. But if I passed out, she'd take me. I couldn't let that happen. With a massive effort of will, I managed to take a step back. I was standing in Lat's blood, pieces of his head squelching under my flimsy shoes.

She laughed. "Don't be silly. Now, be a good boy and come with me."

"Tegan—"

Diane shot her a single, dismissive glance. "Tegan's dead meat. I've put a lot of effort into retrieving you, Abdi. I found Lat and waited for him to lead me here." She glanced at Tegan again. "I didn't expect this. But it's all the better, for my purposes. Where's Dr. Carmen?"

I managed another step backward, nearly enough to get me to the driver's section. "Go away."

"I want Dr. Carmen, Abdi. My reputation is in *tatters*."

"Good!"

She came forward, picking her way daintily through the carnage. "Abdi, you've fallen in with bad company. I can see it's going to take a long time to rectify your behavior. But it's all right. I'll help you."

"Help me?" I repeated.

The worst thing was, part of me wanted to believe her. Part of me wanted to be punished for being so bad, to go back to a place where I didn't have to make decisions or choose my own actions. Part of me wanted to please Diane. Then I wouldn't be hurt. Then everything would be all right, for always.

But the rest of me remembered what it had been like to be under Diane's control.

Tegan was unconscious; Zaneisha and Hanad were too far away. I had to do this myself. I had to face what she'd done, so that I could fight her.

"Help me?" I said, my voice gaining strength. "Diane, you raped me."

250

I'd hoped that saying it might discomfort her, that naming what she'd done would make her hesitate long enough for me to make my move.

But Diane didn't flinch. "I raped you?" she said, tilting her head. "We had sex. You seemed to enjoy it."

Be a good boy, Abdi.

"You made me."

Don't make me hurt you.

"How? I didn't hold you down. I didn't drug you. You didn't exactly fight me."

And that was true. I hadn't pushed her away. I hadn't tried to fight. How could I, with an implant in my neck that she controlled? In the end, I'd been almost grateful that at least what she'd done that night hadn't been painful. Her hands, her body; she'd made it feel good. She'd made me ashamed of myself for what she'd done to me.

"I was your prisoner. I wasn't able to say no," I said.

"You're confused," she said gently.

"You can't lie to me, Diane. I know what you did. You raped me." It was easier to say that second time, and I gathered my strength. "I won't go back. You'll have to kill me."

Diane's mouth abandoned that sweet smile. "The crap I don't have time for," she muttered, and pointed her gun at Tegan. "You're going to come with me, or I'll do her like I did Lat." Her eyes glinted. "I might kill her anyway. We'll have so much more fun without your little girlfriend."

She was expecting me to come at her—I could see it in the set of her shoulders, the way she held the gun at Tegan's head, but looked a challenge at me. She didn't just want me captured; she wanted me humiliated.

Broken. Controlled.

But I'd learned better than to throw myself headfirst at obstacles and either batter them down or fall trying. That was Tegan's way, and it was all right for her, because she was good at it. My way was to think around the problem. And while she'd argued with me, I'd been thinking.

I lunged, but backward, not forward, into the space between the driver and passenger seats. Diane's gun swung up to point at me as my left hand found the ignition button. My right hand slammed the accelerator, and then, as the ambulance surged forward, the brake.

Tegan was strapped in. I was lying in the footwell, bracing myself.

Diane was standing in the aisle, both hands on her gun. She fell, in an ungainly tangle of limbs—the first time I'd ever seen her do anything less than strong and graceful. I didn't have time to relish the moment; I was up the second she went down, scrambling through the gap on my hands and knees, reaching desperately for the gun she was still gripping in one hand.

She smacked me across the face with it. Pain exploded through my skull, but she'd gotten me used to pain. Instead of falling back, I kneed her in the gut and hooked my fingers, clawing for her eyes. We scrabbled for dominance on the wet ambulance floor, hitting whatever soft targets we could reach. I was stronger than I'd ever been, and in the midst of my fury

I felt a wild triumph that I'd finally managed to hurt her. For a moment, I dared to hope that I might win.

But she was trained and experienced, and I had only rage to back me up. Lat had been relatively gentle with me. Diane had no such restraint. She got an elbow into my solar plexus, knocking out my air, and then flipped me facedown, forcing my cheek against the floor.

I tried to throw her off, but she pressed her full weight against my back.

"Nice try," she hissed, and ground her gun muzzle into the implant wound.

I didn't have the breath to scream. A strained, mewling sound escaped as the agony washed through me, every little wire reacting to the jabbing pressure. Even when she took the gun away, I was sick with the sensation, unable to move. Crouching, she dragged my head up by my dirty collar and pointed at Tegan with her gun.

"You lose," she said, her voice rich with satisfaction. "Now watch this."

One last spasm of fear and hate shoved me sideways, dragging at her gun arm. Diane cursed, wrapped her arm around my neck, and yanked back.

"I said watch!" she said, and kneed my side. "Oh yes, Abdi, I want you to see this. See what happens when you're bad."

I screwed my eyes shut. I had just enough defiance left to know that I wouldn't comply.

She could kill Tegan, and I couldn't stop her.

But she couldn't make me watch.

"Let him go," Hanad's voice suggested, and Diane moved so fast I couldn't even follow what happened. One second I was being choked on a filthy ambulance floor, and the next I was some form of upright, a gun muzzle digging into the side of my head. My eyes popped open involuntarily. Marie was clutching containers in her lap, almost invisible behind Ashenafi's bulk. Zaneisha and Hanad were standing with their guns aimed at Diane.

"Put your weapons down, or I'll kill him," Diane said, adding, in the same calm voice, "Washington, you traitor, I'm going to testify at your posthumous court-martial with the greatest of pleasure."

"Let him go, or I'll kill you," Hanad said, just as pleasantly. Zaneisha didn't even bother to speak, her gun tracking Diane as she forced me out of the ambulance. I stumbled, nearly dropping on the jump down, but she pulled me up again and backed us toward the alley entrance.

It was raining hard, heavy drops that struck at my bare arms. My mind was clearing again, a sharp, bright feeling that I knew wouldn't last. There were lots of ways for Diane to win this, but not many for us; the longer she managed to delay, the better the chances that we'd get caught. I couldn't allow her to take me back, but I could make her think that I would to save the others.

A plan of action suggested itself and I took it up before my brain had time to gray out again. When she headed for the exit to the alley, Hanad and Zaneisha following, I walked with her, as easily as I could with my head throbbing and an arm around my neck.

Diane felt the change in my gait. "Good boy," she murmured. "I knew you'd come back to me."

Two steps from the corner. One step.

"I'd rather die," I said, and dropped all my weight at once.

She was much more skilled than me, but I was heavier; the sudden shift dragged at her arm and removed my usefulness as a human shield. I heard a couple of shots stifled by silencers—quiet, deadly puffs of air—and then I was lying on the cobblestones, Diane yelling an alarm as she ran down the street.

There were strong hands on my arms, and I hit out for a moment, panicking at the touch, until I realized that Zaneisha was just trying to get me up. I stumbled back to the ambulance on feet that felt as heavy and dead as lumps of frozen meat.

Someone had dumped Lat's body outside. I got one last look at him, the stump of his neck horrifying and almost pathetic, before Zaneisha boosted me wholesale into the ambulance.

Inside, everything seemed etched in an unnatural light, and small motions were magnified. The vibration of the engine as Ashenafi peeled out of the alley was like hammers pounding at my bones. The blood was so many beautiful shades of red—crimson for the most part, shading into a red so dark it was almost black for the thicker globs. On the walls, smears had already dried to a clear ruby, a wash of almost transparent color over the sterile white. My pale brown pants were drenched with wet brick red.

I'd escaped again.

But I'd never be free of what she'd done.

I lost some time, I think, because the next thing I knew

Zaneisha was kneeling beside me, heedless of the blood seeping into her pants, and draping a blanket around my shoulders. Marie was straddling Tegan's back and working on her wound with Hanad's assistance, swearing viciously.

"Is Tegan all right?" I said through my chattering teeth.

"She'll be fine," Zaneisha said.

"I hate her," I said. "Diane, not Tegan. I love Tegan, maybe. But Diane I hate." I could hear my voice rise up the scale as if I were listening to someone else practicing vocalizations. "Diane I hate," I sang, putting my voice into it properly and trying the phrase again, an octave lower.

"Let's get up," Zaneisha suggested, and lifted me onto the other bed. "Doctor, I need you."

Marie's face hovered over my own, then cool fingers pressed against my throat and withdrew, before I could slap her away. "Shock," she said, her voice detached. "Give him a sedative; keep him warm."

She was gone again, and Zaneisha's face replaced hers, warm with concern. She flung a reflective blanket over my shoulders, and I huddled into it. I was shivering, my voice thin and tremulous as I whisper-sang my hate for Diane, over and over. "I'm going to give you a shot so that you can sleep," Zaneisha said, and paused. "Abdi? Is that okay?"

I think she was waiting for me to protest, but I was tired of resistance. I nodded. When the hypospray hit my arm and I slid toward sleep, I found myself hoping I wouldn't have to wake up.

Δ ʃ Ω

I was fishing for Lat's head in a pool of pink water.

"Hurry up," Diane said. Her eyes were laser sights, too bright to look at.

"I'm trying," I said, and dipped my hands into the pool again. I knew the head was in there; I just had to reach deeper. But the water was to my elbows, then my biceps, and I still couldn't find it.

"It's there," I said.

"It's there," Diane repeated, mocking, and my mother wore a beautiful dress and gave me new clothes for my birthday.

"We're going to a party," she said. "All you have to do is listen."

"Listen and remember," I said. This wasn't right. I was too tall for these clothes, too tall for this day.

"I'm so proud of you," Hooyo said, and hugged me, heedless of her carefully arranged braids. I could smell expensive perfume on her warm skin. "My brave Abdullah. My smart, careful boy. Seven years old, and already a man."

"I'm seventeen," I said. "I'm Abdi, Hooyo." I was wearing my old clothes anyway, awkward and uncomfortable, the shoes too tight on my feet. But everyone thought I was seven. Maybe I was. They were all tall, much taller than me. I saw the man my mother had asked me to watch for and took my computer near him to play my game.

Really, I was listening. His name was Abdullah Haid, and he was very important, and I had to tell Hooyo everything he said. If I remembered it all, I would get a sweet and a new game for my computer.

"Hello, boy," he said, and he was Diane. "Don't be *bad*. You'll have to be *punished*."

257

I was running, running, with something behind me that I couldn't see. My brother, Halim, ran with me. "You should know how to shoot," he said, stronger and older from his time at college. "Every man should know how to shoot."

The thing behind me was a shark. I was in the pink water. Halim handed me his gun. "Two shots, center mass," he said. "Then you'll know it's dead."

There were no earbuds to deaden the sound. It should be quiet underwater, but I could hear every sound. The shark opened her mouth, wide and wider. I took aim.

Lat's head was in her jaws, his eyes opening. "I have to save her," he said.

"I'm dreaming," I said, and tried to put the gun down.

"Have you found that head, yet?" Diane said, and I plunged my hands into the pink water, trying so hard to please her.

Δ ∫ Ω

When I woke, I opened my eyes to the universe.

Hovering above me was a black sky, with tiny pinpricks to indicate stars. Our own sun dominated the middle of the scene, a roiling ball of liquid orange power, and Mercury zipped around it, a little gray dot almost too small and fast to see. Then came Venus, yellow with its sulfuric atmosphere, and Earth, its blues and greens overlaid with wisps of white cloud as it sparkled like a jewel, single moon curling around it as it circled the sun. Mars was a smaller dark red dot, with two tiny black moons. I passed backward through a ring of asteroids and debris so fast it made me start, and then came the gas giants—vast Jupiter, with its cloud of moons, then Saturn, with its tilted rotation and its gorgeous rings. After that came the ice giants, Uranus and Neptune, slowly inscribing their long years around the sun in cold solitude.

The sun seemed to shrink into the middle of the scene. I was falling faster and faster, through the Kuiper Belt of ice asteroids and dwarf planets, through the scattered disk of comets, and then speeding through blackness until the Oort cloud exploded around me, icy planets and comets whizzing in their eccentric orbits around the tiny pinprick of light that was the focus of all this motion, the source of all life on Earth.

My body thrumming with mingled terror and joy, I jerked away from the infinite night.

Birdsong sounded, and rosy golden light illuminated white walls.

I was lying, naked and covered in sweat, in a perfectly ordinary bed in a perfectly ordinary room, and I was almost disappointed when I realized what had happened. The spacescape had been projected on the walls and ceiling as a treat for a waking sleeper. It was an alarm clock, nothing more. It was only my disorientation from the nightmares that had made it seem so real.

I made a mental note to find out what Zaneisha had given me in the ambulance and to stay away from it from now on. My dreams were already bad enough—I didn't need that particular sedative-induced hallucinogenic edge.

I hadn't thought about my seventh birthday for a while. My first step into politics.

I lay there, trying to remember my mother's exact expression, the warm glint in her eyes. Her face was slipping away from me, and that wasn't right—the smooth portrait she'd presented to Diane wasn't really her. My father was easier to remember—dark, clipped hair going gray, deep wrinkles around his eyes from decades of squinting through sunlight on water. I could remember Sahra easily, the energetic brat, and Ifrah's forthright eyes, and Halim, tall and broad.

As a special treat to make up for missing my fifteenth birthday, he'd taken me to the shooting range the French soldiers had left behind. But Hooyo had been furious when she found out after the fact.

"My sons are not going to use tools of violence!" she'd shouted. It was one of the few times I'd ever seen her lose her temper.

"It's a useful skill, Hooyo," Halim argued back. "Not everywhere is as safe as Djibouti."

"Oh, he goes off to university and he comes home and thinks he can teach his mother right and wrong!"

"You have a driver who carries a gun," Halim said, and I made a face at him. Couldn't he see that the best thing was to let her shout out the anger, and then present his own arguments, quietly and rationally?

"But I don't carry one myself," Hooyo told him. "I don't want you carrying one, either. The Prophet prohibits aggression."

"'Fight in the way of Allah against those who fight against you,'" Halim quoted.

"'But be not aggressive,'" Hooyo said pointedly. "'Surely

Allah loves not the aggressors.' Carrying a weapon is an act of aggression."

Halim's eyes fell on me. "What about the atheists?" he said, pointing. "Abdi isn't a believer. He can carry a gun."

Thank you, Halim, I thought. What an unsubtle attempt to shift the focus onto my own filial transgressions.

Hooyo shook her head. "Abdi will come back to God," she said. She was so certain about it that I found myself getting annoyed.

"No, I won't," I said. "Hooyo, you know I don't believe."

Her eyes narrowed. "You are fifteen years old. You don't know who you are or who you will become."

"Well, I know I don't want a gun," I said, controlling my frustration. The whole adventure had been hot and noisy, with Halim making fun of me for missing the target even at the closest range. "I'm sorry, Hooyo. I won't go back to the firing range."

She touched my arm. "Thank you, Abdi. Now, go up to your room while I speak to your brother. I'm sure you have schoolwork."

Behind her back, Halim made a gesture at me that would have earned him a much longer telling off if she'd seen it. I grinned at him and ran up the polished wooden stairs to my room. I was going to rehearse, not study. My cousin's wedding was in a few days, and he wanted me to sing.

I'd sung for my cousin, but the world had noticed. The scholarship offer had come from Australia. And I'd decided to go, far overseas, to a place much less safe than Djibouti.

I sat up, no longer willing to reminisce.

"Good morning, sir," the house computer said pleasantly. "Would you care to review today's headlines?"

"Why not?"

"I'm sorry, I didn't understand that."

"House, show headlines."

That was closer to the programming. The projection displayed lines of text, actual headlines. The house owner was apparently old-fashioned.

The one at the top read NEW REVIVALS REVEALED!

I tensed. "Show more." The story was the focus of thousands of 'casts, and they were all saying essentially the same thing. The Australian government had announced the successful revival of two patients. One had initially died in a sudden accident, and the other had been frozen before he could be killed by a childhood cancer. I scanned a few 'cast synopses to pick up the facts, then ordered footage of the revelation to play.

The official press conference was a choreographed wrestling match, the journalists all surging to get at the revivees. The press had obviously been warned against shouting or speaking out of turn; they asked their questions in voices vibrating with restraint. The revivees sat, one on either side of President Cox, and smiled nervously. The boy who'd had cancer had family members still living. One middle-aged woman stood behind her older brother, now thirty years younger than she was, and wept and wept.

I watched them through different 'casts, different angles, picking out 'casts to watch again so that I could catch every nuance. The cancer revivee was twelve. The older one, the accident victim, was nineteen, a photogenic woman with a long jaw and glossy red hair, a black tattoo of a spider visible on her wrist when she gestured. She'd been frozen for ninety-six years. Like Tegan, she had donated her body to science without caveat. Like Tegan, that gave the government a certain ownership of her, yet to be legally contested. I watched her careful face and deliberate gestures, and wondered what she would do. Or if she could do anything.

President Cox patted her hand over and over, the same motion captured by a dozen bumblecams. He was animated, but dignified, as he spoke of new hope, new worlds, with this last obstacle between humanity and her future removed.

Two of them. Both so young, as Tegan was young.

Someone knocked on the door, and I pulled the sheets up to my chest. Where were my clothes?

"Come in," I called, and only then remembered that I'd been drenched in Lat's blood. No wonder my filthy clothes had been stripped away, though I wasn't sure I wanted to know who had done the stripping.

Hanad came in, carrying Marie. They made an odd pair, she politely trying to pretend she didn't need his assistance, he moving with panache to deposit her on the end of my bed.

Marie pushed her hair out of her eyes. "I wanted to check up on you."

"I'm all right," I said, edging away from her. "I'm fine."

"Tegan will live," she said.

My breath whooshed out in a sigh that was almost a sob. I covered my face with my hands for a few moments, inhaling and exhaling in that small, warm cave. When I emerged again, Marie was watching me, her eyes grave.

"When can I see her?" I asked.

"I thought we should talk first."

"Yes, ma'am," I said, and tried not to sound as grim as I felt. The sheet fell to my waist, and I grabbed it again. "Uh, perhaps I could get some clothes, first?"

"In the wall," Hanad said. "House, show wardrobe."

Part of the wall peeled back, to show an array of clothing in several styles, from the flowing tunics and leggings favored by people here in their leisure hours to the more elaborate shirt-and-trouser combinations used in business settings. While Marie politely turned her head, I scrambled into a pink tunic and some trousers. They were a little baggy around the waist, but not too bad. "What is this place?" I asked.

Hanad rubbed his eyes. "Our safe house. A rich man owns it. He has one in Sydney, Noosa, Adelaide—many places. He likes privacy, and he likes comfort. A friend of mine told me about it." He chuckled. "The rich man will not be happy when he discovers we've been here."

So Hanad trusted us enough now to take us to the safe house he'd avoided before—that was a good sign. Or maybe he hadn't had the luxury of choice.

"What about Joph and Eduardo?"

"The water's still high," he said. "They're all right in the main cave. But they can't get out, and we can't get in."

It had been raining, I remembered, thick drops beating on my arms. Dirty rainwater, but still cleaner than the other fluids that had coated my skin.

Marie made an impatient movement, and Hanad left, winking at me as he went.

I was certain she wasn't here for a medical checkup. "I feel fine," I said, testing.

"Good," she said. "In the ambulance, you said you loved Tegan."

"Did I?"

"You know you did. Abdi, you must understand it can't work. You're going to Djibouti, and no matter what you want, she can't go with you. It's not fair of you to ask."

"Go on," I said. She had a speech prepared. She might as well make it.

"I'm her guardian," Marie said, half angrily. "I've done a half-pie job of it, but I am. I have to look out for her emotional state as well as her physical health. I see how she looks at you. I see how you look back. You can tell me you love her, and I'll believe it."

"You should," I said. "It's true."

"But you're *no good* for her. Have you told her how you feel? Because if you haven't, don't. It's not fair. She needs structure, calm. She needs to be settled in a place that can be home, at least for a while. No more risks."

"I think that Tegan wants to take risks," I said. "I think she wants to push her limits and always has."

Marie struck the bed with a closed fist, hard. "That may be, but she's not going to do it with you! Can't you see how vulnerable she is? You turn up, mysterious and intense—and a musician, of all things! It's as if you were designed to appeal to her! Can't you see how easy it would be for you to use her, when it's easy for you to use everyone?"

I couldn't control my flinch, and Marie saw it. Her voice

became softer, more persuasive. She might be nice, but she could be as ruthless as I was.

"I'm not saying you have to be separated forever. I'm only asking you, for her own good, to please back off and let her make her own choices for a while, without your influence."

"Certainly," I said, so furious I could barely speak. "If you'll do the same. I thought Tegan had made it very clear she didn't want anyone else speaking for her, ever."

"I…" Marie said, then, "Look, I'll talk to her, too, of course I will. I just wanted to say to you first—"

"That I should lie to her? Deceive her about how I feel? No. I'll lie to anyone *but* her, Dr. Carmen. Can you say the same?"

She opened her mouth, then closed it again.

"What's the truth behind the revival process?" I said, and watched her face fold in on itself. I'd planned to be more meticulous about this—to think through what was only a vague suspicion, and then broach the subject carefully. But I was sick of planning. Maybe I could follow Bethari and Tegan, and just blurt out what I was thinking.

"Why is it only young people who have been successfully revived, Dr. Carmen? Can you bring only young people back to life? Cryonics or not, are the older people who die dead forever?"

The questions hung in the air like thunderclouds, pregnant with violent possibility.

"Yes," Marie said. "Every adult person who is currently cryopreserved is permanently dead."

CHAPTER
NINETEEN
Accelerando

It was clearly the first time Marie had said it out loud. Her already strained face tightened up further, as if voicing the idea made it much more real. She'd been holding this secret for...how long? Days, certainly. Weeks, months, perhaps. Unable to trust anyone with this knowledge, her whole career suddenly a waste.

"Are you all right?" I asked.

"No," she said, and closed her eyes. "Abdi, I am not all right."

"Let me get you..." I said. "House, bathroom."

A hidden door glowed a soft green. I rummaged through the bathroom, finding a glass I could fill with water and a plush washcloth I could wet down. Marie refused the first but wiped the second over her face and neck, relaxing a little as she did.

She still looked tense, but I was no longer worried that she might simply break apart.

"I think that you were just much kinder to me than I deserve," she said, placing the damp washcloth in her lap.

"You and your family deserve a lot of kindness from me." The phrase came out without thought; I was still reeling from the confirmation of my suspicions. The implications! Were Marie and I really the only people to know?

But Marie appeared struck by my choice of words. "My family," she repeated. "Yes. I'm sorry. I shouldn't have talked to you like that. I had no right."

I sat back down. "You had some right. It's confusing, Tegan and me. I don't know what we are." I shook my head. "It doesn't matter right now. Does anyone else know that it's only young people getting revived? Do *they* know?" I didn't need to specify the *they*. Marie and I probably shared some nightmares.

Marie pinched her lip between her teeth. "I can't think so, or Cox wouldn't have held that press conference. How did *you* know?"

"I could see that you were anxious about it, that's all. You had to be hiding something, something much bigger than just knowing two more people were revived. And then I saw the new revivals, and I thought, they look so young...and Tegan's young. Tegan said that she'd once seen another man, in his early twenties, but he hadn't been successfully revived."

"Nicolas Fisher. No."

"They want you back," I said slowly. "Diane asked me, 'Where's Dr. Carmen?' If they can't work out what's going wrong, they must be frantic without you. Tegan's not necessary anymore, though they'd probably like to have her. And me, to be their thirdie speaker to the masses. But it's actually you they're hunting. You're the one they really need."

Marie glanced at her mutilated feet and treated me to a

slow, vicious smile. "Well, they can't have me. My contract is null and void." She sighed, collapsing a little. "I don't know what to do. They'll work it out eventually; they have all my case notes, most of my research. When it comes out, there's going to be an appalling backlash."

"We might be able to do something with the information."

"Such as what?"

"I'm not sure yet. But it's secret, and it will upset people; that makes it valuable."

Marie looked taken aback.

"I had an unusual education," I told her. I wasn't going to tell her that I was beginning to recognize just how unusual it was, how much my mother's good intentions and own eager participation might have distorted my growth. Like an emotional bonsai.

But though I was beginning to question its effects, that training might be very useful right now. "To start with, we ought to make sure more people than just we two have this knowledge. Complete with some of the medical details, too."

"The human brain is—"

I shook my head. "Not now. We should tell everyone at once."

"Everyone? Hanad? Zaneisha?"

"I trust Zaneisha," I said, and realized it was true. "And Hanad...I don't trust. Not completely. But I think we can trust him with this." Especially since Joph was still with Eduardo. I really didn't want Hanad to get suspicious about our withholding information.

"You're the expert," Marie said, and if there was doubt in her voice, she seemed willing enough to comply. "Tegan's asleep, and I won't wake her. But the others are preparing a meal. Are you hungry?"

For a moment, I felt again the visceral, churning sickness of blood all over my body. My muscles ached, and there were sharp, sore points I didn't want to investigate too closely, for fear of what had done the damage. Diane's teeth and nails? Or Lat's splintered bones?

But my brain needed fuel as surely as my body did.

"Sure," I said. "I could eat."

The house guided us to the kitchen, upstairs, where natural light flooded through large windows. There were trees outside to screen us from the nearest neighbors, who were apparently some distance off. And grass. Fresh green grass, kept that way from what had to be a private water source.

I reassessed the wealth of the man who owned this place and put him several places higher on the scale of "obscenely rich." My respect for Bethari increased, too; even though she knew the place was empty and no human guards were inside, getting through this security system had to have been something of a challenge.

The kitchen was a collection of varying food taboos at work. Hanad and Zaneisha were making a pasta bake. Ashenafi was grilling lamb steaks, while Thulani cut up pork on the enormous kitchen island. Bethari was at the table, industriously slicing carrots. She smiled at me when I came in. Hesitantly, I returned it.

Most Australians were vegetarian, but to Marie's credit, she looked only mildly horrified by the fact that the safe house's absent owner was a meat-eating pervert and that most of the men were happy to take full advantage of his secret stash. She picked at her portion of pasta bake while we ate. The rich scent of the cooked meat made my mouth water. I'd been reluctantly following my host country's food customs for the better part of eighteen months. One of those steaks would taste great going down—and play havoc with my digestion. I gave in to my urges and had three bites of the lamb, hoping I wouldn't have to pay for it later.

I waited until Hanad had eaten his fill and pushed his plate away before I looked at Marie. "Dr. Carmen has something to tell us," I said.

Marie chewed on her lips with more energy than she'd devoted to her meal.

"It's…the medicine is complicated," she said. "But in brief, it is my professional opinion that there will never be a successful cryorevival of a fully adult human. The Ark Project is therefore useless, and colonies on planets similar to Earth will never be founded."

Zaneisha choked on a broccoli stem. Bethari put down her fork very carefully.

"Um," I said, "try a little less brief than that."

"All right," Marie said, shoving her hair out of the way. She wasn't being deliberately obfuscating—just trying to dumb down the explanation to the point where we'd know what she was saying. Apparently the first time she'd told Tegan about how exactly she'd been brought back to life, Tegan had lost track of the explanation about two sentences in. "The largest obstacle to successful and widespread cryorevival is the potential for damage to the brain."

"I thought that tardigrade solution preserved it perfectly," I said. They'd been using it for over a century, after all—Tegan had been one of the first test subjects.

"Oh, yes. The preservation is complete. It's the revival that's problematic. The...er, let's say the thawing process results in minute cellular expansion. For most of the body, this is not a problem—either the damage is surmountable or cloned organs can be supplied. But for the brain, which is so complex, it's another matter. I believed I had hit upon a solution. It's a combination of techniques that relies upon slow warming and microvesselectomy, with the addition of—"

"You had a solution," Hanad cut in, before the explanation could get any more technical.

"Er, yes. I tested it on Tegan—who we know was successful—and on a slightly older young man who had volunteered before cryorevival contracts customarily stated that no revival could be attempted until the procedure had a tested and audited ninety-seven percent success rate." A shadow passed over her face. "At least, that's what they told me. It wasn't until much later I learned that they were using the early cases to test viability for the Ark Project."

"I saw him," said a voice from the doorway. "And I think they're still doing it. That woman who died ninety-six years ago—I bet she's there as a control case."

"Tegan!" Marie said. Zaneisha and I both got to our feet—she smoothly, me dropping my fork on the lush carpet.

Tegan had wrapped a blanket over her clothes, bare feet flashing as she padded toward the table. That hectic flush in her cheeks had died, and she wriggled her fingers at me in a wave before assessing the room with a level stare. "Hi," she offered.

"You should be resting," Marie told her. Tegan responded to

this motherly gesture with a smile so sweet I had to blink very hard and mutter something about too much chili in the pasta. Bethari rolled her eyes at me.

"Sit down before you fall down," Zaneisha ordered, and I dragged up another chair for Tegan.

That it was beside mine wasn't pure coincidence.

"You look much better conscious," Hanad observed.

Tegan shrugged, lowering herself carefully into the chair. "Doesn't everyone?"

"Ah, but you are the Snow White. The Sleeping Beauty." He pronounced the name with almost clownish gusto, but his eyes were sharp.

"Those are just fairy tales. I'm a real girl. I mutter and drool and wriggle in my sleep. Ask Abdi."

Oh, that wasn't fair. The heat of my blush swept over me from throat to hairline, and I forked up more food to avoid Hanad's inquisitive glance. Technically, the whole world knew we'd slept together—emphasis on the slept, and she did drool—but it was more real when these tough men were having trouble concealing their amusement.

"I understand that I should thank you for saving my life."

Thulani said something in Portuguese that made Ashenafi stifle a laugh, but Hanad returned her direct gaze. "Thanks are unnecessary. A bank transfer is required."

"Joph will pay," Bethari said quickly. "As soon as we're back together."

Hanad spread his hands in generous agreement. "Until she does, we have this wonderful meal, and the good doctor was telling us a story about the not-so-living dead. You say you saw this test case, Miss Tegan?"

"Yes. Just after I woke up. I didn't believe Marie when she told me I'd been dead for so long. When I tried to escape I checked out one of the institution rooms. There was a man on the bed."

"Nicolas Fisher," Marie said. "He had a hole in his heart that no one had diagnosed. He was only twenty-six when he died."

"He looked younger."

"He was in very good condition," Marie said sadly. "We all thought he was an excellent test case."

"But he didn't really come back to life," Tegan said.

"That would be a matter for the philosophers," Marie told her. "Or possibly the priests. As a mere medical professional, I can tell you Mr. Fisher showed no cognitive function, whereas you were—"

"A perfect guinea pig?"

"Something like that, yes. Although if I'd been allowed to test my process on guinea pigs, this might never have happened."

"No animal testing?" Tegan asked, blinking.

"Of course not," Bethari said, sounding faintly shocked.

"You know, every time I think I'm getting used to the future…" Tegan waved her hand. "Sorry, Marie. Go on?"

Marie nodded. "There's…a fallow period, to use an agricultural metaphor. After the revival itself takes place and we repair whatever caused the patient to opt for cryonics in the first place, the protocol is to keep patients in a medical coma for at least six weeks. We work on muscle regrowth, fix any nonfatal problems—oh, lots of things. And while that's happening, the brain also recovers and adjusts. Or in Mr. Fisher's case, doesn't. I now believe that would be true of all adults."

Marie pushed her plate away. "I was…reluctant to continue my work after capture. Eventually SADU gained my compliance, if not my goodwill. They gave me a limited team to assist and brought me many more patients. Most of them were like Tegan, officially donated to science. Others were patients who their families had volunteered for the program, knowing that they wouldn't be able to pay for their preservation any longer. They took the chance that I could help them." She looked at her hands. Long, sensitive fingers. Surgeon's hands.

Tegan put her own hand over Marie's and squeezed. Marie smiled at her, a trembling, fragile quaver. "I tried," she said. "Not for SADU. I tried for the people they gave me to revive, because they were my patients, however they came into my hands. I refined the revival technique. I concentrated on the fallow period. I attempted to insist on the best possible care."

"But it didn't work," Hanad said.

"No," Marie said. "On most of them, it didn't work. There was either complete brain death or a few remnants of involuntary activity, but no cognitive function. No response to stimulus."

Hanad frowned. "Didn't they notice that it was just the young people who lived?"

"Oh, but some of them died, too. Improper preservation, undiagnosed disorders we couldn't fix…at least one died because of an error I made in the microvesselectomy. I was so tired. Always working. And the team they gave me were…

well, few reputable professionals would work for SADU. They weren't up to my usual standards of assistants."

"But you said they have your notes," I said.

"Yes. The pattern is there. Eventually they'll see it. Maybe their doctors already have and are trying to find a solution, fix the problem without telling anyone else. But I don't think the president would have hosted that conference if he were aware of the flaw; the people in charge must not know yet."

Tegan was frowning. "So the revival process works for, what, under-eighteens?"

"Not...quite. Brain function doesn't respect political lines or social conventions concerning adulthood. The human brain takes some time to fully mature, peaking in the midtwenties. It varies a little, depending on the individual's biology. Before that point, the brain is...let's say, very elastic. An immature brain that retains that elasticity is better able to reroute around the microdamage that occurs during cryorevival. The damage still exists, but the brain can adapt to it."

Tegan put a hand to her head. "I have damage in my brain?"

"Tiny holes," Marie said reassuringly. "Very, very small."

"That's not as comforting as you think it is!"

"All those refugees," I said. "Everyone was most horrified about the children, but it's their parents we should have been mourning."

That shut everyone up. I don't know what they were thinking, but I was seeing the ranks of cryocontainers, the faces of the people who had gone into them hoping for something better, and would never come out again.

"Not to mention those people who have friends and family members in cryonic suspension, waiting for cures for what was killing them," Marie said at last. "Cryonics has been practiced since before Tegan's time. Nearly every suspension has been of a sick or recently dead adult, waiting for a life that was supposed to be one day viable."

"And you're sure it'll never work?" I asked. "With a different solution, a different technique?"

Marie shook her head. "It's the hardware that's the problem, not the software. We'd have to remake the adult brain. And while that might be possible in a few hundred years, it's presently far out of our reach. Frankly, by the time we could manage that, we'd be better off opting for an electrical consciousness upload anyway. Immortality, in a global network or an android body."

Zaneisha frowned. "Well, that's creepy," Tegan said.

It made sense that they, who lived so much in their bodies, would find the idea off-putting, but I was intrigued. What kind of music could you make if you had a vastly expanded mind and total conscious control?

Tegan was gnawing on her lip. "So, obviously, we have to tell people before anyone else gets frozen. We can get in touch with the media."

"I've got a few contacts we could approach," Bethari said. "If we start with a preliminary report that teases a few facts—"

"Slow down," I said. "We have to think about this."

Tegan lifted her chin. "Why do we—"

"Because we do," I said, hardly aware of her startled look.

Observe. Consider. *Empathize.* "Tegan, we tell the world, and then what happens?"

"People stop opting for cryonics. And the Ark Project is scrap," Marie said matter-of-factly.

"And this government probably gets ejected," Tegan said, lips curving. "Gotta say, I'm looking forward to that. I mean, I wish they'd been brought down for being torturous scumbags, but I'll take a massive failure of their flagship project instead."

"And what happens to those who have already been frozen?" I asked.

"Burial or cremation or…whatever their belief systems require, I imagine," Marie said. "Some will doubtless opt to keep their family members preserved, hoping that I'm wrong. Those still under the age of brain maturity can continue in a cryonic state until cures are found for their conditions."

"You think they're going to bury the refugees?" I asked pointedly. "The ones who were frozen for being an illegal drain on Australia's resources?"

Hanad snorted.

"And then there are the refugee kids, the ones who *can* be revived," I continued remorselessly. "If the Ark Project isn't going ahead, will they bring them back to life? Marie, just how expensive is your revival process?"

Marie's lips parted in dismay. "Very," she said. "Obviously, with greater volume it becomes less expensive per case…."

"But the volume goes down sharply if you exclude everyone in their midtwenties and above, so it's going to cost a lot." I barely waited for her confirming nod. "Do we really expect the government—whichever government—to bring them back at great cost, and then what? Put them in the camps to be a continuing expense? No. They won't do that. They'll make noises about doing it one day, when circumstances have changed, when the money's there. But they won't go through with it."

Bethari was staring at me. "Aren't you upset?"

I blinked at her. "Yes." My disgust and rage were snarling under my skin, expanding so that I thought I might explode from the pressure.

"But you sound so…"

"This is how Abdi does upset," Tegan said. "He sounds perfectly rational and calm while he lays out all the terrible things that can happen, and underneath, he's exploding."

I should have felt uncomfortable that I was so predictable to her, but instead I was, for a moment, purely glad that someone understood me that well.

Bethari was looking at me, head tilted as if I were an interesting new program with unusual code.

"So the problem with raising the refugee children is expense," Hanad said, ignoring the byplay. "The expense of revival, the continued expense of preservation."

"Yes," I said.

"So why would the government not cut their expenses for good and just turn the power off?" he asked.

I stared at him, stunned. "No," I said. "No, they wouldn't do that. It would be mass murder." Murder of children sleeping in boxes the government had pressed their parents into accepting for them, no less.

"They're slavers already," he said practically. "If they don't see these children as people worth caring about, why not cut their losses?"

"No one would stand for it," Tegan said. "I mean, I know Australia doesn't have the best track record, but the government couldn't do that and get away with it." She looked uncertainly at me. "Right?"

Her doubt was contagious. "I don't…"

"What if they *could* get away with it, by saying it was someone else?" Bethari asked. Her eyes were bright with tears. "What if they could blame simultaneous blackouts on the terrorists who had already used their deadly EMP device?"

"Oh," I said, the possibilities abruptly clear. "It would be especially easy to blame Save Tegan if the government had any evidence of Lat's plan to attack the president. Which they do, because I *gave it to them*."

"Can we get a warning to Lat?" Tegan asked, and I realized that she didn't know.

I took a deep breath. "Lat's dead," I said, as gently as I could. "He came to help you, Tegan." No need to mention just what form he'd wanted that help to take, not yet. "But Diane came, too. She killed him."

Tegan made a strangled, squeaking noise and pressed her hands over her mouth. Her eyes went round and enormous, like two dark moons.

"I'm sorry," I added, and discovered it was true. I hadn't liked Lat. In fact, I'd wanted him to die more times than I could count. But the reality of his death was so horrible that it had cured me of that impulse. Now the only person I wanted to die was Diane. Other than that, I was sick of death—the mess of it, the horror of life and possibility for change forever extinguished in those shattering moments. And I hated seeing Tegan hurt.

"What are we going to do?" Bethari asked. Her voice was shaky. "We have to do *something*."

"I think we have to get the truth out," Marie said. "Like Tegan did before. A public 'cast."

"How much good did that really do?" I was thinking it, but it was Tegan who'd said it. With the initial shock over, her face had gone grim. Under the table, I groped for her hand with mine and felt the small, rough palm squeeze back with desperate strength. She sighed. "I thought that when we first told people about the Ark Project that something would happen. It looked like things were happening."

"You raised awareness," Marie said.

"I didn't get what I wanted, Marie. I wanted the government to put a halt to the indentured-labor part of the Ark Project, and to stop treating refugees like livestock that have inconveniently wandered over from the next pasture."

"I started smuggling because I wanted the medicine patent restrictions lifted," I said. "That's why I told Tegan to put it in her 'cast. And that didn't happen, either."

"No. We got imprisoned, tortured—people slapped my name on their own political movements without any way to check if I'd be okay with what they said and did. So maybe telling people what's going on straightaway isn't our best bet."

"But we have to tell the world," Marie said. "There are

people effectively committing suicide right now. People who gave money to the Ark Project in exchange for being cryonically preserved expect to wake up again, and they never will. Don't you care about them?"

Tegan's eyes met mine, and we had a moment of perfect accord. I could see her remembering the sponsors who had crowded around us, watching us sing and make music, listening to our rehearsed speeches. Were we worried that some of the richest people in those rooms had happily funded slave labor and gotten themselves frozen, ready to enjoy a new world where others would labor for their benefit? Did we care about them?

Did I care about Ruby Simons, who had tried to buy me for a night?

"Not really," I said.

"Screw them," Tegan agreed.

"You can't mean that," Bethari said. Her voice was flat and cold. "I never thought I'd hear you two dismiss human life."

"You weren't where we were, Bethi," Tegan said. She sounded stung.

"They're slavers!" I said, over top of her.

"But they don't *know* they're slavers," Bethari pointed out. She flushed when I blinked at her. "Well, some of them might know and just don't care. But a lot of those people believe what the government's been telling them. They really do think the refugees are happy to go; they sincerely believe this is the best option for everyone. It's not their fault they have the money to take advantage of it. Joph has money. Abdi's family has money."

"Joph would never take advantage of slave labor," I said.

282

"She might if she didn't know it existed," Bethari said.

"She'd find out," Tegan said angrily. "These people are just being stupid."

"I don't know," I said. I was thinking back to the footage Joph had shown me in the garden, to the conversation I'd over-head between Pink Dress and her friends. My memory faithfully served up every word.

Those people hadn't seemed stupid, and far from evil. Just lacking a lot of information and maybe a wider view. They were concerned with what touched them closest. For most people, you had to make something come home to make it real.

"We were on the inside, Tegan. To us it seems very clear. But the media machine they built around us was convincing. It had to be to make them love us so much."

Bethari nodded. "I knew you two, of all people, would never be in favor of indentured labor. But even I was taken aback when you two first started being broadcast," she said. "I wondered, just for a second, if we really had gotten it all wrong the first time." She seemed to collapse a little, her scarf sagging. "And I'm just sick of death, whoever it is that's dying. Aren't you? I put together the EMP. I did something I knew was dangerous for what I thought was the greater good, and people died because of it. How is this different?"

There was a brief silence, where Hanad and his men looked carefully away, and Tegan's grip on my hand grew warm. I couldn't meet Bethari's eyes.

"So if we tell the world, we could stop more rich people from choosing to die," Tegan said.

"But we risk the government turning off cryocontainers for those refugees who *could* be revived," I said. "And blaming us."

"That's only a theory," Bethari said quickly.

"They'd do it," I said. There was a weird buzzing in my ears, but I forced the words out: "It makes sense. It's the practical thing to do."

Bethari braced her hands on the table. "So we tell the world that as well! Warn them that if the power goes, it's government murder, not us! Then the refugees will be protected."

"They'd spin it," I said. "They'd say that we said it to divert suspicion to the government, when we meant to use the EMP all along."

"Is that *practical*, too?"

I dropped my head into my free hand. "Yes," I said. My voice cracked on the word. "I have to think. There has to be some way to make this work out."

Marie was folding and unfolding her hands. "Rich or poor, these are my patients. I have a responsibility. Bethari is right; we have to do something."

"You can do whatever you like," Hanad said, in a tone that indicated a final decision. "But Abdi comes with me. We have spent enough time on this firster foolishness."

"No!" Tegan said. "You can't just take him!"

Hanad frowned. Thulani's left hand slipped out of sight, and Zaneisha's shoulders shifted. I could feel the potential for sudden violence riding the air like a storm. Under the table, I gripped Tegan's hand tighter, squeezing for silence.

"But this is new information," I said. "I have to think...."

"Your girl is cured," Hanad said. "The rain has stopped, and the water levels in the tunnels are dropping. In the morning, we take advantage of commuter crush to hide ourselves. We collect Eduardo and our money, and then I am taking you back to Djibouti. There will always be a reason to stay, if you let it be so. You cannot fix this country." He shook his head, disapproving. "I don't think anyone can. But whether they can or not, your place is at home."

Home, I thought. The amber earth and the black rock, the bright clothes and the busy streets. The city and the sea and the light and heat. Home was where I could never be cold again.

Hanad must have seen the yearning in my face, because his expression shifted, and Thulani relaxed. "Good, then," he said, and took his plate to the counter as if the matter were settled.

I felt, to my shame, an immense rush of relief. This could be someone else's problem. I could return home to my family and leave Australia's issues to Australia.

But I knew I wouldn't, not without a fight. I could read it in Bethari's strained features, in Tegan's huge eyes, in the urgent whispering of my own straining heart.

"I have to think about this," I repeated. To Hanad, it must have sounded like a futile protest he could safely ignore. But Tegan squeezed my hand, and Bethari met my eyes across the kitchen table. They knew me; they knew that I wasn't done with Australia yet.

Not quite yet.

CHAPTER TWENTY
Dolce

After the conference broke up, Marie had one of the men take her back to her room, beckoning emphatically for Tegan to follow.

Zaneisha raised one eyebrow at the dishes that the men had left piled on the bench, at Bethari still picking at her meal, and then looked at me.

"All right," I grumbled. Reese Chang had at least shown me how to clean up; apparently the Talented Alien foster-placement program had been very firm on chores making a Talented Alien minor feel like part of the family.

If Hanad got his way, I'd go back to my family and never have to do these chores again.

Or maybe I would. My parents had sold their house. They must have laid off the staff, too, or at least reduced their number. Who would have gone? Miriam, who held spirited discussions with my mother on Christianity versus Islam? (They tended to both gang up on my father, since in their view any faith was better than none.)

Benjamin, who'd been our driver and honorary uncle since before I was born? And if my mother had lost her position, what did that mean for our family? Clearly, she still had friends, or she wouldn't have found Hanad, but fewer government contracts would be available to my father. There would be fewer perks in general.

I loaded the dishes into the cleaner and wiped down the grilling machine while my mind picked at these questions. I'd thought of going home as returning to a sanctuary, but what if the sanctuary was gone?

Then my family would still be there. That was the most important thing.

It was all too easy to believe that the comforts of my home life were a right, not a privilege I'd been lucky to have. Maybe this was how it began, I thought uncomfortably. You started hiring people to serve you, and then it felt very natural to assume that of course they'd want to do it on another planet.

I'd never assume that people wanted to serve without pay, without freedom or dignity. But I could understand every step in the thought process that took people there.

It was an uneasy realization. I found the controls for the house vacuum and started cleaning the floor.

Δ ∫ Ω

It was late, but my brain was going too fast to sleep. I knew this state of tension; I needed something to occupy the front of my mind while the back worked on the problem of what to say, to whom, when.

Looking for entertainment, I went to the house library, because naturally, this privacy-loving billionaire had a third floor underneath the bedrooms that included a library. The little room was full of books actually printed on paper, instead of normal electronic copies.

I poked around the histories, but they were all Australian. There was a small biography section, and I hesitated over a book about the musician Fairuz, who was one of my idols, but in the end I went for the collection of old action thrillers. They were in a glass cabinet, carefully presented in a way that was incongruous with their battered pages and silly covers. Everyone else I knew thought these stories were trash, too ridiculous and sensationalistic to occupy a moment's thinking. But I liked them, the heedless pace, the way the heroes always knew exactly what to do, their physical courage, and their rough codes of honor.

I felt empathy for the house owner, who had kept these classics safe. Immediately afterward, the guilt struck. That was the problem with empathy—once you felt an understanding with someone, it was harder to do things that might hurt or upset them.

I took the book anyway.

Lying on my bed a few hours later, carefully turning the pages, I contemplated the wisdom of the engineers who had made electronic books possible. There was a tactile pleasure to the flimsy book, though. It smelled good, a pleasant mix of paper and what I thought might have been tobacco. The dry whisper of pages was almost soothing, and just before the hero was about to make a move on the computer scientist he had rescued from an indeterminately evil international crime syndicate, I fell asleep.

"Hey," someone whispered into my dreams, and I started up.

It was Tegan, wrapped in another sheet. Most of her hair had been tamed into two neat braids, but there were a few loose strands she'd missed. The house computer had dimmed the lights while I slept, but there was still enough to make her out, a white ghost in the night. I squirmed over on the bed, giving her space to sit down. "Sorry to wake you," she said.

There was something moving at the back of my head, some bright idea or partial solution that had tried to wriggle its way loose while I slept. I couldn't resent Tegan for waking me up, but I did wish she'd waited a few minutes more.

"You are the worst patient," I pointed out. "What would Dr. Carmen say about this?"

"That I'm the worst patient," she said, and picked up the book. "Is this good?"

"I like it. It's very old-fashioned, though."

Tegan grinned. "Like me."

"For someone who just turned 117, you're remarkably forward-looking."

"Not always," she said, and tugged viciously on one of her braids. "I was thinking more about what's going to happen if we put the word out. You're right. It's going to be a nightmare. Do you really think they'll let the refugee kids rot?"

"I don't know for sure. But I think they might. The big problem is that the refugees are going to get swallowed up in all the other issues. As long as people thought their relatives could come back at some point when there was a cure for bone cancer or Alzheimer's disease, then they were all for pursuing cryonics. But now, from their point of view, government research policy for the last fifteen years has been a massive waste of money and time—not to mention the trillions of dollars spent on a starship that won't be going anywhere. They won't forgive their hopes being betrayed."

"So they won't worry about the refugee kids?"

"Oh, they probably will. But for most people, their own families and their own concerns are going to be the first priority. That's how it works."

That's how it works for me, I almost said. But that wasn't true, not anymore. I loved my family. I didn't want to cause them more pain. But I'd do it if I could help those children in the process.

Tegan nodded gloomily and picked at the hem of her blanket. "I just really want something to punch," she said. "But this one's a political problem. It's up to you."

"Me?"

"Sure. I'm Action Girl. You're Thought Boy."

"Huh," I said, and let my head fall back on the pillow. "I think my powers are rusty."

There were no easy answers in politics. I knew there had to be a solution that would keep the most people safe at the least cost—and that was a dangerous path to choose, because then you really were valuing one life over another and making assessments of *acceptable collateral damage*. It was the logic that had led the Australian government to institute the

No Migrant policy, because it wanted to put its people first, at the cost of thousands of refugees. It was the logic that had led Hurfest and Lat to employ the EMP. They'd indirectly killed a few innocent people so that Tegan and I could be spokespeople and symbols, and hopefully save many more.

Nathan Phillip Cox was protecting his own interests, though, and those of his cronies. And I was ready to make personal sacrifices in order to help others.

Those motivations made some difference, I thought. Maybe even enough of one to count.

But no part of this was simple.

Tegan lay down beside me, close enough that a thick lock of her hair lay across my collarbone. We weren't otherwise touching, but I could feel the heat of her body, a glow that warmed my side. "Zaneisha told me Diane took you hostage after she shot Lat."

"Yeah."

"I really hate her."

"Yeah." I picked up the strand of hair and wound it around my finger. I thought it was her hair, at least—the extensions had been seamlessly added, but it wouldn't be the same to be touching that, somehow.

"You said Lat came to help me," she said.

I hesitated. Truth or lie—the truth that would hurt her or the lie that might bring her some comfort?

Truth. Always truth, for Tegan, who could bear pain, but couldn't stand deception. "He came to rescue you from us. He thought he was helping, I suppose."

"But?"

"But he was going to take you to the hospital, knowing it would mean giving you back to SADU. He thought you could be put in cryosuspension if you couldn't be saved."

Tegan's exhale of breath was more than a sigh but less than a sob. "I would have hated him for that," she said.

I had to be fair. "I think he knew that. I think your life was more important to him." Lat, at least, had tried to do things for the right reasons.

"Did you think about it? Taking me back, if Marie couldn't save me?"

"Sure," I admitted. "But you said you'd rather die."

She touched my hand lightly. "Thank you."

"Diane," I began, then stopped. This was very difficult. But I could make a start. "She...she did some stuff to me that was... not sanctioned, I think. Because she thought it would be fun. Because she likes to control people, and she thought this was a way she could control me. When I saw her last night, I felt like she'd made me feel then."

That was as much as I wanted to say right then, and I think Tegan knew it. She brushed my hand again, and I wrapped my fingers around hers. I was here, and she was with me, and that was enough for now.

We lay there in the dim light, resting together.

Eventually, Tegan broke the silence. "I was thinking. You and I could tell the world about the flaw in the revival process from Djibouti."

I sat up. "Are you serious?"

"I think it's the best option. If you can persuade Hanad to take me and Marie along."

"I can do that," I promised. "Joph wants to come, too. But... really? You're sure?"

"I talked to Marie," she said firmly. "I'm sure." She gave me a sidelong look, almost shy. "I gave her all the sensible arguments: Djibouti is out of Australian reach; we'd be safe there; she'd have lots of interesting work to do. But my real reasons aren't sensible. I'm trying to be honest about this. I don't know if we can work everything out. I don't know if we'll stay together. But I want a chance to try to make a new life, and I want you in it."

For once, I was lost for words. They tangled in my mouth, and the only way I could get my feelings out was by kissing her.

She laughed against my lips and kissed me back, bright and fierce. This wasn't tinged with the fear of our first kisses in the dark, or the way I'd poured myself into her in that underground complex, desperate to forget everything about Diane's touch. This was joy we were sharing and a promise of more to come.

My shirt came off, and I wasn't sure whether it was she or me who'd first started tugging at it. My skin buzzed at every point of contact, my body responding in ways I was sure she'd noticed. *I should probably suggest that she leave*, I thought. If she stayed, I had the feeling we might do some things that probably weren't healthy for someone recovering from a life-threatening illness, especially when she had a cracked rib.

And some things that weren't healthy for me to do with a girl when her mother and scary bodyguard were sleeping in the same house.

"Ow," she mumbled against my mouth, and I took my hands away from her sides.

"Rib?"

"Rib," she agreed, and watched, eyes gleaming, as I carefully settled myself down on her undamaged side. "Are we taking a break?"

"I wanted to show you something," I said, fighting to get my breath back. I signaled the house and watched Tegan's eyes grow even larger as she took in the same alarm-clock sequence that had thrilled and mystified me. She gasped as the asteroid belt engulfed us, then again as Jupiter's giant red spot swelled and shifted. When the Oort cloud spun dizzily around the room and the display began to dim, she shivered and curled up against me once more.

"That's amazing," she breathed. "It's incredible, that we can make pictures of the galaxy, but we'll never see it. I mean, it's just like…there's this whole universe out there, and humanity was going to go visit it, but now because cryonics doesn't work we can't."

I hadn't even thought of that. It was sad, all that unused potential.

"What do you think will happen to the *Resolution*?" she asked.

My eyes opened into the darkness where the solar system had spun. "That's it," I said quietly. The thought that had been trying to wriggle free had finally shaken itself loose.

The *Resolution*'s skeleton was built, hanging in orbit, with a year of full-scale construction to go. The cryonic revival process had been refined. Why were we all assuming the Ark Project had to die?

Because adults couldn't be revived.

But young people could.

My thoughts expanded, pinwheeled, exploded into new possibilities and the framework of a plan so audacious I was almost afraid to say anything. I considered side effects, looked at probable consequences, thought about the many risks, the definite costs, and all the lives at stake.

It wasn't simple. But it was possible that I could make it happen.

"Tegan," I said quietly.

"You've had an idea," she said. "You have that face."

"Yes. Tell me: What do we want, most urgently?"

"The refugee kids to be safe," she said promptly.

"And what does the government want, most urgently?"

"Power, I suppose. To stay in power. And to govern well, which they probably think they're doing right now."

"What if we could get what we want?" I asked. "By giving them—or at least appearing to give them—what they want."

"House, lights," Tegan said, and sat up, looking closely at my face in the sudden illumination. "What kind of idea is this, Abdi? Can we save everyone?"

"Not everyone," I said. "I don't think that's possible."

"But we can save those refugee kids?"

"If it works. Maybe. Yes."

"All right," she said. "Why don't you tell me all about it?"

CHAPTER TWENTY-ONE
Finale

"Wow," Tegan said, when my mouth finally ran down.

"It's risky," I said. "And the ethics..."

"Oh, it's totally skeezy," she said, and saw my confusion. "Ah, past-timer slang, I guess. Dodgy. Dishonest?"

"Dishonest," I agreed. "And on top of that...if we, if *I* do this, people will die."

She looked grave. "Yes."

I was glad that she didn't try to soften it, that she acknowledged the strongest objection to my plan head-on. But at the same time, I felt her agreement strike hard. I had to get up and pace around the room, swinging my arms as my mind roiled.

"How is that different from what we condemned Lat and Hurfest for?" I asked. "When they used the EMP generator, people died. They thought the ends justified the means, too."

Tegan grimaced. "The people *we're* talking about are probably going to die anyway. And we know that the ones who have already been frozen can't be brought back."

"But more and more people are choosing to be frozen. They're going into death with a hope that I'll betray."

"They made the choice," Tegan said simply. "It was never guaranteed that they'd be revived. They took the chance, knowing that there was only one successful test case." She touched her breastbone.

"And now there are three successful cases," I said, still striding. "People who were waiting for confirmation will get frozen now. Not even the colonizers and slavers going on the *Resolution*. Just ordinary people who want a chance at a better life in the future. Can we do anything to help *them*?"

"I was thinking about that," Tegan said. "We could start some sort of campaign, encourage people to choose life now. Carpe diem, all that." She visibly steeled herself. "I could be a symbol again."

"No," I said, pausing in my steps. "I can do that. You've done enough."

"But…"

"You wanted a new life," I said firmly. "A new life where you're not being used. That's what we're going to get you. But this plan, Tegan…are you sure it's the best thing to do?"

"I'm completely sure," Tegan said. "Trust me, Abdi. This is the right action, at the right moment. And it's action only you can take. I'd lose my temper and start yelling or cursing or quoting Bethari at them." She gave me a half smile. "I'm no diplomat, and I can't lie very well. This has to be you."

I felt a weight drop into my stomach, like an anchor into deep water. "Me, the liar."

"You, the guy who saved thousands of lives in his superspy mission to get medicine where it was needed. Do you remember what you told me before I started making that 'cast, talking to all those people?"

I did. She'd been terrified of that big an audience, convinced that all the words would come out wrong, ashamed of some of the things she'd sworn to reveal.

"You said, 'You can do this.'"

I flopped down on the foot of the bed. "Did you believe me?"

"No. But you were right; I could." She leaned over and kissed me, a soft, reassuring pressure. "You can do this, Abdi. Go and change the world."

Δ ʃ Ω

Bethari needed some effort to wake, but once she was up, she took about ten seconds to grasp the implications.

"Oh," she said, and sat down heavily. "That's...wow."

"I think it's the best we can do," I said. I kept my voice neutral—no attempted manipulation, no trying to argue her around. We needed Bethari for the plan to work, but I was going to let her decide for herself. I wouldn't make Hurfest's mistake and use her skills against her will.

"And if we pull it off, you could stay in Australia and help people from here," Tegan said.

Bethari hesitated. "And my mother?"

"Releasing Captain Miyahputri will be my first demand," I said. *That wasn't manipulation*, I thought. *That was the truth.*

"Thank you," Bethari said. There were tears glistening in her eyes, and she dabbed them with the corner of her headscarf. "All right. What do you need from me?"

"Come with us," I said. "Zaneisha might need some convincing."

We found Zaneisha eating a breakfast of leftover pasta bake, topped with what I thought was a dehydrated egg scramble. When I started talking, she put her fork down and focused on me with intimidating intensity. She listened all the way through, didn't ask any questions, and said, "The library would be the most secure venue. I'll see what I can do about defenses."

"Thank you," I said.

"Have you talked to Dr. Carmen yet?"

"No," I said, and grimaced.

"Do it now," she advised, and looked over my shoulder at Tegan. "And Tegan? You should do the talking."

Marie was in Tegan's bedroom and wasn't happy that Tegan was out of it. But when she saw our faces she stopped scolding. She listened all the way through, her expression becoming smoother as we went.

I knew her well enough now to know that wasn't a good sign.

"I'm a doctor," she said, when Tegan was done. "I can't do things I know will hurt people."

"I know," Tegan said. "We won't be actually causing the harm, but..."

"But we won't be preventing all of it. We could wait," Marie suggested, but not as if she really thought it was an option. "Get to safety, then think of a better plan."

"The more time we spend doing nothing, the more people get hurt," Tegan told her. "This is the best possible moment for this to go as well as it possibly can."

"That's what Carl and Lat said to justify their assassination plans," Marie noted.

I flinched, as arguments lined up behind my tongue. I made them stay there, unheard. Marie looked at me, at Bethari, and finally at Tegan. She reached out and stroked Tegan's hair back from her face, fingers lingering on her forehead.

"I suppose everyone wants to help the people closest to them," she said quietly. "I'll help you."

I exhaled. And steeled myself for the next conversation.

Bethari's computer beeped at her. "Prayer," she said. "Gotta go."

It was an unwelcome reminder of time ticking onward. The men would also be at dawn prayer. When they emerged, they would want to go.

Tegan put her hand on mine and traced her fingers over the knobbly bone on the outside of my wrist. My skin shivered pleasantly.

"What if he says no?" I asked. "What if he leaves and tries to take me with him?"

"Then you'll go with him," she said firmly. "We can't fight them."

I tried to smile. "I never thought I'd hear you say that."

"You're having a strong effect on me. No, you'll go. And I'll try to play your part." She looked doubtful, and I tried not to copy her expression. "SADU made me lie for six months. I figure I can use those skills to hit back."

SADU had trained and trained her, making Tegan rehearse every gesture and expression until none of her real feelings seeped through the seamless mask. We didn't have time to do that now. I didn't say any of that, though I was sure she was thinking it, too.

After all, Hanad might say yes.

$$\Delta \int \Omega$$

"No," said Hanad. "I do not get involved with politics."

"I think you get involved with politics all the time," I said. "Your job is very political."

"It has political sides, which I do my best to avoid," he conceded. "Are you packed?"

"You know I don't have anything to pack, and you know that I'm not going with you right now," I said.

"Your mother would want you to come with me."

"My mother would be wrong." The words felt impossible in my mouth. He was right; my mother would want me to get myself home. She'd accept my bringing my ragtag companions and my firster girlfriend with me if I had to, but above all, she'd want me staying quiet and keeping safe. But I couldn't do that. Not with so much at stake.

"I am leaving now," Hanad said, in a tone that indicated he was coming to the end of his patience.

"Then you can pick up Eduardo and Joph and leave for the coast," I said, in the manner of someone offering a massive concession. "Wait for us where you've stashed your boat. When it's done, we'll meet you. You can take me and Tegan and Marie to Djibouti. And Joph, too." Zaneisha had elected to stay with Bethari.

"Tegan," he said, and leaned against the bench. "All this effort and risk for a skinny white firster girl. She's not even Muslim."

"Neither am I," I pointed out, which Hanad dismissed with an irritatingly familiar gesture. Everyone except my father was certain I'd come back to God eventually. "Anyway, it's not for Tegan. You know that."

"Mm," he said, noncommittal. I wished I'd taken up Zaneisha's offer to have her there for this interview. But if it came to a fight, she was completely outnumbered, and I'd thought it best to present this to Hanad privately, man to man.

He sat there for a moment that stretched out until I thought I would scream. But silence was also a tool. "I will give you the coordinates. If you do not appear, Joph Montgomery will pay us and be abandoned there, for whoever finds her. I will wait one hour. *One.*"

I exhaled with relief.

"There will be an extra charge for three extra passengers. Fewer supplies, more crowding…"

"Thank you," I said, trying not to think about how I would pay him. "You're a good man."

"Not always. When I can afford it." He clapped me on the shoulder, and my knees nearly buckled. "*You* are a good man, I think. May God keep you safe."

"Thank you," I repeated, because being rude about someone's religion was something I was trying to avoid these days.

"And when you get tired of Tegan, I will introduce you to my daughters."

"Uh," I said.

"They're beautiful," he promised. "And brave, and very clever." He delivered another assault to my shoulder and left the kitchen, whistling.

Zaneisha brushed by him and leaned against the bench. "Are you ready?"

"Not yet," I said, and looked her straight in the eye. "I need something from you, first."

Δ ʃ Ω

At 7:45 AM, in the subbasement serenity of the house library, we began.

I took a moment for myself, long enough for my heart to judder and settle, like something that had convulsed in the waves and then drifted slowly to the ocean floor. I discovered a quiet place, a kind of heightened calm that seemed to make time slow and stretch, leaving me unhurried and secure. I was still intensely angry, but it wasn't wild rage to be wasted in shouting and stupid violent gestures; it was anger honed to a bright, sharp edge.

And I was ready to cut with it.

I looked at Bethari and gave the go signal. There was no delay getting through to President Cox this time.

"Abdi," he said, his voice oozing delight. "Did you see the press conference? How are you feeling? I really am hopeful that—"

"I have Dr. Marie Carmen here," I said, cutting him off

303

midplatitude. "She is going to explain why the Ark Project as it currently stands is medically unviable."

I signaled Marie before Cox could react, and she began to speak. This was the technical explanation she hadn't given us—for the benefit of those medical advisers doubtless being brought into the conversation as she spoke. But she finished with plain words, simply put: "Anyone aged over twenty-five when they went into cryonic suspension is never coming out of it."

He'd had time to adjust while she spoke. The voice returned, as smooth as ever. "Dr. Carmen, is it possible that you've been swayed by other concerns? I don't mean to question your medical expertise, but..."

"Then don't," Marie said. "I am the world's leading expert on cryonics, specifically on revival technique. I'm not lying, though my conclusions can—and should—be ascertained by experimentation and observation."

"But you won't want to do that, will you?" I said. "That would let every stinking alley-cat secret out of your big, dirty bag."

There was a muffled sound and a distant yell and then the president returned to the line. "Open video," he growled. "If you're going to destroy me, at least do it eye to eye."

Bethari looked away from her computer long enough to shake her head, but I ignored her, made sure Marie was out of camera range, and signed for video to begin.

Cox, who always looked as if he were about to laugh with jovial amiability, wasn't laughing now.

"You listen to me, you little thirdie shit," he said, his voice no longer smooth and warm. "You pull another media stunt like your girlfriend did the last time, and I will bury you. You might be able to drag me down with this, but I'll still have friends. Powerful, dangerous friends. I will personally see to it that you rot in the deepest hole they can find long before I ever take my first step toward falling from grace. If you've got any interest in your own health, you whiny—"

"It was those friends I was thinking of telling first, actually," I said. "Isn't one of them Ms. Valda Simons? The most prosecution-proof woman in the country? So strange, how every time the police find a witness they just disappear."

"What's Valda Simons got to do with…" he started, and then stopped.

"I met her, you know, she and her daughter, Ruby," I told him. "Ruby told me she was so excited about the Ark Project, so eager to arrive on this shiny new planet, that she was going into cryosuspension the next day, before she turned thirty. She didn't want to arrive when she was, quote, old and boring."

During the brief time I'd known her, Ruby had come across as vain, callous, and selfish. But unknowingly ending her own life was such a waste of her potential to grow and change. And her mother, that steely-eyed woman with the commanding presence—she wouldn't forgive the man who'd persuaded her daughter to cut her life short.

Cox's face grew red and white splotches like a moldy carpet. "But Valda is such a good friend of yours," I said. "I'm sure she'll understand. Won't blame you, or order any regrettable actions she couldn't take back."

"You can't," he said unsteadily. "You...no." His mouth was loose, his eyes blank as he gazed upon some inner vision of horror.

I didn't need Tegan's waving arms to know this was the time to give him the good news. "Don't worry, Mr. President. I'm going to help you."

Intelligence sparked in his eyes again and hope with it.

"I'm going to keep this little secret to myself. You can release the information how you choose: a slow process of gradual bad-news announcements or a brave announcement that you've discovered something the army tried to keep from you. Hell, even keep the whole thing secret and dump the problem in your successor's lap. Should you lose the election next year—or in three years—it would be a nice gift for the leader of your opposition, wouldn't it?"

"What do you want?" he said bluntly. Deals and bargains, that was a language he understood.

I did, too. My mother's education, flawed as it might have been, had seen to that. And I was going to break him with it.

Bethari jumped to her feet and gave me the signal. Time for contingency plans, damn it. Well, I'd known the risks of using the video options. But I couldn't afford to seem desperate or hurried now.

"I want Captain Miyahputri released from custody and left to go her own way, unobserved. I want freedom and safety for myself and my associates," I said, deliberate and measured. "I want every refugee in cryosuspension under the age of twenty-five to be delivered, still preserved, to Djibouti City, where they will be cared for under the jurisdiction of people I can trust."

"You can't be seri—"

"And I want the *Resolution*," I concluded. "You can sign management of the project over to the current Djibouti government. Publicly."

"You want a multitrillion-dollar starship built by a world superpower handed over to a tiny thirdie nation?" he exploded. "Are you out of your mind?"

"I probably have post-traumatic stress," I said blandly. "Would you like me to tell the world how I acquired it? I've tacked that account onto the records invisibly uploaded to several thousand databases. If I don't give the approved code word at the appointed time every day, the information Dr. Carmen has discovered becomes *highly* visible."

And that was the great lie I had to tell. No backups existed, no invisible uploads had taken place. The only people who knew what Dr. Carmen knew were in this room or on the way out of the country. If our plan went wrong, I hoped Hanad or one of his crew might speak out. Joph would certainly try. But it was a thin hope to rest a plan on.

Which was why I had the thing Cox couldn't see, held ready in my lap.

"You're bluffing," he growled, and my heart nearly parted in my chest.

But there was a flicker at the corner of his eye, a ruffle in the otherwise gruff composure.

"You know I'm not," I said coolly. "I'm not an idiot, Mr. President. I wouldn't have contacted you without making certain preparations."

He paused.

I kept my face perfect. I had smuggled medicine for nearly a year under the nose of my teachers and guardian. I had helped Tegan Oglietti outface a religious zealot and persuade a world to hear her story.

She was right.

I could do this.

And in the face of my monumental silence, he broke. "I can release Captain Miyahputri and guarantee your freedom and safety," he began tentatively. "Perhaps even the refugees. The *Resolution*, however—"

"Is not negotiable. None of my terms are negotiable." I watched his face, saw his resolve harden. Time to give him something. "I understand that the Australian public may be disgruntled by the move, but you can spin it any way you choose, Mr. President. Call it a joint venture, if you wish—no one will dispute that. They'll think it's brilliant. *You* paraded me all over the country; *you* made me the face of your project to the rich and famous. You made them love me, and they *do*."

His mouth sagged open.

"Keep calling me your ambassador, and I won't reveal it's a lie," I said, gentle but inexorable. "Djibouti is the termination point of the Great Rift Valley, did you know? Tell the world that the birthplace of humanity will be the launching point of humanity's voyage to the stars. Very symbolic. And being able to give investors some of their money back may soothe their anger. After all, what use is the *Resolution* to you now?"

"What use is it to you?" he countered. "What can you possibly do with it?"

"Fly it," I said.

There was a crash from upstairs, and the house computer hummed.

"Warning. Unauthorized entry," it warned, the walls turning a soft red.

Zaneisha pushed the other women behind the sturdy bookshelf she and Bethari had arranged earlier, and ducked behind it herself, her gun cradled in her hands. We'd learned from earlier mistakes. No visible hostages.

Just me, in front of the computer, with Zaneisha's present to me in my lap.

Diane burst into the room. She was backed by soldiers in shiny black gear who cleared the doorway and stopped. Their faces were covered with helmets, but hers was clear, her braids pulled back in a tight queue down her back. She scanned the room, saw nothing to threaten her, and focused on me.

"Abdi!" she said. "You're being very naughty. Stop it!"

Cox looked pleasant and avuncular once more. "Are the terms negotiable now?" he asked.

I watched Diane for a moment and then turned back to the screen. My back was crawling with the urge to spin back again, but I could see part of her face over the shoulder of the image of me on my screen. She looked amused and just slightly affronted that I'd dared to turn my back on her. "No," I said. "Remember the password, Mr. President. If this woman and her colleagues don't leave immediately, I might just forget to use it. If you don't fulfill all of my conditions, I certainly won't."

Diane laughed. "Abdi, don't be silly. I can get any password out of you within an hour."

Cox raised an eyebrow. "Well, Mr. Taalib?"

"Well, Mr. President? Look at me. You wanted to see my face while we talked; here it is. Do you see anything in it that will break in an hour? Break in a day? Eventually, yes, she could torture me into compliance. But you're on a deadline, Mr. President. And I won't let her take me back."

I raised the gun in my lap and watched the screen-Abdi push the muzzle into the soft skin under his chin. "No brain," I said softly. "No password."

Cox's eyes widened. "There's no need for this precipitate action."

"Diane knows there is. I told her that I'd rather die than be under her control again. I don't bluff, Mr. President." A lie, a lie, an enormous lie. The big lies were the ones people believed most often.

Especially when you could mix them with truth. I'd told Zaneisha the bolt-gun was a prop. But if it became necessary, I would pull that trigger.

Watching Cox hesitate and think, I felt like I was swaying over a wide-mouthed canyon, with jagged rocks waiting eagerly to receive my broken body. A breath of air from this man's lips, and I would live or die.

What I wanted, most in the world, was for no one to have this kind of power over me ever again.

His gaze refocused. He looked puzzled, now, more disbelieving than angry. "I thought someone was pulling your strings—Dr. Carmen, perhaps. That you were the face and someone else

310

was the brains. But this is really all you, isn't it? I'm actually negotiating with a child."

My lip curled. "I stopped being a child some time ago." I ground the gun muzzle deeper into my flesh. "Do we have a deal, Mr. President?"

"We have a deal," he said, and looked over my shoulder. "Fall back, men." In the screen, the soldiers shifted, holstering their weapons. My hands, so steady all this time, trembled with relief. I would live. We would all live.

The soldiers were moving away, but Diane lingered. "Sir, I must protest. We don't negotiate with terrorists."

"I am acting in the interests of the nation, Agent. Withdraw from the premises and allow this man and Dr. Carmen free exit. Where is Dr. Carmen, may I ask?"

"Somewhere else," I said, seeing Diane's eyes narrow. "You surely don't think we'd speak from the same location?"

"She has to be here, sir. And Tegan, too, and Washington, and whoever else. The rest of the house is clear; they must be in this room. Let me search it. He'll give up the password to keep them safe."

"I order you to fall back, Agent," Cox said.

I turned around to watch her closely, my hands still shaking. "I will die before you get a chance to touch them," I told her. "You will never lay a finger on me."

I saw her recognize that I wasn't bluffing, watched her confront and reject her failure. "Let's see," she said, and as Cox shouted uselessly, as Zaneisha Washington hurled herself over the bookshelf, Diane brought up her gun.

But my gun was already aimed. My brother had taught me how, and my mother had scolded us, and I hated violence, but I would not let Diane win. My fumbling, twitching finger tightened on the trigger.

The sound of the shots tore the room apart.

Two shots, Halim had taught me, so you can be sure your enemy is dead.

Diane staggered back, her eyes blank with astonishment, as her gun fell from limp fingers. "What?" she said. "No..."

And she fell, bloody, to the floor.

I exhaled in a long, shuddering moan and jerked my weapon down. The president cursed. "I ordered her back, Mr. Taalib," he said. "You heard that, yes?"

My voice sounded mechanical in my ringing ears. "I heard. Yes. Her decision, not yours."

Marie's surgeon's instincts had pushed her out of hiding, but while she was trying to check the blood flow, the pool spreading under Diane's body looked conclusive.

And even if they froze her, she couldn't come back.

"Quite. Well. I assume you'll get in contact with me again, to discuss the details."

"Yes," I said, dragging my gaze away from Diane's body.

The sides of Cox's mouth had sagged in subtle relaxation. "Do you really think you can do it?" His voice was unmodulated now, sincere in its curiosity. "Settle a planet with a crew and cargo of teenagers?"

"We'll do it," I told him. "Just stay out of our way."

312

CHAPTER
TWENTY-TWO
Coda

I rose on legs as wobbly as a newborn animal and shuffled over to stare into the dead face of my enemy. Diane's eyes were still open in disbelief. At the very end, she'd been so shocked that anyone could hurt her.

Tegan approached. "Let's put this down," she suggested, and eased the gun out of my hand. I'd forgotten I was still holding it.

"You hate guns," I said. And I had just shot someone with one. Everything was echoing. I didn't really have time to go into shock, but I was worried I might anyway.

"They're useful sometimes," Tegan said, but she put the weapon down on a shelf and came back to snake her arm around me. "Marie, what are you doing?"

"Nothing useful," Marie admitted, and sat back. Her hands and knees were wet and red.

"She's dead?" I asked. "She's definitely dead?"

"Definitely," Marie said.

"Good," I said, and my knees buckled. Tegan eased me to the ground, her arm steady around my waist. I hid my head against her shoulder and took a deep breath, then another. My voice hitched on the third, and tears pressed hotly against my eyelids.

It was different, being vulnerable in front of Tegan. I didn't feel so ashamed of my weakness, this way. I stayed in her arms for a long moment, while Zaneisha dragged Diane's body out of sight. I was grateful for that.

But I didn't have time to cry for long. I blinked back the tears, but it took a few more seconds before the raw, jagged clasp on my throat eased enough for me to speak.

"Bethari, please set up the call," I said at last.

"Now?" she asked doubtfully, but her fingers were already jabbing at the air. "All right. When you're ready."

I scrubbed at my face with the heels of my hands, and stood up. "Ready. Go."

Once I managed to get through the layers of bureaucracy, my target appeared on-screen quickly. It was past midnight in Djibouti, and I'd feared I might have to rouse him from bed, but he appeared in a dark shirt with wide lapels. Working late.

"Peace be upon you, sir," I said, in respectful Arabic.

"Peace and God's mercy be with you," said President Abdullah Haid in the same tongue. "How are you finding Australia?"

"Unwelcoming. I'd like to come home."

"You'd be very welcome, but I suspect you didn't call so that I could tell you that."

"No, sir. I'm bringing some gifts with me. I hope you'll accept them."

He folded his hands under his short-clipped beard with the neatness of the practiced diplomat. "That sounds interesting, Abdi. Why don't you tell me all about it?"

Δ ∫ Ω

It was a lengthy conversation.

We switched to English so that the others could follow and Marie could give her evidence. He asked questions, and I remembered that he'd been a practicing medical doctor before he went into politics. But unlike Nathan Cox, President Haid could see the advantages to Djibouti and to his party immediately. It was he who brought up the possibility of an East Africa Alliance meeting to discuss the benefits of combining resources. "The Great Rift Valley," he said thoughtfully. "Yes. The second birth of mankind, perhaps? Not a bad phrase, in English." He flicked his hand dismissively. "I'll have people work on it."

I brightened. "So that's a yes, sir?"

He spread his hands. "Perhaps. There are many things to discuss."

"Sir, we don't have much time."

"Which is your fault," he commented.

I didn't argue, because it was true. I'd done it on purpose— the more time for either government to think it over, the more chance of their coming up with a way to wriggle out of the deal or try to impose extra conditions. The real bargain was between the Australian president and me, but it couldn't

315

appear that way. It was absolutely crucial that Djibouti take public ownership of the Ark Project.

"I take it we don't get the money with the starship."

"No, sir. It's been privately funded since—"

"Yes, since your last escapade. All right."

I startled. "Ah…"

"I said yes. We'll take the ship. I suspect we can raise more money for this expedition, and if we can't, well, there will be a Djiboutian presence in space. That's worth a little inconvenience. Now, these frozen refugees…"

"They come with the ship, sir," I said, as firmly as I dared. "It's a combination package."

The president tapped his fingers on his lips. "And they're coming with all the equipment they need to remain viable?"

"Yes, sir. I'll make sure of that."

"And you want to wake them up."

His tone was doubting, and I faltered. "Well, yes."

"How?" he asked, implacable.

"I'd be happy to donate my time and services, sir," Marie said, appearing over my shoulder.

"Dr. Carmen, hello again. While we would welcome a surgeon of your caliber, I'm afraid that unless you can also donate billions of dollars, we may not be able to accommodate Abdi's desire. These children went to sleep believing they would wake on a distant planet. It's possible they can still do that, but any other option is unlikely."

Bethari muttered something, but Tegan shushed her.

"They didn't get a real choice," I said. "We need to see if those kids truly wanted to go."

"We have to let them know that their parents won't be waking up," Tegan broke in.

I nodded. "And there's no way to find out whether those kids would choose to stay or go—unless we wake them up and ask them."

President Haid looked weary. "You know Djibouti has a refugee problem of its own, Abdi. It has been less pressing since Somalia and Ethiopia became stable states, but the water disputes in Chad are sending a number of displaced persons our way. As far as refugee processing and accommodation go, the currently breathing have to be our first concern."

I had known, but only in the abstract. It hadn't been a pressing concern for me until now. "Yes, sir," I said, ashamed.

"Until my finance people start looking at this, I can't even guarantee that you'll be able to launch. Nigeria will be interested in investing, certainly, and probably Mongolia and Japan, too, if only to get the jump on China. But I can tell you right now that if we *can* launch, we'll barely be able to afford to finish construction *and* train your crew *and* stock the starship *and* put together the infrastructure needed to facilitate all this. Infrastructure may sound boring to you, but it's vital and not cheap." He rubbed at his nose. "We won't have the resources to wake and care for these children as well."

"What are you saying?" Tegan asked.

But I already knew. My hopes were sinking before the

president spoke again: "Wake them, and they stay on this planet, with all the privation that entails. Let them sleep, and they might—might—have a chance of waking up somewhere better. Either way, Abdi, they won't be able to choose. You have to make the choice for them."

I think he was being as kind as he could possibly be, under the circumstances, but leaving the answer in my hands still felt like a horrible thing to do.

Making that decision was physically painful. I felt the weight of it settle in my gut, cramping my belly and sending a deep, heavy feeling through my bones. I wanted Tegan or Bethari to say something, come up with a crucial argument or brilliant idea that would solve everything. Maybe they were waiting for me to do the same thing. But no inspiration struck, no lightning bolt clean and crisp through my mind to make the problem dissolve like salt in water.

The worst part was realizing that this wasn't the last time this was going to happen. I'd thought choosing to keep the government's secret in order to get the refugee kids out had been the last difficult choice I'd have to make, but that had been naive. If I truly wanted the *Resolution* to fly, if I was going to be a part of making sure she did, I was going to have to make decisions like this often. I'd have to compromise and haggle and choose between bad options and worse ones, over and over again.

I thought it was probably worth it, but I couldn't be sure.

Was that what it meant to be free of people having power over me? Did I have to trade it for having power over others?

"Let them sleep," I said, my mouth twisting at the taste of

the words. "At least...until we know more, until we can plan better. Maybe there's an answer we haven't found yet."

"Maybe there is," he said kindly. "I will pray for it. You'll forgive me if I leave you now; I suddenly seem to have a great deal to do." He hesitated, his eyes ranging over me and the luxury of my surroundings. "I hope you don't expect to leverage this opportunity to put your mother back in power."

"She can do that herself," I said, and he laughed.

"She probably can. You're certainly her son. Well played, Abdi. I'll see you again." His eyes went thoughtful. "Sooner, rather than later."

"I'm leaving today, sir."

"Good. May God grant you a safe journey." He waved goodbye, and the connection ended.

"Amen to that," Tegan murmured.

Δ ∫ Ω

In the car, Bethari started on the code that would make the bluff a partial reality, putting Marie's testimony of the cryo-revival process on several servers that would message prominent 'casters worldwide if they didn't receive passworded verification every day.

Including Carl Hurfest. I didn't like him, but whatever his motivations, he had organized my rescue. If Cox double-crossed me, Hurfest could have the story.

"It's not quite as complicated as what you told Cox would happen," Bethari explained. "Easier to interrupt, too, if they can

319

find and disrupt the servers. You'd better set up more independently. And when you've got the time, update the feeds. Make the story personal. Do a 'cast—"

"Not a 'cast," I said. I was thinking of the adventure novel I'd read, of its swift pace and easy solutions that papered over all the ethical gaps. "A book, I think. I'll write a book."

"You sure you don't want to come with us?" Tegan asked Bethari. She was holding my hand, as she had for the entire trip, and I squeezed it in response to the plaintive note in her voice.

Tegan was leaving almost everything she'd ever known behind, for the second time. She'd lost her family and friends, but she'd still had the land. Now she had a new family and friends, but she was losing the land. And this time, it was by her choice.

All I could do was hold her hand and hope that she was ultimately happy about the decision. And quietly swear to do everything I could to make that so.

"My mother won't leave," Bethari said. "And I won't leave her. When will the last of the refugees arrive?"

It was an obvious attempt to change the subject and I went with it. "I'm going to give Cox a two-month deadline to get the last of them onto a ship. A month after that, they should all be en route to where the Australian government can't claim them anymore."

"You know he's going to hold some of them hostage to your continuing to keep his secret," Bethari said.

"I know," I said. "But when the last refugees they actually ship are in friendly hands, we'll tell the world about the revival age rule."

"Three months, while more foolish people choose suspension," Marie said, turning to look back at us. She held up her hands as I opened my mouth. "I know, this is the best we can do. But you realize the families of those people aren't going to think we're heroes? They're going to want to know why we didn't reveal this immediately."

"And we'll tell them everything," Tegan said fiercely. "We'll tell them that their leaders knew and did nothing—that after torturing and using us, their leaders threatened us and bribed us so that they could stay in power. That their president values his own hide over his citizens' lives. We're not heroes, Marie. But we won't be the villains, either. This government's going down."

"And I'll get people organized," Bethari said. "I still have a lot of contacts; SADU can't have found them all. I think we can put some plans together to encourage people to avoid cryonics."

"I could give you some copy," Tegan said. "I won't be a spokesperson, but I can write it down, what it feels like to wake up like I did. How awful the recovery process is."

Bethari's eyes were shining. "I can definitely use that. Good plan, Teeg—you write it; I'll say it."

"Australians who choose cryonics now won't have access to the *Resolution* anymore," I said. "Make a lot of that, all right? Emphasize that if they sleep now, they'll wake up in the same world, with all the problems they left behind and didn't fix. Get some rumors going about the revival process failing in some subjects, get people thinking that it's not worth the risk. Oh, and try to spread some doubt about the ages of the successful revivals, so that it's not such a massive shock when we—"

Bethari was smiling at me. "You should have been a journalist," she said.

"I'm a politician," I said, shaking my head. "That's enough trouble for one lifetime."

Δ ʃ Ω

Wilsons Promontory thrust out into Bass Strait like a barbed thorn into a thumb. It was a wild place, scarcely populated, and the small cove where Hanad's ship was moored was half an hour from the nearest road. It was a tough hike, through scraggly brush, with Zaneisha carrying Marie. Marie looked justifiably frustrated about it. Her feet were healing, but it would be several weeks before she could put any weight on them, much less walk of her own volition. I was hoping my brother, Halim, with his knack for medical machinery, could help her with some assistive tech.

When we got down to the meeting spot, Joph hugged Tegan so hard that Tegan had to remind her of the cracked rib. "You look so much better," she exclaimed. "I mean, not that you could look much worse."

"Thanks, Joph," Tegan told her, somewhat breathlessly.

"Anytime, Teeg!" She embraced me next, and I grunted with the force. "Hanad filled me in. Did the plan work?"

"Yes," I said, and then remembered the choice I'd had to make. "Partially, I suppose. We'll see."

"Good luck." She looked mournful. "I'm really going to miss you."

My insides lurched. "But aren't you coming?" I said.

"I…what?"

"We talked about it, in Bendigo. I said I could use another sister, and you said that sounded nice."

"Abdi," she said, and stopped, perhaps the first time I'd ever seen Joph Montgomery at a loss for words. I could feel my stomach crunching into a tight ball. "I…That's sweet, and I love you for it. But I didn't know you were serious. I'm a lesbian who was born male-bodied. It's fine here; no one cares. But in your country…am I wrong in thinking that people like me aren't so welcome?"

"Not always," I admitted. "I mean, you being a girl, people will get that, but you being a girl who still likes girls…people have these ideas about what men and women should be. But it's legal."

She shook her head. "Legal isn't the same as comfortable."

"You could help change that?" I suggested, knowing it was a stupid hope.

"I wouldn't even know how. And I bet there are people already working for change. They don't need me coming in and telling them what to do." Joph looked at my face and added, "Australia isn't always on the wrong side, you know."

"I know." I somehow managed to smile. "One of my best friends is Australian."

She laughed and kissed my cheek. "We'll talk," she said. "I'm going to make things better here, and you…you're going to change the world. We're going to be amazing, just wait."

"You're already amazing," I said, and had to let go of her. Hanad was walking up to us, and I didn't want to cry in front of him.

"Ah, good," he said, looking more pleased to see us than I'd expected. "If we leave now, we can just catch the tide."

"Right now?" Tegan asked.

"Yes," he said, and flicked his hand at me in a question.

"She's coming," I said firmly. "And Dr. Carmen, too."

"Just these two?"

"Yes. I'll pay you back, somehow."

He sighed. "No charge."

"Thank you," Tegan said, very sincerely. I suspected her of irony, but she managed to keep it out of her voice.

"I'm getting sentimental in my old age. Call it my contribution to your little revolution." He pointed at me. "I still don't like politics," he warned, and then cocked his head at Zaneisha.

"I have to see these two home safely," she said, indicating Joph and Bethari, and I felt disappointment stab me. When had I come to like her? I wasn't sure, but I was sorry to see her go. "You may see me again," she added, looking at Tegan. "I have one or two things to take care of, but then a change of scenery might be an excellent idea."

"The job offer stays open," Hanad said genially. "Not forever. But for some time."

"I don't think I'd care for your current line of work," she told him.

His teeth flashed. "Oh, I suspect new opportunities will shortly be opening for me." He turned to look at Joph and Bethari, Tegan and me. "Make your good-byes," he said. "I'll wait, but not for long." He walked down to the small yellow inflatable boat that would take us out to the ship and stood with his arms folded, looking out at the sea.

I did cry then, hugging Joph again. Zaneisha shook hands

324

with me and Marie, very solemnly, and squeezed Tegan tightly, whispering something in her ear that made Tegan smile tremulously through her tears.

Bethari and I looked at each other. I opened my arms.

"Why not?" she said, and hugged me before she moved on to Tegan. The two girls clung to each other so long I was worried that Hanad would come back to hurry us on. Then Joph caught my hand and dragged me toward them, and we became a tangle of limbs, the four of us holding one another up.

We made promises we might not be able to keep, promises about visiting and keeping in touch and always being friends. But we meant those promises, that was the important thing, and we all knew we'd do our best to keep them.

It was Zaneisha who broke us apart with a quiet remark and Marie's gentle encouragement that got me and Tegan to the boat. The sea wind tumbled Tegan's hair into a dark tornado and whipped Marie's across her face in straight lines as Hanad and I rowed. Facing backward, I could watch Joph, hand in hand with Bethari, with Zaneisha standing behind them.

The ship was beautiful, with solar panels incorporated into her sleek lines, and, I was relieved to note, a highly illegal diesel motor mounted under her stern. We'd be using wind power most of the way, but that motor would get us out of Australian reach much faster. I helped Hanad winch up the inflatable, there was a shout from the side as Thulani weighed anchor, and the engine chuckled as we got under way. Tegan and Marie sat at the stern, looking out over the waves to the dwindling cliffs of the Australian coast and the three figures standing lonely on the beach.

They faded into the dimming light, and then the cliffs faded with them until there was the barest outline of black against the midnight-blue twilight sky, and then we could see no land at all.

Still, the women watched where the shore had been, as the stars came out and the breeze died down, and we moved on through the deep waters.

At last, Tegan let out a breath and turned around. There were fresh tear tracks down her cheeks, but her smile was wide as she reached out her hand. I took it in both of mine.

"Are you ready?" I asked.

"For what?"

"The next chapter. Another beginning."

"Do you know what I've realized?" Tegan asked. "I just keep getting beginnings. I think that's what life is, one beginning after another. But it's really the middles that count—all the things we do with the middles of our lives."

"I don't think we're going to have any trouble keeping ourselves busy with this middle," I said.

"We have a lot to do," she agreed.

I wrapped my arm around her shoulders. "How do you keep going?" It was a question I'd wanted to ask her for a long time. "No matter how hard it is, you never seem to lose hope."

She glanced up at me. "I lose hope all the time. And then I find it again. How about you?"

"I lost it for a while," I said. It was hard to remember how, with Tegan warm beside me and the wide sea open around us. "But I'm hopeful now. I'm happy now."

Tegan kissed me, slow and sweet. "Abdi," she said when she pulled away, "would you sing me something?"

I smiled. "Requests?"

Her eyes were shaded, but her voice was clear. "'Here Comes the Sun.'"

It wasn't a performance, and it wasn't a pretense. No one was making me sing or her listen. It was a choice we made between us. And because she asked me to, and because I wanted to, I sang the song I'd once hated for the girl I loved.

Δ ʃ Ω

It's nearly time for this story to be told. We have all but one boatload of the refugee children in hand, and the *Resolution* was officially signed over to Djibouti last week. Bethari is ready to distribute the truth about the revival process as soon as I've finished writing it.

Tegan was right. We get lots of beginnings and lots of middles, twisted together and piled on top of one another, until we're confused about which goes where. And we get a lot of endings, too, which in a way are all practice for the final ending we can't anticipate.

I hope that final ending is a long way off, for Tegan and me, for Bethari and Joph and Zaneisha and Marie, and for the children we managed to save from selfishness and greed.

But I'll leave you with this: the two of us sailing into the night, Tegan thinking about the future, and me singing about hope.

As endings go, I think it's a good one.

Acknowledgments

My first sequel! So exciting. Sincere thanks go to the lovely Alvina Ling for giving me the chance to write this book, to my awesome editors, Connie Hsu and Allison Moore, for pushing me that extra bit on every draft (MORE FEELINGS), and to my excellent agent Barry Goldblatt for his generosity and general willingness to let me rave at him over IM.

Support, encouragement, and excellent advice were provided by the stalwart Robyn Fleming, Melanie Reese, Carla Lee, Willow, Chally Kacelnik, Kirti Kamboj, Matt Powell, Sumayyah Daud, Sarah Rees Brennan, Katie Scott, and almost certainly other people whom I am shamefully forgetting. Thank you all, so much.

I did much of the editing for this book in free time snatched from my teacher training at the New Zealand Graduate School of Education. I'm grateful for the supportive staff and my lovely colleagues.

This is my fourth book; it is long past time for me to thank my readers for making that possible. Thank you; I am truly grateful to you for enabling me to do this work I love.

And finally, I owe a great deal of this book's existence to my parents, who let me live with them for the year during which I wrote most of it. They never asked for rent and only occasionally complained about the way I cluttered up the place. Thanks, Mum and Dad, for that and for everything else.